I0754840

MIDNIGHT, AT THE WAR

BOOKS BY DEVI S. LASKAR

FICTION

Circa

The Atlas of Reds and Blues

POETRY

Self-Portraits Ex Machina

Anastasia Maps

Gas & Food, No Lodging

ANTHOLOGIES

Taboos & Transgressions: Stories of Wrongdoings
(coedited with Luanne Smith
and Kerry Neville)

Graffiti
(coedited with Pallavi Dhawan
and Tamika Thompson)

MIDNIGHT, AT THE WAR

a novel

DEVI S. LASKAR

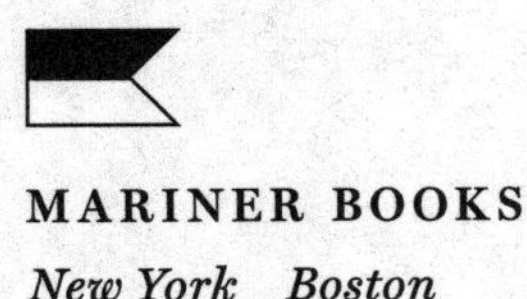

MARINER BOOKS
New York Boston

hc.com

FIRST EDITION

Library of Congress Cataloging-in-Publication Data has been applied for.

ISBN 978-0-06-328943-7

Printed in the United States of America

26 27 28 29 30 LBC 5 4 3 2 1

For my family

I broke the myth and I broke.

—From "I Didn't Apologize to the Well,"
by Mahmoud Darwish

To dwell is to leave a trace.

—From "Fast," by Jorie Graham

MIDNIGHT, AT THE WAR

Prologue

[NEW YORK, MARCH 2003] — IN THE BEGINNING I TRAVELED IN the hushed hours between midnight and dawn. I savored the quiet that fell over a city when the sky was at its darkest and its streets were nearly empty—all conflict diminished by the loom of night. In the beginning I pictured myself as seasoned and savvy, attempting to beat the rush, aiming to arrive early to the next emerging crisis. But after what happened to my colleagues Johanna and Margot struggling to exit Damascus two Septembers ago, I unceremoniously switched to day traveling, relishing the company of strangers and bright-eyed airport attendants, happy to be noticed for my high-tops and denim jacket, remembered, searched, and even questioned.

Today is no different. No matter the city or the angle of shadow cast from the sundial or the skyscraper, the routine on my day of departure remains steadfast. I inevitably check and double-check that I have enough pens and reporters' notepads to get by the first months, and stuff the suitcase with extras (pencils, hard candies, Scotch tape, paper clips) with which to barter; I make sure I have extra batteries and an adapter for my tape recorder, though I rarely use the device. I remember how my former translator, Rafiq, had long admired it, and I resolve to gift it to him if I ever see him again. I repack my satchel with its reinforced shoulder strap, an effort to utilize every inch. Today I slide in a few of Virginia's books, slim volumes of poetry she won once during a college trivia contest. Some things of hers to carry with me wherever I go. I finger my mother's opal ring, which I wear on a simple silver chain. I triple-check travel documents and the validity of my passport with extra pages sewn into the back like an epilogue to a story that is yet to be written. I call the airline to make certain that a departure is taking place. Since September 11, things that I once took for granted are no longer assured. I pace by the window until an airport limousine, inevitably delayed because of the afternoon rush, arrives.

Today is no different, and relief courses through my veins when the airline agent confirms the flight, her voice nasally and bored. Now I check my watch, then stare at the apartments across the street from Ford's condominium. I've made myself at home—especially now that he's gone out of town and I've stopped answering the phone. This is the kind of woman I am these days: married to my handsome husband, Sebastian, but camping out at my old flame Ford's apartment across town. Married to one man but sleeping in another's bed—often with him in it. Twice I pick up the phone to call Seb but I hang up before I complete dialing. Twice I begin to write Ford a note, but I rip up sheets of hotel stationery that he uses for scratch paper and deposit my false starts in the trash. I don't want to share what I now know. This is the kind of woman I am, carrying secrets at once big and small.

Across the street, everyone is out, even the grandmother on the seventh floor. I have named her Edith because of the Wharton-style hat she dons every time she leaves the apartment she shares with a middle-aged man, presumably her son, and a pair of beagles. I don't know for certain, but I think the building across the street doesn't allow pets. The beagles are the only pair I've ever noticed. My money is on Edith: In all the time I have observed her, this grandmotherly face has remained somber and stony, a woman who regularly stares into an abyss of grief but has the strength to look away.

I know that look.

Today is like every other international departure except that I have no mother to say goodbye to, no mother to wish me bon voyage.

I

One

[APRIL 2001] — THE FLIGHT IS NOT FULL, AND I FALL ASLEEP across the empty row despite my best intentions to see the mysterious world at night from my window seat. I wake to find my shawl draped over me and the oval-shaped light from the window coursing across my face. The sun feels good. I close my eyes and the light from the window creates a converging pattern of red lines on my eyelids. They are missives, plentiful like a sky full of paper planes. Come home. Your mother is dying. Come home. Your husband needs you. Come home. Your family needs you. Come home. There are plenty of stories and news assignments to be had in America, in New York. We have all survived Y2K and millennium doomsday scenarios; the future is limitless—if you leave your foreign assignment behind and return. Come home.

But I know a thing or two. I love my job. I am only as good as my last good story. I love cataloging the present with my practiced eye and transforming it into history, however rough. I've earned the privilege to do this job.

If I were a man no one would be telling me to come home.

A plane change in Cairo, and then off to my destination. Customs is perfunctory, and a young man holding up a sign with my newspaper's name and ELENA KEPPLER meets me just outside the translucent sliding doors. I smile. "That's me," I say, pointing to the sign. "You can call me Rita." He looks puzzled and I show him my press badge, something I love to do as it eases the tension in every situation where the face they expect to see does not match the name on the placard. He introduces himself: Rafiq Sayed. My new driver and translator. He is young and round, bearded, with glasses that make him look studious. He wears Western clothes: a collared shirt and beige slacks, closed-toe shoes.

I look around and, for fun, count the number of children milling about (fourteen) and the number of nonblack bags on the carousel (six).

We are quiet as I take everything in.

Rafiq asks, "How was your flight?"

"Great," I say, my go-to word when I can't or don't want to tell the truth. It is the slightly better version of "Fine" that everyone in America says in automatic response when someone asks how they are. "Managed to get some sleep."

We gather my bags and head toward the parking lot, then we exit the airport checkpoint and venture toward the center of the city. This place resembles the Indian subcontinent: the dust on the roads, the muddy brick and stone architecture of the buildings, and the types of cars, compact, older models; the winding layout of the side streets. I see mosques from my window and vast, open-air tent city markets, a hospital, apartment complexes, and the entrance to a garden, in the distance animals grazing. Ahead a construction site, yellow and red cranes beak forward like birds of paradise.

It smells like spices and sweat—and food cooking nearby. Minus the continuous addition of incense on the streets, from the Kali mandirs along the paths. There are Kali mandirs everywhere in Kolkata, in every neighborhood, the miniature black clay goddess dressed in shimmering silk with a necklace of clay heads around her neck. But I am not in India, I am thousands of miles away. I am in [--------], but I could have been in Kolkata, Mumbai, or Delhi. This place neither smells nor looks like the sterile, paved, unoccupied streets of America—my brain can't help but compare each place I've lived in America with this crowded, bustling present. The American cities where I've lived, with the exception of New York, are ordered, homogenous.

Like India, here there is always the undertone of something burning. Maybe that's what I smell now. Someone in the distance is burning something to the ground as people go about their lives, shopping for dinner ingredients and picking up their children from school. People are not the only subjects of my stories; whatever the subject, it has the odor of something burning. The questions rise through me: Who set this world on fire, and why? Where? How much more damage do you expect? What are your preventative measures to keep this from happening again? How much of this world has been burned to the ground already? What are your losses? Who is in charge, and what is their arrangement with their adversaries? And how much longer before the fire spreads to where all these innocent people stand now? Who is responsible for the fire? Who oversees the matches and the gasoline? How many were harmed by the previous fires? What are the names of those who were burned? How much did the fire obliterate? What are your plans to contain the fire that is burning out of control now? These are always the questions. The reporter merely substitutes the word *fire* for *war, government, police, corruption, racism, misogyny, assault, trafficking, famine, displacement,* or *drugs.*

Even as I enter this new world and new assignment, I miss India. I miss how I've spent the last year in the land of my mother's birth. I had written the bulk of my stories outside the capital, and this had worked in my favor. My immediate boss, Hughes, had been fine with the arrangement I had set up for myself. But Rich, also on the international desk and a peer of Hughes, was a bastard in the last month after the high court in India had handed down a ruling banning headscarves for Muslim girls at the local university. Rich didn't like that I had covered that particular story from afar, and he insisted I move to Delhi and set up residence where almost all of the other international reporters lived. Rich didn't like that I was doing a good job, that readers and peers had been complimenting my work. Rich doesn't like that there are women in the newsroom, and he has held that belief since we were both in Florida. Rich doesn't like that someone, probably the managing editor, gave me a shot at a coveted position.

"The paper needs a physical presence, Keppler," he had said, the line cutting in and out when he stopped to take a breath. "You're not even in the same state, for god's sake."

I'd corrected him about my name, but he ignored me.

I liked my role as a ghost, going places to cover events but always returning to haunt Calcutta. I pumped out stories about the drought in Mumbai, about the voting irregularities in Bihar, about the exploitation of textile workers in Orissa; about the Indian government eschewing the British spelling and pronunciation of the cities of India, transforming Calcutta back, finally, to Kolkata, Bombay to Mumbai, Madras to Chennai. I had a tiny office, I squatted in the Reuters spacious floor on Taratala Road (near the house where my great-aunt grew up, in Behala, that was sold to settle my great-uncle's considerable gambling debts after he died). The wire service guys were friendly, always buying me masala cha and offering to help.

On any given assignment, I had spoken to officials on the phone and then donned a baggy neutral-colored salwar kameez and affixed a sparkly bindi to my face. I hitched rides, had chances to see the issues for myself. I blended in and was a spectator, a witness. I looked like every other interested bystander, only I was holding a small pad and a pen. I untucked my press badge and spoke to them in fluent Bengali or a child's version of Hindi. Nine times out of every eleven, they agreed to speak to me on the record, they congratulated me for the job I was sent to India to do. Unlike Americans, they didn't balk at my pointed questions or examine my credentials, or ask me more than once where I was from and who'd taught me English.

In fact, Rich was the first person to ask me, loudly and slowly, my first day in the Florida newsroom if I spoke English. I was glad I was able to answer him flippantly in the moment in front of everyone, without missing a beat. "It is my second language," I'd said in my best southern drawl, and everyone but Rich had laughed. But later, in the bathroom, I had shut the door to the stall and felt my face flush with heat and hot tears sting the corners of my eyes. As much as I despise Rich, it is the Indian government liaison, Mr. Sharma, who I wish would acquire an untreatable rash. The villainous Mr. Sharma as I liked to call him behind his back, mostly because of his cartoonish mustache and thick brows, tried to feel me up at lunch one day not too long ago. When I didn't reciprocate, he complained repeatedly to Hughes of my purported mistakes, my bad attitude, my unprofessionalism. Hughes asked me four times if something had happened, and I played it off as sour grapes that I hadn't used Mr. Sharma for the upcoming Bhopal accident anniversary story. I knew better than to tell Hughes or anyone else about Mr. Sharma's roving hands: It would have confirmed their suspicions that women weren't cut out for this kind of job.

Mr. Sharma was probably one of the reasons for my expulsion, one of the excuses for my probation and this new trial position in [--------]. I missed a big story: the statues. Over and again, I was told to cover the news with an impartial eye, as in Impartial I. Yet there are eyes back in New York who look from afar and try to impose what they claim to see from thousands of miles away—not trusting the reporter on the ground, so to speak.

When the Taliban threatened to bomb the Buddhas of Bamiyan, the sixth-century statues carved into the central Afghan mountains, none of the editors in New York took the warning seriously. For one thing, the site could not be reached at a moment's notice. It's northwest of Kabul and a long journey, especially from Kolkata or Delhi. Second, no one believed it could even happen: These Buddhist reliefs were almost fourteen hundred years old and had been there for public viewing without incident for nearly a millennium. Yet the men who orchestrated the destruction were angered by a restoration group's stance that funding would be used solely to repair and restore the statues; it would not be used for the feeding and care of the hungry children in the nearby village and the thousands of residents in the region. At that point the sanctions imposed by the United Nations had already had an impact throughout Afghanistan.

I asked Hughes if he wanted me to go cover the story, but he'd said no. Then Rich called back the next day and said for me to be ready and go on a moment's notice, that this could be a really good one. Rich and, to a lesser extent Hughes, had looked at the threat like children would look at a bully on the other side of a tall fence. From their vantage points, the bully was all talk and there was no anticipation of any action. The newspaper editors wanted to compete with cable TV broadcasters, and in this new era of twenty-four-hour coverage, they wanted a blow-by-blow description.

Still, everyone was caught unaware. On a Monday, just as these men had warned, the Taliban used dynamite and guns and blew off the faces of these two Buddhist reliefs, much to the horror of the people who had come to repair them. There was one video of the bombing, taken by a restoration worker when he realized the Taliban was going through with the threat, since none of the news stations were there yet. The world watched the grainy video the following day on all the channels, after it was verified. Rich's call came after the video was published. Sadly, the world is concerned with old relics in history only after they are threatened. The lining, in silver: Now suddenly everyone around the world is questioning their government. What are you doing to protect our past? What are you doing to protect our monuments and the marks of our civilization?

In response to the Taliban's action, many Buddhist societies around the world announced plans to build replicas of the destroyed statues and place them on public display in a show of unity. In places such as New Zealand and Poland, China, Hong Kong, Sri Lanka, and India; and inside the United States in Hawai'i, California, and Illinois. I was able to interview via telephone a film crew from India that captured the reliefs with their noses blown off and a member of the restoration group from Sri Lanka who had returned home. One of the film crew returned to Delhi, and I was able to interview him in person. I had written two stories. The lede for the second story: "Rakesh Bhatia never dreamed he'd become an eyewitness to the destruction of history on the eve of his 20th birthday."

Still, Hughes had not been satisfied. "You did know this was happening? Your crystal ball is polished, right?"

Another phone call with New York—this time Hughes and Rich on the line together. I stood at a busy corner of the floor where reporters like me were trying to phone back to their home countries. The stench of body odor and tension permeated the air. "What, that they were going to blow up the faces? No."

I heard Rich in the background. "Mike Barrett is going to land in . . ." Hughes clamped a hand over the receiver to muffle the noise. On my end, a percussion of voices near and far.

A moment or two passed. "I've got to go if you want that follow-up story," I said into the phone, the line hissing indiscriminately. Some of my colleagues looked over at me. I must have been shouting.

"Next time your crystal ball says—" Hughes began.

"Next time?" I interrupted. "I'm in the middle of a sexual assault story. Remember the girl on the bus?" A teenager had been raped on Delhi public transport and died later from her injuries. There were nine people on the bus, including the driver, and no one had intervened on behalf of the five-foot-one fifteen-year-old on her way home. The teenager had just started high school. The police had been quick in finding and detaining all the passengers and the bus driver, but there were no answers to the reporters' questions at the daily press briefing. I'm not an ambulance chaser, though perhaps this is what Hughes wants. Someone who drops everything or someone who can do six things at once. There are threats like the potential destruction of Buddhist statues all the time. I hadn't guessed correctly. I'd missed a big story. "You said the girl on the bus was a priority." There was a rumor that an English tourist had been molested on a Delhi bus but that she was unwilling to go public. I needed to track down the tourist.

Hughes interrupted back. "Next time, we will have a chance to do better than this coverage . . ."

But I stopped listening. I had found witnesses to the bombing and still, that was not enough.

Meanwhile, the paper's longtime Middle East correspondent David Richards had been killed. Kidnapping. There was extensive coverage and now a plan to replace him. The two Mikes were being considered: Mike Barrett and Michael Reyn. I could hear the debate all the way from Delhi. They'd never consider me, even if Mr. Sharma hadn't tried to feel me up and then cover his tracks. The only reason I even got the India assignment is because of all the recent strife in Kolkata and because my Bengali was damn near fluent, and probably because their first choice, Josh Weaver-White, had a problem with his passport.

But I also knew what "I can't promise" meant when Hughes had said it. It was code that he was going to float up my name, that he was going to make it happen. The paper shuffling was a tell, too. My editor shuffled the papers on his desk like a deck of oversized cards, and that sound meant he was mulling something, trying to unravel a complex knot.

"You can try me out in Egypt and [--------], until all the boys decide which Mike to amplify." My weak attempt at humor had been met with a pause and then a chuckle.

"Okay, Rita, I'll put in a request. Let's find some good work out there."

I breathed out as soon as I was off the phone, happy to have kicked my problems down the road like empty soda cans. I didn't have to go back to New York, and I didn't have to face my husband or my parents.

I focus again on the present. [--------] is a fabled city-state in the region, but riddled with recent political upheaval, an emerging conservatism, and an increasingly anti-Western sentiment. Rafiq drives me to the heart of the city. The hotel is in the bustling city center, which I love. To be in the core of a city, to hear its heartbeat and to see the streams of people coursing through the streets, morning and night, is the greatest gift. The proximity almost guarantees that Rich won't ride me about my location. It is not too far from the government buildings and the river that cuts through this metropolis like a lightning bolt through a thunderous sky. Also not too far from the local newspaper offices, where some of the editors have already been arrested. Wire services report that government security forces are rounding up protesters and those vocalizing dissent—jailing them. The hotel is a modest building, three stories with a maroon awning that looks freshly laundered and has a certain joie de vivre emanating.

Rafiq says, "This is where most of the foreign journalists stay." His English is crisp, textbook.

"Great," I repeat. Maybe I can make a friend or two. My best friend from college and fellow reporter, Virginia, is so far away.

Rafiq pats his belly. "Many come here for breakfast," he says, drawing attention to the adjoining restaurant.

"Well, I won't have far to walk," I say, pointing to my worn shoes.

Rafiq smiles and trains his gaze toward the local market and says there is a bustling business, manned by vendors in kiosks, all along the square and near the museum, one of the biggest in the region. "You can get almost everything," he says. "Even in your size."

For a Bengali girl, I'm a five-foot-seven giant. Well, half-Bengali. I look taller because of my build, and the way my curly hair is usually piled into a big bun on top of my head. I've got my dad's frame and my mother's face; and I have inherited her youthful appearance, so I belie my age of thirty-seven years and six and a half months.

We enter through the revolving door, and inside it is palatial, resplendent in plush fabrics, giant chandeliers. The air smells like a flower shop overrun with roses and gardenias and jasmine. "Gorgeous," I say.

"That's what David said too." Rafiq's smile wanes. "He wouldn't leave this hotel, even after the second threat."

There is never a split second when I can't recall how David had died. It rushes forward in my mind: the kidnapping on the street, the ransom demand, and in the end, the dead reporter when that demand was not immediately met. It came on the heels of two other highly publicized kidnappings, one of an American university president and the other of a well-known philanthropist who made his home in the region.

A shiver crawls down the length of my spine. I turn to study Rafiq as we queue up behind a camera crew waiting to check in. There is still some baby fat on his face, and he looks as though he just started shaving a week ago. My radar does not register anything wrong. "My condolences to you on the loss of your friend," I say.

He bows his head slightly. "Thank you." Tears moisten his eyes for a moment. "Did you know David?"

I shake my head. "Just by reputation."

We reach the front of the line, and a well-dressed man asks to see my passport.

"Miss Keppler," he says. "Welcome."

I smile. "I use my family name. It's Das." This statement is halfway between true and false. My name is Elena Indrakshi Keppler. But I have always been Rita, nicknamed by my brother when I was born. The story is that Adam, whom our mom calls Babu, had been watching *West Side Story* with Mom and Dad and enjoying Rita Moreno's dance sequence, "I Want to Live in America." He had turned to Mom and asked what the actress's name was, then said, "We should call my sister Rita." When asked why, he'd purportedly said, "She's the prettiest, and she dances the best!"

I assumed my mother's surname long ago, on the first day a story written by me appeared in print. Because no one believed me when I said my name was Elena Keppler, no one thought I was telling the truth. From my first byline, I've been Rita Das, much to the consternation of the Kepplers in Madison, Wisconsin, or Syracuse, New York, or Nashville, Tennessee, or wherever Dad's enigmatic family is really from. My mother's genealogy is practically linear in comparison. She hails from a long line of Sens and Dasguptas, Senguptas and SenSharmas, and Guptas. My maternal grandfather shortened his name for convenience. They hadn't been exactly thrilled that I took Mom's name either. It was not appropriate action for a good Bengali girl. Everyone in Sebastian's family is also outraged that I have made no move to modify my byline name since our marriage.

"Of course," the man at the desk says, his face and voice smooth, modulated. He assigns me a room on the third and top floor.

At first Rafiq objects. "What will she do if—when—there is load-shedding?"

Here is a term that I've heard so many times over the course of my life. Rolling and regular power outages in the rest of the world are called load-shedding, from Kolkata to Cairo, from Delhi to Dubai. Only in America is it referred to as a blackout.

The attendant begins to answer, but I interrupt him after I haltingly translate from Arabic his nametag. "It's all right, Mr. Salim," I say. "I am not afraid of stairs."

Rafiq argues anyway and secures the best room on the third floor, the one next to an interior stairwell, impervious, apparently, to outside disturbances, both natural and man-made.

"There is a fire alarm just outside your door," Mr. Salim says. "First sign of trouble, you break the glass."

I smile in appreciation. Mr. Salim hands me a single room key, notices my wedding band, and says, "Should I give you a second key?"

I decline with a shake of my head, then thank him for his efforts. Rafiq and I turn to go.

At the elevator, Rafiq looks at his watch and says, "I will come back for you in an hour."

I can see the tension in his eyes. He doesn't want to leave me, and he doesn't want to be late. I don't know my new translator at all, but I know the look of a man in love. It is the dawn of the twenty-first century, even though I'm in yet another country that favors arranged marriages. "Hot date?" I tease.

Rafiq blushes a little. "It's . . . Miss Das."

"It's Rita," I remind him, settling on the time. "Bring your girlfriend along, I'd love to meet her."

Rafiq tries to shrug off my questions. He looks away, he shrugs his shoulders, he blushes again. I don't even know a name yet; all I know is that he's so lovestruck that he can't even articulate. I don't think I was ever this much in love. Well, maybe with Ford a long time ago when we first met, but years have passed since then, and I'm married now. Sebastian and I are circling an icy patch, but that's what two people with strong personalities do: They circle each other. I think of my parents, and this circling is not outside what I have observed to be normal.

I know I have colossal shoes to fill as David Richards's temporary replacement, especially under these dire circumstances, the kidnapping and the murder. I can tell that Rafiq genuinely cared for David and his wife, Gina. He points out the cafés and shops David and Gina frequented, by the ports. He points out the vendor in the brightly covered kiosk who supplied more than candies and print editions of the newspapers from around the world. [--------] is a city-state that is out of time; it is timeless. I know that the somewhat-distant Cairo is the center, politically, in the region. I know Rafiq and I will shuttle back and forth like worker ants. But I'm glad to be here instead of there. The salty air buoys me, especially after the way I had to leave India; the villainous Mr. Sharma had called me at my Delhi hotel and chortled. The Indian government had revoked my visa at his recommendation.

Rafiq says something now but I don't hear it and ask him to repeat.

He says David's widow, Gina, is an English teacher and has no plans to leave before the end of the school year. She stays with friends and walks every day to her classroom at the nearby international school. "Your husband is joining you, yes?"

"No," I say. "My husband is stationed in Europe. Sometimes he goes back to America." What I don't say is how my marriage has become an international tug-of-war game, each of us pulling, trying to force the other's position. The last several months have been rocky. I'd gone to Europe to meet Sebastian on my brief breaks:

Barcelona, Berlin, Amsterdam. He had successfully begged off coming to India.

Rafiq says something about married couples being in the same field, and I laugh in politeness. "So, your girlfriend isn't in the translation business?"

His face turns the color of ripe tomatoes. He shakes his head.

I bet David Richards and his wife had asked him personal questions, taken him to dinner, known him well. I don't know why he is blushing now like a lovestruck schoolboy. But I am not David. He was a longtime award-winning correspondent out of the Washington, D.C., bureau, and he is dead just four weeks. Hughes had his way, and I am here. Virginia called my hotel and left me a message when I was out: Josh Weaver-White is taking my job in India.

Rafiq is good but young. Whenever I ask for something, he replies, eagerly, "I know a place," and almost by magic, my question gets answered. One day soon after our initial meeting, he comes into the office with a soft cloth package in his hands, a gift for me from his mother, Aya. A head abaya, the color of a shoreline as it abuts a sea. "Just in case you need to cover your hair," he says. "She worries." I smiled at their thoughtfulness.

I had had Mr. Biswas in Kolkata, the old concierge at the apartments where the long-term businessmen and journalists and professors on sabbatical lived, in a Salt Lake neighborhood, near the water tower and the main street where the Mukherjee Sweets shop was open late into the evening. Mr. Biswas worked wonders, though I was not able to return to the neighborhood I hadn't seen since I was eleven. It is my dream to return there with my mother one day. There were Bengalis everywhere, and once I said, "My mom is a Bengali doctor, so I had to do the opposite," and more likely than not I got help. I never mentioned Dad, and everyone assumed he was an Indian man. I never once corrected them, for this was my superhero outfit. I was Clark Kent in India—I blended in as a local, I belonged. No one had to know my dad is white.

Almost everyone I encountered in West Bengal told me proudly, even though I was there to report on bad news, that India had changed, that India was modern now. I never agreed with them outright, but I felt it too. It was a different sort of India than I had witnessed when I was eleven, and I hinted at it every time I called home and Mom answered. "It's not the wild, wild West anymore, Mom. The people are not the vigilantes we encountered." I don't speak to Dad or my brother about my observations—India had frozen for them decades before.

Sebastian had a similar experience in Spain. Once he opened his mouth and spoke to sources in their local intonation and played his dad-the-famous-Spanish-economist card, he rarely encountered any issues. Of course, Seb was a journalist for a prestigious monthly magazine, and his business- and money-reporting was not at the same frenetic pace of daily news. I had tried to call him twice, to let him know I had been expelled from India and that I was now in [--------]. He hadn't answered—at either location, his tiny apartment in Madrid nor the offices that the magazine writers used when they worked out of Spain. I left him a message at work, something insubstantial and funny, and how it would be easier to see each other since I'd changed addresses.

I almost called my father-in-law back in the States but chose my parents instead. Dad answered.

"I went through Cairo and landed here in [--------]," I say by way of greeting.

Dad laughs at what he thinks is a joke. "Did you get kicked out of India already, Elena?"

I play along, though I want to correct him about my name. He has never called me Rita, and he has never approved of my brother's nickname for me. "Actually, yes," I say, trying to keep my voice light.

But Dad is not fooled. "Seriously, are you on your way home?" He sounds excited, hopeful even, at the thought. "Adam and Jennifer are coming over, soon." He calls my brother Adam, not once using the nickname Mom picked out for him.

Home. Home is New York and had been for the past twenty-five years. I had never considered my parents' house my home. My home was Mom, so the emergency room at Memorial Hospital where she worked was my home. Ever since the cancer had returned, her home had been more and more the house she shared with Dad and my brother until he got married, and less and less the hospital. But we have an arrangement, Mom and I: She will not die until she becomes a grandmother, and I promise not to have kids for at least another five years.

"Egypt," I say. "First, then . . ."

"Yes, I know where [--------] is," he interrupts. "Are you unemployed, Elena? Are you in trouble? Do you need money?"

Almost. Maybe. No. "I've been reassigned," I say.

Dad grunts, and I know that noise. He is suspicious and unconvinced. I picture the look on his face: No doubt he is furrowing his brows together to form a caterpillar as he clenches his jaw. "Your mother is getting worse," he says, reminding me that he'd relayed the urgency of my return many times in the past months. His voice does not reflect the look I know is on his face, his voice is smooth like polished stone. "Why didn't they reassign you to New York?"

I am not going to argue or explain, neither works. I hear him clear his throat. If Mom had answered the phone, she would never have asked me to return. "Is Mom there?"

He grunts again. "No. She went back to work."

In my reporter's mind, everything echoes. The present always hearkens to the past. Time is fluid but still propulsive. The next month disappears in this way. My interactions with Sebastian and my parents are fleeting at best, mostly messages, some brief phone calls where we recognize each other's voices and say one funny thing, and then I'm off to do something else. A vocabulary word or an accent instantly throws me into a different time or at least a different time zone: Sebastian saying thank you to me in different languages every time I made the coffee before he woke up. Ford's face pops into my head every time Santana is played, instrumental version or not, on the radio or in the elevators, the easy smile, the way his hands hold his air guitar. Rafiq remains secretive with me. I never did meet her, the mysterious girlfriend. Maybe she held only a temporary place in his heart. Though I did get a first name, that first day, over tea and pastries: Hanan. I was curious at first. Every young Hanan we came across could have been the girlfriend. But Rafiq's eyes never did flicker like tea candles at the sight of any of the three in the following month. There was a Hanan at the press pool briefing in Cairo after the car bombing, another Hanan who was the assistant to the assistant to the national agricultural office when I needed a quick tour of new export crops and a quote, and the Hanan who was a relief worker and had started her own NGO, who was venturing farther and farther with each trip, into camps and areas where the governments had not exactly said no but were frowning. With each meeting, Rafiq played it friendly but cool. I sensed the last Hanan was a possibility; they shook hands for a second too long, but soon after she looked disinterested, and he looked positively bored.

I had known Rafiq's mother, Aya, was looking for a bride, but Rafiq seemed ambivalent at best, so I didn't think too much of it until he shows up at the hotel the first Saturday after I have returned from a quick stint in Amman. He shyly shows me his wedding band and tells me about Luxor, where he traveled with his new wife, Zahra, for the weekend-long honeymoon. "It was a family wedding," he says. "Settled within a few days."

I am shocked but hide behind my smile, issue a hearty congratulations, wonder aloud what I could buy him as a gift. He grins, tells me he wants a ticket for Zahra, so he could take his new bride with him to America. The sun pours through the open window behind him, and the air swirls with dust. I am hoping to have him be my full-time permanent translator, but he says he really wants to leave for the United States by the end of the year. I promise him my help. He had been invaluable to the paper when David Richards had been alive, and I want to keep the newspaper's promise.

Rafiq's short timeline is not unlike my own. I had eloped with Seb, and of course, both our families still smart like a scab freshly torn open every time our wedding comes up in conversation. Even two years later.

As a new husband, though, Rafiq is hardly relaxed or bubbling with information. Every day he comes to work, and he is alert and ready to drive, photograph, translate, whatever is necessary. He is more serious and somber than he had been as a bachelor, and I want to interrogate. I throw out questions the way Dad and Adam used to cast lines into the river on Saturdays when they went fishing, but my bait remains unsuccessful.

I am tired but can't sleep, turn on the TV and begin watching an old *Murder, She Wrote* rerun with Arabic dubbing and English subtitles that do not match. In place of the American ads for toilet paper, hamburgers, laundry detergent, there are ads for women's tailored clothing and a kebab restaurant, and a traveling exhibit at the museum. I remember the plot halfway through the episode and feel heady with power. It reminds me of India the year I turned eleven, before the event that obliterated our lives, how the cousins and aunts crowded around the one TV that my great-aunt had in her flat, to watch an old rerun of *The Bold and the Beautiful*. Months before when I was home sick with the flu, Dad and I had watched soap operas. That one episode was enough to know that I knew these characters' futures. Now the phone rings and I turn down the volume before I answer. "Yes?"

"Hello, darling," Mom says, the noise of the kitchen TV behind her as a man hawks new cars and a low, low price. "Are you living your best life?"

My heart leaps. "The hotel is in the center of town," I report. "And my translator is a newlywed."

"You told me that already," she says. "Don't you remember?"

The brief memory of my eleventh year creates fog, which creates more fog: Now I can't even remember what I ate for lunch today. "Of course I do," I say, cracking my knuckles. I see my distorted reflection in the TV. Then recollections pop back into my mind: The last time I spoke to her was nearly two weeks before. I ate lamb kebabs for lunch. "I was just testing you."

Dad coughs as he picks up the extension, ostensibly from the bedroom. "Elena, your mother won't tell you, but the doctors are hoping that you and your brother can accompany us to the next visit."

Alarm bells ring inside the chambers of my heart. "When? Where? With whom?"

Mom laughs. "It's not that dire, Rita. They'd like to see me this fall." But my mom's laugh is too easygoing.

"No," Dad interrupts. "They want to see you in two weeks, and they think you should stop practicing altogether. They'd like the family to gather."

Mom laughs again and repeats what she said the very first time and on all the subsequent occasions when Dad had wanted her to retire. "My cancer is not contagious. Kindly let me do my work." Her voice cracks at the end, and I feel the corners of my heart pinch together.

From the day I left for India more than a year ago, Mom and I have a magical thinking agreement: She has given me her word, and I have given her my word. My heart beats loudly now in my chest. "Mom, do you need me now?"

But Dad answers, almost shouting. "Yes, she really needs you right now." He sneezes, excuses himself. "The appointment is in the afternoon. If she improves, the next one will be mid-September."

I shake my head, but of course they can't see. "I'll ask Hughes."

"When do you think you can come back for a visit?" Mom's voice is soft.

"October," I say, glancing at the TV. Jessica Fletcher in *Murder, She Wrote* is traipsing across the street in grim pursuit of someone she wants to interrogate. Hughes knows Mom is sick, and he has told me to give him a little notice and I could return. "But I'll ask if I can come sooner."

Dad's humph is pronounced.

"Then it's settled, darling," Mom says. "I'll see you in September."

"You'll do no such thing," Dad says. "Elena, please come home now, even if it's for a few days. Your supervisor will understand."

I hear anxiety in his voice. But it has been the same sound I've heard for years, ever since the doctors detected cancerous cells in her left breast. It is nothing new. "Mom?"

"I'll be fine, Rita," Mom says. "Babu and Jenny are coming tomorrow. Let us know when you finalize *your* plans."

There is a bomb scare near the pyramids and the Sphinx. Security is extremely tight, and at first the threat called in is treated like a prank. But then one of the uniformed police officers gets paranoid and orders an extra sweep. The news spreads like a fire. Rafiq and I are in Cairo for an energy conference, the afternoon session ending early so that the conference goers can visit the nearby Wonder of the World. The conference leaders are all corralled just outside the park. Some of the park goers have left, and Rafiq and I decide to wait. There is a bag, something one would carry a change of clothing in, with a blue handle and some popular label. For a short time, it looked like dynamite and some kind of explosive with a timer and wires.

When I say short time, I mean four hours. For four hours, Egypt holds its breath. Bomb-sniffing dogs and the bomb unit are called in. It is determined that it is a dummy device that was somehow put together inside the park. There are many tourists that day at the pyramids and the Sphinx—the streets are packed full of people dining and drinking and taking in the views. The sun bears down and even the few shaded spots are hot. All the camera angles could not point to a single person carrying a blue-handled bag. Rafiq and I get a closer look: The bag is labeled AMERICAN TOURISTER, but the closer one gets to it one can see that the letters are just off slightly and TOURISTER is misspelled, an extra E in place of the I.

The commander says it appears that this was an elaborate hoax. Rafiq and I nod at each other.

I call Hughes and I convince him at first that this is a nothing story, that the whole point of the bomb scare is to get attention and that we should play it down, that there are so many other things going on in Cairo and in Egypt, in the entire region, that while we could lead with a dummy bomb scare we should have it turn to something really substantial and important. The energy summit, for example, and fossil fuel debates.

Hughes hesitates.

I remind him of the school bus debacle in Florida five years ago: We were both in the newsroom the afternoon a school bus shuttling special needs children back from an event had tapped the back of a sheriff's deputy's car at a red light. No one was hurt. Nothing was damaged. Not even the tiniest of scratches on either vehicle. No one was charged, initially. The media came to know about it only because it involved two government vehicles. It was a slow news day. Channel 7, the NBC affiliate, and Channel 9, the Fox affiliate, jumped on it as if the plight of mankind were at stake. After a long debate in our newsroom that afternoon, there was a vote taken whether to even run a story, and Hughes and I voted to save the space for something more substantive: the repercussions from a radiation accident at a nuclear power plant in Japan. It was Rich's side that won, though, running story after story about the phantom fender-bender for close to a week. The consequences: The poor driver was suspended for a week, the school superintendent called for reform of bus driver requirements, and there was a general commotion in the community about the predicament of disabled children in the Sunshine State. "Let's not repeat," I say to Hughes now.

Hughes clears his throat. There are men in the background speaking loudly, and soon Rich's voice comes on the line. "You're missing the story."

"What story am I missing?" I ask, trying to sound calm. "It wasn't even a real bomb." I picture Ford, leaning back in his seat, the Florida sun setting behind his left shoulder, grinning as he tells me how he yeses his editors to death when he doesn't want to do an assignment.

"Do I have to spell it out for you?" Rich's voice slices through the telephone. "Everybody else has got a big story about this, okay?" He sniffs. "This is a story about how unstable the whole region is."

I roll my eyes but I drop my voice. "No one was hurt, Rich, it wasn't even a real bomb." I pause. "Nothing went off, nothing got damaged; and yes, a lot of people got inconvenienced and now they're going to go home." I cough to give myself a second. "Anyway, this is not an example of instability. It's the opposite: Everything worked, and a crisis was averted."

Rafiq stares at me, mouth slightly open.

I can hear Rich gasp, presumably because I talked back to him. "I'm looking across three TV networks and they're covering the hell out of this!" Rich shouts. "Get me something now!"

The haze of the air smudges the otherwise picturesque sky. "Okay," I say and hang up. The truth is that the commander on the scene did not like my questions and I do not want to ask him again. But I also know if I don't ask him and fashion some kind of story for Rich from those answers that I will no longer be working for the newspaper.

The commander's nostrils flare and he puffs out his chest a little. All his pins and metals puff out a little too. "It is an affront to the people of Egypt and to the world to have their Wonder threatened in this manner."

I glance at the bank of smartly dressed broadcast reporters, mics in hand, and their cameramen, all shooting live with the Sphinx in profile and the three pyramids in the distance. "Since there is no damage and no real attack and you yourself say it was a child's toy that was fashioned to look like a bomb, what is the purpose, do you think?"

Rafiq relays the question.

The commander frowns and the weight of the world looks heavy on his face. "Fear," he says, his voice betraying no emotion. "Whoever did this wishes the people to be afraid, to live in constant fear."

Two

[SUMMER 2001] — IN INDIA, I HAD AN ADVANTAGE: I PULLED OUT the mother card. But here it is a learning curve at the edge of a desert where I cover roadside bombings from a distance. Sometimes I sneak in stories about a school for the blind in dire need of help, and sometimes it is a story about water and its continual shortage. No one in the New York newsroom is interested in history or context. The more human interest stories do not get their own space with their own headlines. Rather, I sneak them in, all the numbers stories that I do now, how many have died in the regional wars, how many of them soldiers, how many civilians, and the special interest groups, children, and women and the old, how much money everything costs, the munitions, the cost of living during these wars, the loss of tourism on the national and regional GDPs. But it's not like America where the old are thrown away, often put into neglectful institutions, often visited by their families as an afterthought a couple of times a year. Here multiple generations live together, the wisdom of the elderly is revered.

I soon fall into a familiar routine. As in India, my little office is inside the wire service bureau on the main boulevard where I squat in the late mornings. It is an older building with blue walls but with a bank of windows, and on the top floor there is a common balcony next to a private business. I get a glimpse of the river that slices through the city, the country, the region, with its greenish blue water. I meet a newspaper vendor who is old and kind and looks out for me. The second weekend after I arrived, we became friends when he sold me the Sunday magazine that held my last India story in its glossy pages: a retrospective on the Indian government's lackluster efforts to hold Union Carbide to account and provide compensation and medical care to the families of more than the initial eight thousand dead and estimated half-million wounded from the 1984 gas leak and chemical accident at a pesticide production plant in Bhopal. Corporate hands pointed their fingers at the government, and the government pointed its fingers back, each accusing the other publicly. Some remediation efforts had begun but all the promises to clean up and provide aid were literally standing still. I had interviewed some of the chronically ill, and the sight of their broken bodies and their broken spirits is something I will carry with me for the rest of my life. I had spoken with doctors who still treated those injured by their exposure to methyl isocyanate, who said their patients' suffering was infinite. I had quoted the head of an independent environmental group saying their testing indicated that the landfills were unstable and that toxic waste was filtering into the ground water supply: "Where do you go when everything around you is poisoned, and you're too sick to flee?" This purported "accident" had metastasized into a multigenerational environmental disaster. There were rumors of employee sabotage and industrial negligence.

Here at the war, the vendor's name is Mr. Mohammed, and he whispers what he's heard and seen. He's a good eavesdropper, an older man with a wiry frame, kind eyes that hide behind thick glasses. He often tips me off as to what is happening around town and around the region: a skirmish over water, a cholera outbreak, a dam collapse; a food shortage because of regional famine and war, because of neglect and indifference; a clash over boundaries on remote mountains or a desert that could lead to the war broadening its scope and size. Refugees pouring in. Roadside bombings and café bombings are infrequent, but the number of displaced persons increases each month. More and more, the [--------] government rounds up and arrests its critics, those dissenting from policies that place educational and workplace opportunities for girls and women out of reach. It seems like every Friday there are coordinated demonstrations across the region, and heavily armed police arrest as many protesters as they can, their wagons full of young men but some women too.

So many stories and not enough time. Rich again hammering me for doing some stories from afar. "You need to get in there, Keppler. We're not paying you to sit seaside and have lunch with your friends."

In my defense I see my colleagues from another newspaper, Johanna Becker and Margot Durand, on the job. We end up at the same sites because of the car bombings in Syria and in Lebanon, for an uprising in Iraq, for the continual violence in Gaza and the West Bank. So many dead, so many more wounded and displaced, homes destroyed as well as places of worship, roads and bridges rendered useless, marketplaces bombed and closed for good.

But Rich appreciates none of that reporting. He gloms on to the one day where we were on our way to something else, something less traumatic and mind-numbing. There is one photo of us eating lunch, and although it did look like a seaside hotel, it was a convincing backdrop used for a movie that was being shot in the area, a thriller picture. The movie production crew had run out of days and money and settled for the desert town on the outer rim of Jordan. After a quick lunch, Margot set the timer and we posed as if we were seaside, the salt air flavoring our skin. Rafiq waved in one of the photos. When the cameras were turned off, we peered behind the backdrop to find the Jabal al Adhriyat mountain range in the distance, a desert before us, a sea of sand. Margot had published the photographs through the wire along with others, which was the only way Rich had come to know about the impromptu meal.

The phone rings one evening. "Here I thought you'd disappeared," Ford says, his voice lazy, the words slurring. "Instead, I find out you're on vacation."

So Ford had seen the photo too. My heart beats rapidly at the sound of his voice. I had not spoken to him in more than a year, before I left for India. I had not seen him since just before Sebastian and I got married two years ago. I laugh at the sound of his drunken speech, and I hear in my own voice the sound of genuine delight. "Nice thought. But it's fiction." I wonder what he wants.

"Johanna looked good," he says. The volume of the TV in the background diminishes. "I hope you don't have any plans," he adds. "I can be there in a couple of days. You could show me around."

Ah. He is bored and alone and wants me. Rafiq walks in the door and points to the notebook in his hands. I look at his face. There is stress in his eyes, and I glance at the clock. Ninety minutes until deadline. In this moment, the love of the job outweighs my love for Ford. "Sorry, I can't."

The silence is so lengthy I think he's hung up. "Another time," he says finally.

I can hear the surprise in his tone. Usually, I don't refuse him. Of course, this is the first time Ford has asked since I got married. Sebastian's face flashes before my eyes and I'm glad I've said no. I tuck away this phone call, something I will later report to Virginia.

I don't miss any stories, but it takes a while for me to be out in front of the days, to feel as though I'm prepared for whatever may happen next. The adjustment is slower than in India. It doesn't help that Rich yells into the phone, that Hughes is somewhat displeased. I lean into what I know. I know how to make friends with the other reporters, and soon enough, because of them, I have a favorite tailor, I have a favorite café. My clothes from India work well here, long-sleeved kurti tops and baggy pants with deep pockets. I don't buy scarves from the marketplace, except as gifts that I tuck away in my bag to take home. I always have the gifted abaya with me, in case Rafiq and I are out in rural areas where the custom of women covering their hair in public is observed. I know how to cram, and soon enough I have several key phrases in Arabic memorized; Rafiq quizzes me as we drive.

Still, I love this life. I don't want to return to New York. It is a bad taste in my mouth. Dad leaves messages that I ignore, while my husband's remarks have been more precise. "It's been two years," Sebastian said during our call two days ago when he was in Madrid and I in [--------]. "Shouldn't we think about being in the same city, at least?"

I smiled into the receiver and projected as much warmth as I could muster. "Visit me on your days off," I said. "Come try out where I am." A rare afternoon off, and I'd whittle it away at the market, buy guavas and pygmy bananas, come back to the hotel, change into my pajamas, and watch a soccer match on TV.

"There's a wine festival coming up, and you'd love it," he countered. "I found this great beach and seaside hotel where we could stay."

I successfully demurred.

As much as I love Spain, where he is now, and New York, where he sometimes lives, and California, where his family had settled down, I am not ready to be domestic or domesticated. I love my job. The best parts are asking the pointed questions, beating the deadlines, making sense out of chaos and informing the public. I thought I had made my position clear when we eloped and then ran away to Italy.

"I have stuff to do," I had said, taking my seat in the gondola, the sun in my face, checking the trendy new watch Sebastian had bought me in the duty-free shop en route.

"*We* have stuff to do," he replied as the gondolier set off to see Venice. He took my hand in his and our shiny wedding bands clinked. "We will make it work."

The first few months after we married were loose and easy, a breeze through an apple orchard on a crisp fall day. We laughed between ourselves at the outside world's dismay, at its presumptions. We dropped in and out of each other's orbit, and our reunions were sweet. I felt desired: I frequently caught him staring at me, a smile on his face as if he had just opened the best gift.

I finally returned phone calls. "Mom is so mad that she couldn't give you a proper wedding," Adam said. Mom wouldn't talk to me that day, and no doubt Adam was seated across from our parents in their kitchen. No doubt they had been stewing over their coffees, snapping at each other.

"What's that?" I asked, still dizzy and delirious from my whirlwind courtship with Sebastian, our two-week tour of Venice, Positano, Pompeii, and Rome. "Proper for whom?"

Adam clucked, then chuckled. "Dad is happy you saved him money."

I heard their collective laughter in the background and knew that I'd be forgiven. One day.

Seb's parents had been more direct. "Is there a reason you couldn't wait?" his mother, a well-known philanthropist, asked. "Will I be a grandmother sooner than I anticipated?"

I laughed in reply but said nothing.

Then nine months passed and there was no baby, and everyone settled down, established a routine of protracted whines and complaints. It stopped being fun the first time I came home to New York to find Sebastian packing his suitcase, the stereo blasting "Immigrant Song." "I've got to leave in two hours," he said, shouting over Robert Plant's voice. "You could come back with me."

But I was tired from the journey and the stories about the serial killer in Florida and wanted something carefree. "You could work from here," I said.

"You made me promise never to ask you that." He stared with the eyes of a stranger. "So don't ask me."

He zipped up his luggage, took one long look around, left a bruising kiss on my lips, and then he was gone.

The ground beneath Sebastian and me has been shifting for the past several months in this similar fashion. His family's biological clock is ticking. Seb is the oldest, and they want grandchildren. But I am the only one inhabiting my body. Motherhood would be an irrevocable change, one I cannot afford as I shift and adapt from one assignment to another, from one place to another. Michael Reyn's wife gave birth to twins last year and it didn't change his life one bit—but his wife, Catherine, who had just received a plum assignment in Rome the year before, was sent back to New York and has been sidelined. I am tired of the phone calls every week, and I am tired of the circular arguments with Seb. I am tired that neither of us can change the other's mind. I am tired of his grand gestures—a room of pink roses delivered to me after a particularly nasty fight several hours ago. I wonder what Mr. Salim thinks is going on as he and the other hotel staff carry all the clear glass vases to the third floor. I call Seb to thank him for the flowers.

"Now will you come here?" he asks.

I survey the blooms and thorns all around me, the fragrance is of nostalgia. "Why send me something that's going to die?" I ask, picturing my parents and their rituals and gift giving. The sky outside sports the palette of a sunset.

Seb hangs up in response.

All roads lead back to Ford. My first big love, the one who taught me how to survive and thrive in the real-life journalism world. The one who has all the connections. The one who keeps getting away. It was because of Ford that I'd met my hero. I had met Johanna Becker years before, at an awards ceremony. I wasn't up for anything. I was on Ford's arm, wearing a twilight-blue sari and silver-colored sandals; my hair was twisted into a chignon. The sari had a hundred tiny mirrors stitched on the material and I felt as though I had a hundred eyes, looking everywhere, noting everything. Typically, these awards were held in Chicago and there was a grand ball. Typically, afterward, a group of us would change quickly and go out for deep dish and hotdogs, more than happy to wolf down Chicago-style dogs and grin at each other with celery seeds stuck in our teeth. But this year, someone in the management echelon had become ill and the whole affair shifted to New York. Another grand hotel ballroom of mirrored walls and chandeliers, seemingly a sea of circular tables—each with an oversized clear vase sporting yellow chrysanthemums—with white tablecloths and white plates and cheap crystal glasses, and white-cushioned straight-back chairs. From above the ballroom where the crowd was gathered at the mezzanine for wine and hors d'oeuvres, the layout below looked like a field of English daisies. Ford was going to accept an award for his in-depth coverage of a World Series MLB team and how they'd rallied around the pitcher whose six-year-old son was gravely ill but expected to survive. The Atlanta Braves claimed victory in six games, besting the Cleveland Indians. Ford had skillfully woven in the large-scale protests about the franchises' use of Native American names and mascots, and the Braves fans' obsessive use of the tomahawk chop during the home games.

I chose to ignore the pretty women who all lingered a moment too long over my escort, directed our attention out the window at the giant Union Jack flying over the British consulate next door. I chose to talk about the crown jewels and Big Ben and mused aloud, "Wouldn't it be lovely if the English government apologized and returned the Koh-i-Noor to India?"

Ford was amused, in high spirits in his tuxedo, as he tended to be when he was the center of attention.

"Darling, this sort of affair is just my cup of tea," I said, though I usually didn't like these sorts of events.

"Darling," he replied, his hand brushing the small of my back.

The organizer of the event, a stocky management type for a prestigious magazine, came toward us and I quickly stopped with the high tea and crumpets act. I was introduced to Johanna, who had a crispness about her, a green-eyed eagle dressed in Chanel. She had just returned from Bosnia. She was the print version of Christiane Amanpour and was to be honored for bringing the breakup of Yugoslavia, the war, the ethnic cleansing, and the regional destabilization to Western readers. Like Amanpour, she had defied her bosses and camped out in the region, and each week during the years-long siege of Sarajevo she humanized the death toll (eleven thousand and counting) in a city that just eleven years before had been the site of the Olympics.

"It's an honor to meet you," I said, shaking her hand. I meant it.

She grinned and her teeth gleamed like a row of perfect pearls.

On her left was a tall blond who looked familiar. Johanna introduced us. Margot. The newish photographer on Team Johanna would also receive an award, for her breathtaking photographs of the children of the war, tentative as they clutched their familiar toys, as they saw their childhoods disappear in a haze of guns and smoke and rubble and dust. We made small talk about their stays in New York, where they were headed off to next, Germany for Johanna.

"I think I'm still married," she said with a laugh. "Hopefully Dieter will be at the front door to greet me."

I laughed in return.

Margot was off to France to see her grandmother. "The milestone birthday is in a few years, but every year is a milestone," she said.

I nodded.

Margot leaned in and said, "I finally remember! I've seen you before."

I leaned back and smiled at her. I am a veritable encyclopedia of names and faces who has always been able to recall the connections, ever since I was a child. But I was certain we'd never been formally introduced. I looked away for a second and recalibrated with the couple standing by the bar. They were a two-journalist household, Christian and Candace: The wife worked for a business periodical and the husband was among the awardees this evening for his coverage of the financial crisis in Japan and China and the waves of consequences around the globe. To their left was a famous broadcast journalist, Kevin, who had covered the hooligans in England during a recent soccer match that had resulted in many injuries and deaths and his longtime girlfriend Leah, a writer for a big magazine in Florida. I turned back and looked at the organizer to whom Ford had introduced me three years before, John Parker Nelson. He had three names—like every NPR correspondent—but he was also the president of the body that organized these awards, a part-time academic, and the full-time head of a media think tank. "Where would that be?" I asked slowly.

Ford and John started talking sports, and Johanna chimed in about her experiences covering pop-up soccer games in the war-torn areas.

"University," Margot said. From her pocket, she produced two peppermints wrapped in clear plastic the shape of a pillow and offered me one.

I didn't remember her from J-school. Besides Virginia and me, there were only two other girls in the daily news track. I would have remembered her. I knew there were more girls in the media and technology track, though I thought I knew all the girls. She did look familiar, but I really didn't recall where I'd seen her, and this troubled me. My almost photographic memory had gotten me out of trouble many, many times.

I took the candy and nodded my thanks. "Sloan Hall?" I asked, the three-storied converted chemistry building where the bulk of the journalism classes were held. The professors had hobbit-like offices on the third floor, all with tiny picture windows. The writing classes were held generally on the second floor, and the basement and first floor had media labs and darkrooms and were generally reserved for the computers that were big and bulky and already out of date but were like what the bigger newspapers used. My mind hopped to my professor, Jane Monroe, and J-school from long ago: Keep smiling. Firm but pleasant. The first time I (or any of us women) complained about harassment or inequity I would be sent home. The blaming game was at an all-time high, especially at newspapers. I witnessed many a male supervisor "date" a female employee, and usually the women were fired or forced to quit when the relationship ended. I witnessed many an editor order a female reporter into their office and chastise her for wanting to leave early to pick up her child from soccer practice or the student infirmary. The most egregious example in Florida was when one of the editors, Derrick Anderson, pointed his finger one Tuesday afternoon at my colleague Angela Mason in front of ten people and called her into his office. The door was left open, and his voice reverberated as he told her she should have aborted her baby, that she had no business being a mother and wanting to continue work as a daily news reporter.

"And Cassidy Hall," Margot said. The nice auditorium where

the J-school held events, speakers, graduation exercises within the school. "I was a couple of years behind you. I was there when you won the Grantham Prize."

The Grantham Prize. Our senior year, Virginia and I had covered the appalling report released by a national research group, alleging that date rapes occurred so much more frequently than had been previously reported. That, in fact, the number of women who had experienced date rape was more likely to be one in three, and that statistic was conservative. We had found women to speak to, on the condition we change their names when we printed the story. There is so much stigma surrounding date rape and reporting assault, so much victim blaming and shaming.

Our editor had agreed, and Virginia and I decided to give every girl the same name, a name that didn't belong to any of the women we interviewed: Lisa. We gave them all the same home state, and we made them all local, since none of the women had grown up anywhere near the university or this side of the Mason-Dixon Line. So there was Lisa D., a senior from Wilmington; and Lisa M., a freshman from Fuquay-Varina; and Lisa T., a sophomore from Asheville; and Lisa J., from Greensboro; and finally, Lisa P., a junior from Pittsboro. We had interviewed far more women than we could quote—and naming each of the women Lisa had this magical effect of inclusivity and empathy: We were all Lisa. Their stories were sadly similar: Men they had decided to trust, men whom they judged to be safe, had betrayed them in the worst possible way—and they didn't know how to recover, how to walk among the living again, without fear. The lede I wrote for the sidebar, a story about numbers: "The next time you see a group of ten girls at lunch or at the park, know that at least three of them have most likely been sexually assaulted." From that time I learned from Virginia to walk down a night-darkened street with a hand balled over the bows of my keys, the blades jutting forward as a potential weapon,

"I'm sorry we didn't know each other," I said, looking down to make sure the pleats of my sari hadn't unraveled.

"Plenty of time for that," Margot replied, grinning. She held out her palm and I almost laughed as I placed the empty wrapper in it. "I don't think you have any pockets."

Ford leaned into me, murmured in my ear, "Darling, I think they're getting started."

I wait at this corner for Rafiq and Zahra. We have another appointment with the consulate. They are uncharacteristically late. I look at my watch again and realize I'm uncharacteristically early. We are attempting to finish the application that the newspaper started with Rafiq more than two years ago, to get him (and now his new bride) safely into the United States. I'll watch the embassy staffer go through the machinations of explanations and we'll all collectively refrain from rolling our eyes. We know the drill, and we have been here on several occasions. Nothing changes. Hours are wasted.

I look around but there is no café to duck into and grab a quick cup of something hot. As I wait, I count the number of women walking with their children (seven) and the number of shops with their doors open (thirteen). I look closer at the string of shops but nothing appears to be a coffee- or teahouse. The sky is a never-ending blue. There is a sense of peace: people walking about, living their daily lives, the air surprisingly clear and the ambient noise at a minimum, a few voices, a child's laugh, a bit of traffic a couple of blocks over, and in the distance several vehicles sounding their horns. I check my watch again and breathe in, calm. Then three black jeeps with neither license plates nor discernible identifying features pull onto the street, wheels squealing in unison, and seconds later, men in black clothing with mirrored glasses and bandannas over their faces jump out. In one fluid motion they grab a modestly clad woman and her two children off the sidewalk—push them into the middle vehicle, then speed away. The shrieks of women and children resound. Cries of protest and screams echo on the street as normalcy shatters. The cars are gone, and several men have run into the street. One runs after the cars, but they vanish. I cut across to the bookshop where the owner who had been no more than a few feet from the woman and her two children is sweeping. I identify myself and ask him what he saw.

"I've seen her, the little girl in the pink dress with a big smile," he says, pointing ahead on the left. His English is somewhat fractured. "She goes to the school over there."

I thank him, then ask, "Does this happen often here?"

The shopkeeper stares past me, broom in hand, but does not reply.

I thank him again and begin to run in the direction he indicated. I know the drill in America but not here. In America, when someone is stolen off the street the best chance of finding him or her is in the first hour. Years ago, the FBI agent working the case of a carjacking turned child kidnapping (the baby was asleep in a car seat as the father went into a gas station mini-mart to buy Cheerwine and a roll of Sweet Tarts) told me that at the press briefing. The first hour is when the perpetrators make the most mistakes. After that, as the clock strikes into the future, the likelihood of finding the abducted unharmed and returning them safely to their family diminishes significantly. (At that point twenty-nine minutes had flown by. The baby's photo was aired, a description of the car was broadcast. The father was in the middle of an acrimonious divorce with a socialite and had taken the baby boy for the night. Fingers wagged and pointed, and the car thief heard the news on the car radio, no doubt. Several minutes later, the thief ditched the baby by a twenty-four-hour car wash restroom and ditched the vehicle at a construction site by the highway and a mall and disappeared into the moonless night.)

Rafiq and Zahra pull up across the street.

I called out that a woman and two children were abducted moments before, describe the vehicles.

"We passed three cars," Zahra says, adding that they took the highway and disappeared. Rafiq makes a sign to park the car, his face fraught with worry.

I point toward the school.

Zahra's eyes are huge on her face. Her voice is serene, though, when she says she will find a phone and postpone the interview at the consulate.

Moments later, Rafiq, his face shiny with perspiration, joins me at the front door of the school. It is propped open to give the strong odor of glue a chance to escape. We walk in and see children elbow-deep in an art project, birthing papier-mâché animals. A woman wearing a powder-blue headscarf and black-rimmed glasses approaches.

We introduce ourselves, ask if she heard anything moments before down the street, and tell her what the man at the shop said. "Is there a student absent today?"

She hesitates. "Maryam and Nylah, they are sisters."

"Their mother brings them?" Rafiq asks, his face shiny with effort.

"Their aunt," she says. "Their mother works."

Rafiq's face sags a little.

"Do they always come at this time?" I get Rafiq to ask.

She nods. "They are late this morning."

I mumble to Rafiq that I wish we had a photo.

He nods imperceptibly and asks softly but the woman shakes her head.

No.

Zahra is standing at the threshold of the school, and the woman looks past Rafiq toward the form at the door. Her face brightens in recognition.

Rafiq and I turn toward Zahra as she asks, "I thought Hanan would come."

The woman's face crumples a little. "Your friends here are asking about her nieces."

Rafiq says, "I'm her husband."

I ask Rafiq and Zahra, "You know Hanan? Hanan is the aunt?"

Zahra says, "You know her too." From months before, she says. Hanan was the social worker with the NGO trying to get more tents and water at the camps.

I look at Rafiq, whose face is impassive but still sweaty. I stare past Zahra and see a police vehicle, then a few uniformed men walking on the other side of the boulevard.

Zahra clicks her tongue to the roof of her mouth. "Wait," she says, and she takes her purse out, unclasps the main hook, and rifles through the contents. After a long moment, she pulls out a pair of photographs and a piece of paper. She plants herself in between Rafiq and me. The top photo is of Zahra with what appears to be her father and Rafiq and a young relative. There is another photo from the same day, with people gathered around a table eating dessert. The piece of paper is a newsletter, and next to a headline in Arabic is a picture of a woman in a headscarf and several children clustered around her. I recognize her immediately. I met her months ago. How the war had shrunk her, physically, emotionally.

"Is this recent? Why would anyone take her?" I ask.

A policeman walks in. The room goes silent, the children all stop where they are and watch.

Zahra stuffs the photos back in her bag.

The policeman addresses Rafiq first, who answers with bewilderment in his voice that we have all just arrived. I ask Rafiq if he can get Hanan's address.

It is Zahra who slyly confirms where Hanan's family lives. The policeman dismisses us, and we leave after he extracts a promise that we cannot name the school or the young girls until he gives us permission. We agree. The teachers and children resume their activities.

Back in the car, I ask Zahra, "When did you see her last?"

"Two weeks ago," Zahra says. "We are supposed to meet tomorrow." There is a donation of women's sanitary napkins and other menstruation products coming from France. Hanan had made a list of the camps and other shelters where the supplies were low and needed assistance. Zahra had previously held Hanan's position but now worked at the local university, in the office of the university president.

"I'm sorry," I say, then ask as gently as I can: "Maybe we could speak with her family?"

Zahra says, "I don't think they will be interested." She pauses. "They are very different from Hanan." Wealthy. Conservative.

"We can try," Rafiq says, shrugging. "I know a pla—"

I put a finger to my lips and the phrase dies in his mouth.

I keep my interview questions short. I am here to assess Hanan's family life and to get the photo that I know Hughes will want. The teenage brother, dressed in blue jeans and a plain black T-shirt, does not stand up when we are welcomed to the sitting room, introduced. Instead, he drags a leg over the arm of the chair and says, "Ciao." In his hand is a comic book of some kind, though he is too far away for me to make out what he's perusing. I can tell both parents are astonished at his rudeness and that both want to say something, but they don't want to say anything in front of me. I'm astonished at their stoicism—how they do not cry, how they are stiff like cardboard cutouts. They order the servants to fetch snacks.

In between sips of tea, I ask them about their grandchildren. Hanan's parents beam with pride. Her father speaks of his grandson Omar, and how their daughter Farah, who works at the French consulate, has taken him to a soccer tournament. That is why Hanan was taking Farah's other children to school. Hanan's mother speaks of Farah as well and her devotion to her children, her many kindnesses. Farah's husband died just after Nylah was born, at the central market bombing when three were killed, sixty-five were injured, and one shopkeeper lost his leg.

"Farah is on her way home," the father says. "She and my grandson will arrive tonight."

I ask about Hanan, and they take turns speaking of her commitment to Maryam and Nylah. "She is like their mother," the father says.

Zahra's pager sounds and she asks to use the phone.

Rafiq is quiet. He does not touch his tea.

"I wish she would live here again with us," the mother says, her voice cracking like glass on the pavement. "She is so independent."

I know enough to know it's not customary for unmarried women to live alone. I ask how far her apartment is from here. Does she take them to school every day?

The father's face sets in stone. "Ten minutes. She stays with her friend." He turns toward his wife. "Simi? Sammi?"

"Yes," the mother says, blushing. Today was her husband's turn to take the girls but he was running late and Hanan volunteered.

I wait for them to say something, anything—voice their fears, their concerns. But they do not say anything, they are lost in their own thoughts as they sip their tea. We fall into an uncomfortable silence. I'm not uncomfortable, I am used to outwaiting the people to whom I've posed hard questions. But clearly, they are waiting for me to leave. It is strange that they do not voice concerns about their daughter or their granddaughters. I catch the father glancing at the clock on the wall and its incessant ticking.

Zahra returns, gently asks on my behalf for a family photo, and the father is quick to ask the son to bring something from the other room, his demand echoing to the tall ceiling. Reluctantly, the boy leaves and returns with a white photo album and hands it to his father. He flips through the pages and pulls out two pictures: one of Hanan with Nylah and Maryam in her lap on the couch now occupied by her parents; another of Hanan in a sage-green headscarf smiling into the camera. At first they offer me both photos, but then the wife murmurs something to the husband. He offers me only the photo of all three of them, in which Hanan's face is partially obscured by Maryam's hair.

"You'll let us know anything you find out, yes?" the mother asks Rafiq.

"Of course," Zahra answers for him. "She's my friend."

I leave them my phone number at the hotel.

Rafiq and I say goodbye and thank them again for their time. Zahra says something to the mother, and they briefly embrace and clasp hands. It is the teenager who jumps up and escorts us to the door. I glance quickly at his hands and find the *Asterix* comic there. We walk back to the car. "What do you think?" Rafiq asks after we exit the gate, the security guard far behind us.

"I don't know," I say, which is my way of saying *I'm not discussing it with you, I don't want my personal opinions to cloud my judgment or color the story*. "What do you think?" I ask, knowing Rafiq only asks when he has something to share.

"They are a typical rich family, they have connections, they have friends, they have alliances," he says. "But something is not . . . correct."

I nod.

Zahra says the page she received was from her friend at the embassy, the daughter of a power broker in the city and in the know about everyone. "The mother is the second wife," Zahra says. "Her son came three months after the first wife died." She pauses. "She's the rich one. That's Hanan's stepmother's house."

I am reminded of the football coach I once did a story on in California. The young girl he married was still in her late teens. Six months later the baby girl came, and of course that tow-haired blond baby resembled the football coach. It was a feel-good story about this coach who had enormous success on the national stage but decided to retire and lead a high school team, settle down with this new wife, and raise their kid. I am reminded of this story because the football coach moved into his young wife's house; she came from a very wealthy family. Something vaguely odd about their situation. But also, it was something completely normal as I consider America, how the older white man gets the second and third chance, gets to start a new life. How if it were an older woman and a younger man, that would be the center of all the gossip. That it is the wife's house is an interesting twist but irrelevant to this story. "How far are we from Hanan's apartment?"

"A few minutes," Rafiq answers quickly, and Zahra's mouth hardens.

"My friend from university, his brother lives in the next building," Rafiq adds even more quickly.

Zahra's smile is thin. "I have an appointment, so drop me by the shopping center and I will make my way."

Rafiq frowns and then smiles.

I am relieved. "Okay." And moments later, my goodbye is warm.

Zahra wordlessly produces an apartment key and hands it to Rafiq before she walks away.

The police have yet to arrive. "I feel very uncomfortable," I say to Rafiq. "It would be one thing for me to do this in my own country and somehow talk my way out of it, but here I feel like I will be deported or jailed."

Rafiq laughs without making a sound. "I will take full responsibility."

I agree, mostly because I do not want this to be another example where I missed a story in the way I had missed the destruction of the Buddhas of Bamiyan.

The flat is empty, but there are telltale signs it has been occupied. It is clear no police have yet searched the place. A stack of plates and a small hill of cups clutter the deep sink. Breadcrumbs of some kind litter the table, and there is the faint odor of kebabs in the kitchen. The fridge door is slightly ajar. I go to close it, but Rafiq beats me there and, instead, opens the door wide. The light inside the fridge flickers, casting a poor strobe over the six-pack of eggs, what looks to be a container of labneh, and a trio of eggplants pocked on one side. He closes the door and opens the freezer above. It is empty, but there is a monster growing as stalagmites and stalactites of ice inch toward each other like a mouth full of sharp teeth. It occurs to me that this apartment belies its simplicity—the fridge is scuffed and its logo removed, but it's clearly American since the icebox has a separate door and, now that I notice it, a place by the front handle to get cold water and ice. The fabric on the low-framed couch is almost velvet, and I remember Margot showing me a photograph of her sister Camille's living room outside Paris. This couch is a replica but in blue. A row of planters hangs on the windowsill facing the back with herbs I don't recognize alongside some mint.

The walls are empty.

Rafiq says, "There used to be a framed painting above the couch." He points. "There. It was a poster. Miró."

Hanan is a fan of Miró, he says. Lately she's been selling some of her Miró-inspired art at the marketplace.

"How many times were you here before?" I ask him, but Rafiq has turned away and is inspecting the hall closet.

I walk into the bedroom where the bed is unmade and there are clothes strewn on the floor. There is no evidence that Hanan has a roommate. Another white photo album splayed on the floor, pages open. I glance around and see the imprint of luggage on the rug. The sun shines through the curtains and the nightstand glistens, clean. I flip through the photos, and they are mostly of Hanan as a child with her mother (same nose, same smile) and her brother or cousin. The photographs are captioned and span time: Hanan as a child in Beirut, Hanan in Jordan, Hanan in the war. There is a square missing—I wonder if it's a photo of Hanan then or now, I wonder if it's a photo of someone Hanan is looking for. I hear a noise in the bathroom and freeze. Rafiq is nowhere, and I call out, "Hanan, are you there?"

I hear the scratching noise again, then I make my way to the bathroom door. I knock a few times, but no one answers. I open the door and see movement out of the left corner, near the shower. I turn my head and there is a cat, her collar sports a nametag: Habibi. I sigh in relief.

Rafiq enters the bedroom and asks, "Did you find her?"

"Just Habibi," I say, pointing at the cat with the look of a miniature Bengal tiger. I remember Hanan telling me about Habibi while I covered a story about the camps on the outskirts of the city, how the cat thought she was a dog and wanted to be walked on a leash. I remember that young woman, full of ideas and attitude, unafraid of anything. I remember how she and Rafiq touched a second too long. They had fooled me with their facial expressions, but clearly, they had been involved.

"Oh yes," Rafiq says, sliding by me and picking up the cat. He rubs the small space between her eyes, and she purrs. "I'd forgotten about her."

Habibi meows, and I say, "I wonder if she's hungry."

Rafiq looks up, a sheen of pain over his face. "I'll take her home. Zahra can look after her."

I want to argue but I have no alternative. "I'll go find her bowl," I say, trying to murmur.

"Last time I checked the bowls were under the table in the kitchen," Rafiq says absentmindedly, his cheek close to Habibi's head.

How much is he hiding from me?

We hear sirens the next block over, and Rafiq signals it's time to leave. We go through the house and shut the doors and windows so that it resembles the way we found it, and then we exit the back door to the alley across the courtyard. Habibi is in the front pocket of Rafiq's backpack where the mesh paneling is. We find ourselves at the tail end of a marketplace with the police cars whizzing past us.

They turn left instead of right.

"They weren't even coming for her," I say. This is not even a priority, and she's the daughter of someone important.

He shrugs, throws on his sunglasses.

"We should visit her place of work," I say.

"Isn't it getting late?" he asks, pointing to his watch. Time is hurtling toward the late afternoon.

I tell him I need him to call and get the ministry's data: how many people have been taken this year alone and if they have any data going back. I make a mental note to check the database and then call New York and see if Mrs. Park, the nice librarian, can dig up any stories from David Richards about kidnappings.

We come down to the center of town and go into the marketplace.

I buy a bag of oranges, my hands trembling, and an extra bag and split the fruit with him, just in case someone asks us later what we were doing in this part of town. I hail a taxi, and Rafiq drives Habibi away.

I call the NGO offices to get their dismayed reaction and a quote. Later, Rafiq comes by the hotel to show me some photographs he'd taken so we can choose which ones to send to Hughes. A uniformed policeman approaches us in the lobby and hands us papers wordlessly. I recognize him as one of the three I had seen in the morning. The policeman shakes hands with Rafiq, then speaks rapidly in Arabic about the case and I miss much of it. Rafiq glances at me a couple of times and I catch a quick nod: He will fill me in. The policeman walks through the rotating door and then circles back and stands before us again. "Will you use my name in your article?" His English is suddenly excellent.

I cannot discern if he wants me to or not. I opt for the truth. "Not unless you provide more information."

I can tell he is astounded that I am not begging him for more information. I remember Hughes's advice about outwaiting a source and asking for something just once. The ransom note. I look just past his shoulder and wait, remembering Rafiq's advice to not stare directly at the police.

A couple of photographers enter the lobby, boisterous and laden with gear.

Finally, the policeman fumbles through his jacket pocket and pulls out the purported ransom note covered in plastic.

"Perfect," Rafiq says, and he opens his satchel for his camera.

"Is it real?" I ask.

"I showed the father," the policeman says, adding that the parents are influential people.

Rafiq nods imperceptibly, then sneezes. I thank the policeman again and say, "Do you have a direct line so I can call you if I have any more questions?"

He pulls out a card, then leaves. Rafiq and I take the escalator to the mezzanine to write the story. "Where's the cat?" I ask.

"In the car," he says. "I bought her some milk."

Hours later I am done: a story about a woman taking her nieces to school and all three are abducted in broad daylight, how commonplace it has become, how there are a hundred questions but few answers. New York provided a story three years before that David Richards had filed about the rise in Westerners and journalists being kidnapped but that the [--------] government had not really been keeping statistics of any kind. Anecdotally, though, it was not a high number, and there is no data being collected about how many women and children, especially girls, disappear each year. (This is just like America, where there is little or no data about the number of missing or murdered of several groups of people, most especially Indigenous women.) Rafiq confirms details through the ministry's office. Then he calls the policeman one last time before I file. Nothing has changed. Rafiq sends me the photos of the street where Hanan and her nieces were taken as well as the ransom note before he leaves for Zahra's. I consider the ease with which I received the information, the policeman's insistence about the veracity of the ransom note; even Rafiq's enthusiasm and the way he knew the inside of Hanan's apartment so well. I was lucky I had Professor Monroe as my first teacher. She was J-school old-school, the first African-American woman to teach journalism at the university. She was an old broad and she never did anything but pound the facts at us. Don't write cutesy, she warned us, the four girls in the class. Write as though you're a man. Declarative sentences. Ask a lot of questions. Ask five times the questions you have room for in your story. Most of the work you're going to do is explanatory unless you can land a job as a police reporter or a court reporter. Most of the job is explaining the rules and how someone has either excelled at them or broken them and what the consequences will be. If it doesn't smell right, exclude it.

The policeman didn't confirm the ransom note's authenticity. He claimed he showed it to Hanan's father, but I didn't witness this interaction. I think of Hanan's parents, I consider her apartment. Something doesn't look right; something doesn't smell right. I decide not to include the ransom demand or the policeman in my story. I submit the photos of the street and Hanan and her nieces but not the note. The lede: "An NGO aid worker and her two nieces were abducted yesterday morning as they walked in the posh Al-Kittab Avenue neighborhood of [--------], blocks away from the U.S. and French embassies. Armed, masked men used three unmarked black cars to kidnap them near the elementary school where the first- and second-grader are students." I do not want to talk to Hughes just yet. I go up to my room and lock the door behind me and take a hot shower, order room service.

A local newspaper prints the ransom note the very next day. In the hotel lobby, Rafiq and I hover over the page and a pair of men read over our shoulders. I glance at them, recognize the one on the left as Ali, a reporter for UPI, but not the second man. "What do you think?" I ask aloud. My stomach is suddenly in knots, and I want to throw up.

"Did you send this to Hughes?" Rafiq asks, then chews his bottom lip.

I shake my head. "There's something off about this."

Ali laughs suddenly and murmurs something to his companion. The second man puts his finger on the page. "It is from a film," he says. His smile illuminates his slender face.

"The note?" I ask.

"A local film," the man says, then murmurs something in Arabic.

Rafiq translates: an Arabic adaptation of the Meg Ryan movie *Proof of Life*.

I breathe out, and the nausea recedes.

Ali taps Rafiq on the shoulder and hands him another paper,

turned to an inside page: a photograph of the policemen outside Maryam's and Nylah's school. "Doesn't he look like the actor from the mystery film?"

There is a commotion in the hotel, raised voices, someone shoves a reporter to the ground and runs away. Without answering Ali, Rafiq runs over and helps the reporter up.

Ali says, "Don't worry."

Soon after, Rafiq and I are in the conference room, two different local papers spread out before us on the table. Victory courses through my body and I feel like I can fly.

Hughes calls early, and Mr. Salim transfers the call to the conference room. "Did you know about this?"

"Yeah," I say as casually as I can. The sunshine streaks across the wall through the gaps in the blinds. "He tried to sell me late yesterday. I wasn't buying."

"Way to be frugal," Hughes says.

That is a great compliment from Hughes. Rich's silence is a compliment too. I am lucky, but I don't have to tell my editors that. Hughes and Rich talk about something else.

Rafiq, abashed, leans over and asks, "How did you know?"

I smile at him. "How did you not know?"

Rafiq pales. "I don't see many films."

I look at him, register the tension in his eyes, and then put every bad thought out of my head. "I hadn't really seen the original film either," I say. "Just a few minutes on an airplane last year."

Rafiq asks again, louder: "How did you know?" Hughes and Rich fall silent.

"It was far too convenient," I say. "When something is too good to be true, it usually falls in the fairy tale department."

Just like the long-ago American baby in the car seat, the two girls, Nylah and Maryam, are dropped off, found safe and unharmed at the gates of a famous garden and park, next to a castle and fort built in the fifteenth century. There is no sign of Hanan. Neither the family nor the actual police issue a statement once the family has the girls back. There is a war in the region: so many large-scale protests, arrests, roadside bombings that Hanan's continued disappearance falls away.

Hughes says, "I want a short that the girls are back home."

That's it. Move on.

I hear about the girls' return only because Zahra mentions it in passing—she is at the hotel, having breakfast with Rafiq at the beginning of the day.

"There is a party to welcome them home, but we are not invited," she says. Everyone wants the story to go away, Zahra says as she smooths the soft green sleeve of her blouse.

Perspiration beads on Rafiq's forehead and above his upper lip. He retrieves a handkerchief from his pocket and wipes his face.

Before I file the short, I want to interview the girls, see if they remember anything at all. No one answers the phone. I tell Rafiq twice about my proposed destination. Nothing happens as he looks away or decides just then that his shoelaces are untied and in need of more stringent tying. On the third try, he drives me reluctantly. There is a hum emanating from inside the home. Clearly, there are many people inside celebrating the girls' return. I try knocking on their door, but no answer. I want to push my way in, but Rafiq shakes his head. "Maybe in America this is okay, but not here," he says.

I think to myself, *It's okay to enter her empty apartment, but it's not okay to enter a house full of people who know her?* Rafiq and I step back onto the street, and I think I see the girls' mother, Farah, through the window, but she quickly retreats from the light and vanishes.

I run into Zahra again, outside the hotel and near a lovely café. I'm killing a little time trying to recall the names and news outlets of everyone going in and out of the hotel doors while waiting for Margot to return from dropping off Johanna at the airport. We have plans to shop at the new Western-style department store that opened recently. The concierge told us the store had an excellent candy selection. There are the Reuters guys, Jean among them, and the couple who belong to Agence France-Presse, the Bernards. The UPI reporter exits the taxi and waves at me before hustling into the hotel. Ali.

I have given Rafiq the afternoon off after our long trek to see the archaeological ruins excavated near the Syrian border. The photos are dramatic, and Rafiq and I share a byline—he received named credit for his photos. The governments were cooperative for the first time since the eighties. Although Syria had no direct claim over the ruins and the Kurds every third day were not recognized as a sovereign territory or sovereign nation, there was still excitement in the air. It was palpable. Even the hardcore reporters who were never excited about anything were excited, and it was a pleasure to be there. Zahra had wanted to come along, and I had said yes. The three of us had a good time: This was not doom and gloom. For us this was a moment when we could celebrate being on planet Earth, being around people who were not challenging history but were instead embracing it and beginning to learn from it. The air was crisp in the early morning hours, and the archaeologists and all their student assistants worked diligently and methodically and quickly just in case some masters of bureaucratic machinery changed their minds. The lede: "Four teams of world-leading archaeologists raced each other and the clock to unearth an ancient city before Syrian government officials changed their minds and revoked their visas."

Presumably today Rafiq and Zahra are going to do some family activities. But then I spot Zahra walking casually from the newspaper kiosks straight toward me. I had literally watched Rafiq depart fifteen minutes before. I do not want to get him into trouble with his new wife, but I do not want to lie to her. I smile as she approaches. There is something about the look on her face, the look in her eyes. Has she been crying?

"Is Rafiq here?" she asks. Her voice is not as modulated as the previous day.

"No, he's not back yet," I answer, and this seems to satisfy her in a way, like I know that he has gone on an errand of some kind, though I know nothing of the sort.

"I have been ill because of Habibi," she says.

Cat allergies are common in America. Truth be told, since I've been in the region, I haven't seen too many house cats or dogs. I did see an aquarium, a rather large one, at the children's hospital. I surmise there are pets there, but I hadn't really run into pet lovers yet. "Someone is fostering the cat?" I ask deliberately, using a word she may not know.

Zahra shrugs half-heartedly; apparently Omar, Hanan's nephew, is in love with the cat.

"Oh, I see," I say.

Her eyes look past me and brighten: There is Rafiq coming out of the hotel as if he'd never left at all.

Three

[SEPTEMBER 3, 2001] — IT WAS VIRGINIA ANNE LAWSON ON THE first day of J-school who shared her sandwich with me at the disorganized welcoming. The picnic was already running late, and there was no food to be seen on the front lawn of Cassidy Hall. It was Virginia who introduced herself as "I'm going to be your next best friend. I can just feel it." And it was true. She was brunette then, with a streak of blond running to the side like lightning. She's taller than me, in better shape than me. She ran all the time, didn't mind staying up late, had odd jobs that were overnight, slept until noon, and sweet-talked the registrar into having all her classes fall between one and five in the afternoon. We watched *MacGyver* together on Wednesday nights and played bar golf. She drank everyone under the table. Our senior year we roomed together.

I was the one who was in touch more, though, after graduation. During the four years we were in school together we were inseparable. For all the projects everyone knew to pair us because no matter what happened, Virginia would always find a way to work with me. Yet we landed at different newspapers right after graduation. We intersected in Florida for a while, and then it took us years of hopping from place to place to get to the same newspaper, now in New York. Since we left college, it has always been my turn to catch up with her to find out about her boyfriends and all the stories she was working on. Virginia Lawson. She belonged to them and everyone who was in her orbit: her work friends, her gym friends, her club friends. She came from a big family but never talked about them except to say "I refuse to go back to the farm." To the best of my knowledge there was no farm; there was a large family somewhere in northern Maryland. Her father had some kind of government job. Her mother taught fifth-graders.

Virginia was the second oldest child and the oldest daughter. I didn't meet her mother until graduation; her father didn't come. Her mother looked just like her—or, rather, Virginia looked just like her mother, Danielle. "We could've been sisters," her mother quipped. My parents said hello and invited everyone to lunch before they left to tour the campus, but Mrs. Lawson declined, saying they were double booked. Her daughter's face was suddenly aflame. Virginia's mom was useful and energetic, packing up Virginia's books and papers with speed—and apologetic that the father was suddenly called away on business.

"He's so disappointed," Danielle said, tucking a loose strand of hair behind her ear.

Virginia's face fell. "That's okay, Mom."

Then she refused to talk about it anymore. Her younger siblings were there too. They were polite and shook my hand. I think the very youngest sister is named Claire. She said, "Sissy talks about you." I didn't know what to say except thank you, since Virginia never really talked about her siblings, except to say that she had had enough of the livestock and she was tired of all the chores.

I call Virginia the first Sunday in September.

She answers on the first ring. "Guess what?" she says by way of hello.

"Chicken butt," I say without thinking. It is almost dinnertime, and my stomach rumbles; the sun has set but there is a pink-orange stain in the sky. I remember I ate lunch, but I forget what I ate several hours ago.

She giggles and then says there's a think tank that's opening a new office in the World Trade Center. "They asked me to come in and give a talk. The great John Parker Nelson called me himself."

I remember meeting him once, while on Ford's arm. Parker Nelson was a news god, a thinker. Like me, Virginia is tired of people like Rich and the constant hassle; and unlike me, she wants to teach eventually, and she wants to go into some kind of nonprofit work or perhaps become some kind of watchdog for journalism. "I definitely have ideas," she says, "so many ideas! I think my talents and my anger and frustration are being wasted in the newsroom."

My turn to giggle. "When's the interview?" I ask.

"A week from Tuesday—doesn't start till nine but you know me: I'm hyperpunctual, I'll show up a half an hour early, get something to drink, find the best bathroom, and then I'll be all ready to go."

Hughes calls shortly after, as if he has been eavesdropping. "Look, I want to do something nice for all of us. We've been working hard. If you could come back today or tomorrow, bring Rafiq with you if you must, then I can book us a table at the Trade Center the following Tuesday. At Wild Blue. We can have a late brunch. I'll bring a surprise guest."

I don't want to out Virginia, but I don't believe in coincidences. "What makes you so eager to go to the Trade Center?"

Hughes chuckles. "I'm the one who made the introductions for Virginia, Rita."

I breathe in a big gulp of relief. "Oh, good."

"I'll try to get her to stick around, and we can all catch up." He pauses. "What do you say?"

The building shakes and the light fixtures above my head creak and groan. "There's shelling," I say. "I have to go! I'll do my best. I think I should stay here and cover this one," I say. The paint cracks all along the ceiling. "The next flight that I can get is Tuesday. I'll just take that one, but I'll try for an earlier one."

"I've already made the reservation," he says, and the static on the telephone increases to an almost unbearable pitch.

I cup my hand on the receiver and count to ten in Bengali, then say loudly, "Let me just cover what the fuck is going on right now outside my hotel. I'll find Rafiq and we'll make a plan."

He hears the hesitation in my voice. "How's your mom feeling? Rita, have you spoken with her?"

"Yes," I say. "She really wants me to come home and I want to come home." I speak as convincingly as I can.

Hughes hawks. "Your dad called . . . he really wants you home."

I open and close my mouth twice. The building shakes as if hit by a powerful earthquake. "I'm in the middle of something right now. You should understand that."

He says, "Just don't want the time to slip."

"Don't worry, I'm not wasting away eating M&M's and watching TV," I say.

He laughs.

I say goodbye and hang up, run downstairs using the interior stairwell, and get Mr. Salim to help me find Rafiq.

I took these jobs as a way to tell the truth even though I knew the filters were white men who didn't know what it was like to fear the street, to be objectified, to be sought as a fantasy, to be heckled, to be catcalled, to be viewed as an outsider, to be blamed for everything going wrong in a stranger's life. I knew the drill even in J-school, when I'd come back with a quote from an old woman or an immigrant man. No matter their years of life experience or the string of letters and degrees after their last name, my male peers and the old white male professors asked me, constantly, "Who is this person? What makes this person an expert? Why can't you just interview somebody normal?"

But it was Ford who first trusted my judgment. He complimented me openly after my first court story, day six of the attempted murder trial of the former beauty queen who had allegedly tried to run over her husband/manager with their Italian coupe after she had found him in the arms of a younger woman. "I liked it," he said, the editors within earshot. "You made her human, instead of a soap opera star."

I blushed a little, and soon after he asked me out.

Ford was older, divorced, with a body of prize-winning stories under his belt. Handsome like a movie star version of a reporter, he exuded fitness and good health. He was funny and calm, with bright blue eyes. He said, "You've got to fight for your perspective, especially in this newsroom, kiddo." This was our first date: at a charming Greek café on the Gulf Coast, the two of us nursing beers and sharing a basket of fries. I had just finished a day-long romp through the Everglades with DEA agents and watched them seize thousands of pounds of marijuana. It was a dog-and-pony show for the media, but it was still interesting to watch. Ford had just finished a preseason MLB roundup and coverage of a preseason game between two New York teams. In the beginning we spent so many hours at the café, at the nearby beach, making out like lovestruck teenagers in the back of his car, watching the sun rise. "I'm crazy about you," he said to me over and again, but never used the word *love*.

I nursed my beer. "How do *you* do that?"

"I yes them to death," he said, flashing a grin. "I agree with everything they say and then do it all my way. The key to success is to come back with a good story."

I smiled.

"You're doing fine." He returned the smile. "You already know what to do."

And with those words of advice, I redoubled my efforts and landed again and again.

Ford was the first person who saw me as human in journalism.

I've made my share of mistakes, but my intent has never been to disparage someone. Professor Monroe had drilled into us our responsibilities to the public. But because I was stubborn, because I was so good at my job and I was rarely wrong, I could not let go of Ford, at least for very long. I was good at leaving him at the crucial moment just before I lost my nerve, good at goodbye gestures, good at making myself promises, good at walking away—literally walking out of his apartment, with my head held high and my eyes on the frozen stars and the various phases of the liquid-yellow moon. Time after time, after another egregious betrayal on his part. As good as I was at leaving, I was better at returning to him after he'd apologized, yet again, and promised, most sincerely, to do better.

"Sweetheart, I won't let you down," he'd said more than once, more than ten times, his hands holding mine gently, his blue eyes filled to the brim but not spilling over, our bodies on the expensive couch in my furnished apartment, so close, as if our limbs and our clothes were knitted together. The kisses were plentiful, and the room spun when I came up for air. I was so good at believing him in those moments. I was so good at preserving the status quo.

But after two weeks or sometimes a month, all the while he was solicitous with me, the pink roses and the sweet notes tucked in between my windshield and the windshield wiper, Ford dated other women. He lied about it unconvincingly: "Don't start, she's a colleague." All the times I caught him in those years, all those women leaving the messages, and the receipts for restaurants and little hotels on the coast, these women showing up at the newspaper parties, and him getting drunk and me leaving for home alone. Later, getting the calls from other reporters at the parties: "Are you okay?" echoing. As reporters, none of them spared me the details: the blow-by-blow descriptions of how he and this one woman sucked face or, when the clock struck midnight, took off their clothes and skinny-dipped in the executive editor's heated pool. He could get away with everything. He was so damn smart. Every few months, it seemed, he would win these accolades, be publicly recognized as a fine writer and journalist.

Everyone tolerated this behavior.

Everyone, including me. Most especially me.

The first time I did something was the only time I'd done something. I was the last to see it, of course. I was practically living with him by then, and I excused it all. The late nights when he didn't return long after deadline or he returned reeking of rum and Coke, his skin flushed, his eyes at half-mast. The strange phone calls at all hours and the messages on the answering machine from strange women, flirty in tone, thanking him or saying they were looking forward to the next night. I didn't believe it, but I didn't sit idly by—every woman who left a number got a call back before I erased the tape. It was Truth or Dare, it was Two Lies and One Truth. I called myself Elena, said I didn't quite understand the message on the machine in my best southern drawl.

The women's question was inevitable but always surprising: "And you are?"

"Oh, I'm Elena, his wife," I always said with a smile. "And *you* are?"

"I'm so sorry" was the typical reply.

By the time I did something, the days were bloated with sorrow. I felt it in my shoulders and on the tops of my feet. By the end of the workday, I started to shuffle like a crone from a fairy tale and scrunch my neck like a tortoise retreating into its mosaic shell. The month before, a child had drowned, a four-year-old who had slipped away from his mother during naptime and jumped into the pool in the backyard. The fire marshal became apoplectic when he realized the parents had bought the safety equipment but never bothered to install it.

"He knew how to float," the father insisted at the news conference as his wife wept openly. He put his tattooed arm around her slender shoulders jutting out like clothes hangers from her kelly-green halter top. "We were taking him for swim lessons."

The second child was a three-year-old boy who, the following Saturday, was also found dead in an ungated pool. The boy had wandered away from a birthday party to the next-door neighbor's yard. The photo we published in the paper showed a chocolate-eyed boy with red hair, grinning in his father's lap.

By the third drowning, I was barely making it out of bed. Three kids, a brother and sister and their playmate, no swim lessons under their belts, had been left unattended next to an ungated pool.

"I had to answer the phone," the babysitter had said to Channel 6, her face sheet white.

When the fourth child had drowned in as many weeks, the fire marshal issued a biting statement to the public on the topic of vigilance. A slew of mothers and friends of mothers, those who had lost their children in the previous weeks, called in to the newsroom. I was tasked with fielding each call since I had reported on and written each story for the past month. Each was a gut punch. Writing obituaries for people who had not learned to read was disturbing to the point where I preferred to curl up alone on Ford's couch after deadline and watch *Hogan's Heroes* reruns than be in my own apartment alone. The first two sets of calls about the drownings weren't directed at me, personally, and I went through the marshal's statement with them, line by line. "He isn't blaming anyone," I said. "He's asking that the public be extra careful." It was Florida. The public got touchy unexpectedly. It was, no doubt, easier for these people to call the newspaper and blame the reporter than it was to face how and why these children had died.

The next two women who called cursed at me and hung up. Both voices sounded similar, and I wondered if the same woman had called twice. The last call came about an hour before I was done for the day. I was amid a discussion with the layout editor. He wanted to include all the cute photos of the dead children and was asking me to cut another couple of inches from my story. "To make room," he said.

My copy editor had come up the steps to the area where the layout guys were, and he looked at the smiling photos and turned green. "If these kids don't change people's minds, nothing will."

It was a typical harried night, deadline looming. We belonged to the confines of a morning paper. Deadlines as late as midnight for the sports guys, especially if there was overtime or a playoff game. But for general news, unless it was the crime of the century, unless it was a trial of the millennium, we had until nine thirty or ten o'clock—that's about as late as the layout and copy editors allowed us to push.

I opened my mouth to keep those two column inches when the layout editor's phone rang, and Chris answered. He handed me the phone and said curtly, "It's for you."

I answered, surprised, and the woman on the other end let out a stream—no, coursing river; no, breaking levee—of curses at me. "I bet you don't have kids!" was the first G-rated sentence she screamed.

I grunted. So much easier for her to blame the messenger than to account for her own loved one's actions or inactions. "Please tell me what I can do—"

"No, no, no!" she screamed, cutting me off. "Nothing you do will bring back my nephew! Nothing you can say will take away my sister's pain!"

I looked at the photos and noticed the three drowned children who were boys.

"Which one is yours?" I asked, my voice low. The fact that I gave her some ownership over her nephew was not lost on anyone. The copy editor and layout editor exchanged glances.

The woman said, her voice hoarse and sad, "Jack." The boy whose photo I had to give up two column inches for.

"I'm leaving it up to you," I said, though it was not her decision, though we had already received the parents' permission. "We are running another story in tomorrow's paper. Do you want us to put his picture in the paper?"

She cried a little. "Yes, please." She wept some more. "If his photo doesn't change people's minds, nothing will."

I thanked her and hung up. I nodded at the two men. There was salt water in the air, and the buzz of the fluorescent bulbs sounded like bees. "I'll find something to cut," I said, then turned around and went downstairs.

Forty minutes later, I was curled up in the fetal position in Ford's apartment. I could not get up to turn on the TV; the remote was just three feet away on the hideous glass coffee table that reminded me of a coffin. The phone rang and I tried to answer, thinking it was Ford calling.

I didn't reach it in time and the answering machine picked up. I recognized the voice; it was the new morning show TV anchor who had just moved up from the Sarasota station to the cable network: Callie or something close to that. Her voice was throaty, hoarse, like she had just smoked a cigarette. "Ford, you still owe me a drink. See you tomorrow after the game." I found myself grinning at the machine and on the verge of uncontrollable laughter. The tears would come much, much later. At that moment, it was all so damn funny. *Elena to the rescue,* I thought to myself. I dialed the number from the boxy black phone on his nightstand.

"Hello, Ford?"

"No, this is his wife, Elena." I tried to sound conversational, in the same way I try to get to know the pizza delivery guys by name, so I can be sure none of them spit on my pepperoni and olive before it reaches my door. "I didn't understand the message you left my husband."

Callie snorted. "He told me he was in between marriages."

I laughed. "That's a good one. He will be between marriages in about six months." I surprised myself at my own conviction. I was selling a bill of goods, but I was selling it to myself as well as Callie. "But he's firmly in this marriage right now."

Callie coughed, mumbled the most insincere apology, then said clearly, "He's been pursuing me for almost six months," and hung up.

I grinned as I erased all the tape, even the message from his father, something about the anniversary of his mother's death. I laughed aloud as I reset the machine to the automated setting that merely stated the number and was not personalized. I smiled as I changed the sheets, smiled as I cleaned furiously. I used the last of his toothpaste to polish the silver in his dining room cupboard. I used his toothbrush to hack away at the stains in the grout by the tub and then rinsed off the brush with dish soap before returning it to the stand in the bathroom. I used his comb to shred the cobwebs starting to form at the corners by the back door, then rinsed it with the last of the balsamic vinegar in his pantry. Then I ordered the most expensive pizza and used Ford's credit card to pay and leave an exorbitant tip for the delivery guy, Gus, that evening, and I sat down to watch the late news.

Ford came back from covering the MLB game hours later, his eyes bright though his face haggard. His clothes were pressed, crisp, hardly worn.

"Are you sick?" I asked, willing my voice to remain sanguine, willing my arms and hands not to cross, willing my face to remain smooth and untroubled. By this time I had eaten half the pizza, all the pepperoni, and left my dirty dish in the sink, put crumbs under the table and in between the mattress and box spring. This was summer, and the air-conditioning in these old buildings was antiquated and unreliable at best. Ants would arrive before morning.

He shook his head. "Tired. A couple of the guys went out for beers after deadline."

I sniffed his hair as I hugged him. He didn't smell of beer. He smelled of nondescript hotel room shampoo. "Bye, love," I said as casually as I could. "I have an early start tomorrow."

He walked away from me and into the kitchen. "Rita, how many times have I told you to please rinse out the dishes?"

"Sorry," I said. "I left you supper."

I heard Ford grunt and the box lid open. "Where's the pepperoni?"

But I didn't answer. I just shut the door behind me and embraced the hot night air. I went home and vomited pepperoni and cheese and two kinds of olive. I thought for sure the nice lady with a baby next door heard me through the walls, but no one knocked or checked on me. I almost called Ford twice to tell him to get a new toothbrush and to check for ants.

Instead, I called in sick and left for the airport. I didn't say a word to my parents when I went home to visit the following day. Still, they somehow knew. Dad left the room the minute he saw my face; he simply mumbled some excuse about a phone call and retreated to his office. Mom said she was needed in the ER but wanted to talk when she returned twelve hours from now. Friends from work were calling my parents' number, asking me if I was all right. When Tracy Franks and Emily Greely and Kelly Hendricks called, I gave them a breezy, just-walked-in-the-door narrative.

My parents' house, a house they'd only been in for the past ten out of twenty-five years, was taking on the properties of a hoarder's paradise: stacks of newspapers, four cats, and an empty fridge except for a half-full can of tuna with the lid peeled back. Then Virginia called and asked if I was all right.

I replied, "Is there a reason not to be?"

Virginia, my favorite political reporter, my favorite person, said, "Well, he got super sloshed last night, and he botched the story about the doubleheader."

Ford was covering a baseball game. How hard was it? Someone won and someone lost. Doubleheader. Someone won and someone lost twice, consecutively. "And was seen sucking the face of a blond bombshell instead of meeting the deadline?"

Virginia laughed. "You're fine."

"Indeed," I said, though I was not fine, though I wasn't going to be fine for a long time, though I would be carrying my grief for years to come. "But please tell me what's going on. It's not like him to drink before the game."

Apparently, Ford had become ill, violently ill. There was vomiting and diarrhea and apparently a bout of dizziness. He missed the end of the first game and the first six innings of the second, managed to return only for the seventh inning stretch, and then of course turned in such a short story that the editors had to use the wire service to fill the huge hole in the paper. Space they had been saving for Ford. After all, the teams in question were ranked first and second respectively, and there was a great deal of anticipation and fantasy league money betting involved. "He's healthy as a horse," Virginia said. "I mean, I've never seen him take a sick day."

I coughed, trying not to laugh or cry into the phone. Virginia was a damn good reporter; she would know immediately. Virginia was my best friend; she could read me instantly. Apparently, he had used the toothbrush, and grout grime and mildew had caused a violent physical reaction.

Even in Ford.

He was human, after all.

I wanted to feel something different from the seesaw of shame and elation. But I didn't.

Even though time has marched firmly into the future, and I've filed half a dozen shorter pieces about the food shortages and the sudden earthquake in the southern part of the region that killed 296, Hughes seems dissatisfied. "What else?"

"There's a proposed shutdown," I say, pitching my story about the government's plan to dismantle the big school for the blind and farm out those poor kids to the four corners of the region where there are local care facilities.

Hughes grunts. "That's compelling," he says carefully, "but what is the American readership going to take away from this? Will throwing money their way change the outcome?"

I pause. "Perhaps." I pause again, swallowing my anger, then quickly tell the story of eight-year-old Aisha who, if moved, will be hundreds of miles away from her widowed mother. I want this story not just because of Aisha and the hundreds of girls and boys like her but because the paper's spotlight is the only chance for this school to garner resources. This is part of the larger problem: drought and food scarcity. These programs are some of the only ways these kids get meals consistently.

I hear Hughes shuffle papers on his desk, then cover the receiver with his hand for a moment to speak to someone. "Okay, write up something." He tells me to keep it short, that he'll speak to someone for a longer piece in the weekend edition. "I'm transferring you to Rich," he says. "He has a question about the story you filed yesterday."

I have complained to Hughes about Rich in the past to no avail. Now is not a good time to revisit my hate for Rich. "Can't wait," I say in my most cheerful voice.

Hughes laughs, then says goodbye.

The phone clicks and hums for a moment and then Rich answers. "Rita, thanks for making the time," he says, his New England accent betraying his contempt for me. I murmur a few pleasantries, then ask him about the story I filed. It was a quick trip without Rafiq; I hitched a ride with the photographers and got in and out. It was about a border between an old Palestinian neighborhood and an Israeli settlement: how the physical boundary markers that had previously been agreed to were shifted overnight, and now construction of new apartment buildings was being completed at record pace. The story about shifting borders was not new, it was an oft reported sequence. What made it new was that someone had literally moved the markers in the dark and then changed their settlement plans accordingly the next morning, as if no one would notice.

"I don't think it's appropriate the way you used 'occupation' in the second graph."

I can't even remember the second paragraph. I am aghast. "What's wrong with it?" I cradle the phone between my shoulder and ear and start shuffling papers on my desk. I remember printing out a hard copy so I could refer to it for just this occasion.

"You're taking sides," he says.

His voice sounds triumphant, as if he's caught me in a giant lie and now he can impose punishment.

"Hardly," I say, flipping through everything but unable to locate anything of value. "I'm pointing out that one side is breaking the rules." I think back to the first day of journalism school. My tall professor who had won a Pulitzer Prize said that if two people are arguing about whether or not it's raining, it's not our job to write both sides, it's our job to go outside and look up.

Rich makes a noise, but I can't make out what it is.

I try rifling through my backpack as well. No luck. "Excuse me?"

"Propaganda," he says. "I don't think this newspaper uses the word 'occupation' except in wedding announcements, as a way of asking what you do for a living."

I hope that he is joking but I suspect that he is not. No one would ever accuse Rich of having a sense of humor. Still, I mimic a chuckle. There are two kinds of reporters in the world: the ones willing to dumb it down for the public and the ones unwilling. "I'm willing to change it," I say, dropping my voice, "but only if I can add three sentences about the last time ordinary Americans were faced with soldiers coming into their homes and occupying their lives was during the War of 1812."

Rich coughs. "That's beside the point."

"Context is king," I say. I think of an article I'd read recently, about how a majority of Americans did not understand what the words Nakba and Intifada meant; did not know Palestinian or regional history; did not know about the Oslo Accords or a proposed Two-State Solution; did not know U.S. history and could not place themselves on a map; could not place their hometown inside the outline of their state, nor place their state inside the familiar outline of the country. At last, I find the paper. It is hiding in between the pages of a report on the state of the landfill just south of the [--------] capital, where there were rats as big as cats spotted, as well as some sort of leak.

There is a long moment of silence, so long that I believe Rich has hung up. Then: "Rita, I have made a note that you objected to my suggestion and don't want the word 'occupation' changed—and I'm sending it over to the copy desk. It's slated for Sunday."

That's new. Then I remember Hughes had said something after Louis Vandermeer had made a giant stink when someone had used the thesaurus six weeks ago and changed the nuance of one of his sentences about the Pentagon's change in policy about military-base land acquisitions. "Thank you, Rich," I say, not knowing what else to say.

"Hang on," he says, and the clicking and humming begin.

It is Hughes again: The M.E. is amenable to a longer piece for the weekend. "Can Rafiq get a photo of the girl you mentioned?"

I recall Aisha's mother is willing to share a photo of her daughter when she was still well, before an illness robbed her of her vision. "I should be able to get a photo of the young lady," I say. "Rafiq can take a few shots of the school. It's a beautiful campus."

Someone interrupts Hughes, and he says he must go.

I summarize the other points of focus for the weekend piece and send it in as an email: private groups providing housing and food, medical care, and education to Afghan girls and women targeted by the Taliban; most of the women were jailed and beaten at some point; some were trafficked because they were dressed in Western clothes and accused of being "bad girls." (No one wants to talk about the rapes that must be happening, no one wants to talk about the steady stream of girls who simply disappear.) Also, there are groups trying to open girls' schools and attempting to keep open two girls' schools in Syria that have been under attack in recent days after the founders were murdered and several members of their family had been trafficked. These schools were doing double duty: educating and also feeding their students during school hours as a way of combating food insecurity in the home. They were taking away yet another reason some families were marrying off their daughters early. The UNICEF reports are devastating.

I pull the quote from the new head of the school and add it to my summary: Fifteen hundred students fed twice a day in one school, supported through all the underground networks. "From Yemen to Afghanistan, families are now resorting to selling their young daughters into marriage because of the severe shortage of water and oil, gas for cooking, eggs, milk, wheat." (And there's no acknowledgment that the effects of global warming and climate change have resulted in more famine, more disease, more refugees.) I want this story, so I can one day write this same story shedding light on Americans who engage in trafficking and child marriage. So many girls disappear every day, in America and around the world, and no one writes about them. Most countries don't even keep count of how many have disappeared, except anecdotally: So-and-so's daughter or niece or mother or sister or aunt. The census data is appalling and reveals gaping holes. I want this story so bad, so I can write a follow-up story, and then another one and another one: a whole chain of stories about the missing girls and women at home and abroad. The more sunlight I can put on the disappearances the more there is a chance that something will change, that someone will care.

That should be of interest to the public.

Four

[SEPTEMBER 9, 2001] — THE AIR IS STALE AND SO HOT. WE WALK on the concrete plaza but really, I'm dragging along until I spy the coffee vendor. I know what is expected of me: Hughes has made that clear. I know that Rafiq knows too. And I know what is expected of him: Hughes has been crystal on that as well. But I'm tired today, everything on my face hurts, my teeth, my lips, my jawbone. I can't continue clenching my jaw and watching Rafiq wallow in whatever is causing the prolonged sighs, the failure to hear my requests on the third or even fourth try. I'm tired of him looking at his watch. I'm tired of his moodiness, the way he stares into the distance.

Mr. Mohammed's stall is closed today. There is a printed sign with painted sunflowers around it, stating he'll be back tomorrow. My mood always sours at the sight of sunflowers. We go to the next kiosk. I pull out my wallet. "I'm hitching a ride," I tell Rafiq as I hand him a coffee from the vendor. "You can go home."

Whatever he is dreaming, Rafiq becomes rigid, a mannequin sporting a steaming hot cup of coffee with milk. He tries to hand me back the coffee. "Am I fired?"

I'm just not in the mood. "No." I wave away his efforts. "Jean from Reuters has found a seat for me," I say, forcing my mouth into a smile. This is both true and untrue: Jean will find me a seat as soon as I ask him. But I haven't asked him yet. I saw Jean at the hotel earlier, and I know if I hurry back, I can still catch him. I turn away and look over my shoulder at Rafiq's still unmoving form. "Have a great day off!"

At the war, the Kush king has died. He had previously survived three assassination attempts, but on this day his body has been found. Not in a cave in the outskirts of some small town in the hills in the nether land between Afghanistan and Pakistan—a body made lifeless by many bullets. He was in fact killed in daylight, at a restaurant in [--------] celebrating his oldest daughter's eleventh birthday. Dozens were killed, including the younger daughter and some of the guests, many of the staff. The wire stories were a cornucopia of facts about his upbringing and his political life, his hands deep into the conflict with the Soviets and his successes. Hughes had relayed something from Reuters about a relative of one or more of the deceased, Mr. Hamid, who may have more information. Hughes wanted me to track him down. Maybe the fact that the birthday-girl daughter is eleven and her life has changed—her father is dead, and she is seriously injured—these facts have placed me squarely under a cloud.

I try again to find Mr. Hamid, the relative of one of the deceased at the café. The first neighborhood has a Hamid family, but it is not the correct family, and the man who had answered the door is closer to my brother's age than the old man I am trying to track down. It is my first real solo venture in a while where I am not conversant enough in the language. I've been immersed in the local dialects for a few weeks now, and the words are starting to echo and ring in my ears as I sleep. I am starting to know more, but I am still a student of the language, and of the nuances.

At the time the Kush king was assassinated, there were a series of bombings across the region. This is my last story before I go home Tuesday to see Mom and Dad.

If I had hitched a ride with Johanna then we would have to divvy up which angles we were pursuing so we wouldn't turn in the exact same story. But I am in the thick of this story with a Reuters photographer—there is no need to divvy up or agree who is covering what. I had managed to catch Jean before he left the hotel. Jean is doing a photo story for the weekend. I am trying to get a quote and confirmation for the next day's piece, and make sure the family that was killed as collateral damage at the café bombing really belonged to him, that it is his important son-in-law and daughter and twin grandkids, a boy and a girl. All the doors on this narrow street are similar, wooden and scarred, with beige exteriors, and flowers in pots on the windowsills on the second floors. If I squinted it could be Europe from a bygone day, but it is not. It is [--------]. It is a drought-stricken day, dust blooming from the ground, the smell of something rotting in the air. Jean adjusts the strap on his equipment bag and says, "My friend Remy told me the house had roses on the sill. Pink roses."

I look up, higher and higher, farther and farther down the street. The street and this neighborhood snake infinitely from where I stand. The windowsills are full: There are daisies and violets and some flower I can't quite remember but know to be in the lily family, only smaller. Then the house, just as Jean's friend Remy had described, with the scarred door and the beige arch and a windowsill full of tiny pink roses.

Pink roses are my mother's favorite. Dad always bought them on the special occasions: birthdays, anniversaries, her first day on the job as an emergency room doctor the fall after we returned from our final trip to India as a family, the day she went into remission. Dad came in the front door, the blooms wrapped in cloudy white tissue and held together with a forest-green sash of a ribbon. Mom's eyes lit up and the grin was unrelenting—though her words were seldom more than "How lovely, thank you." There was a hug and a peck on the cheek. Of course, I came to expect that visual marker, I came to understand that this was the way they communicated, through the ritual of gifts. The act and the art of invention and reinvention. The act of revision would come later. Mom always gave Dad thick sweaters, ordered from an expensive catalog company in Maine, and umbrellas. We had an extensive collection of umbrellas, from red to green to brown, from polka dot to striped, to the kind you would find on the movie set of

My Fair Lady. It was some kind of joke between them. I was not included, though inevitably I inherited the umbrellas and stored them in a clear plastic bin in the hall closet. The roses stopped for a time after India and did not start again until Mom had claimed victory over cancer the first time, when I was in college.

Those were the years that Dad still bought pink roses, but they went to a slew of other women. The credit card bills arrived in the mail and Mom saw the charges from the florist and said, "How lovely. Thank you," and then wrote checks to the credit card companies and threw away the statements.

These roses on the windowsill look like diamonds, petals overlapping, and tiny sharp thorns protruding at the stems. This house has creeping roses, and the roses from the second-floor windowsill have come down the floor and a strand of them hover just above the door. "Here," I say.

I wait until Jean is next to me and then I knock. Slowly the door cracks and an old man's eye peers out. I introduce Jean and myself as softly and quietly as I can in Arabic.

The old man opens the door farther and smiles at my poor efforts. "I speak English," he says.

"Thank you," I say, and I smile back for a moment. I am not a believer in tap-dancing around the pain. I was that kid who could rip the bandage off the skin, knowing it would smart, but knowing it would be over. My brother is the opposite, the child who cried even before the bandage was touched, unable to look. I plunge in and ask if he is Mr. Hamid.

He nods.

"Are you related to this family?" I ask and show him the list of names.

The man pales and nods and then shakes his head. "I am the uncle," he says. "I raised my niece when my brother died."

Despite my best efforts, I feel my lips turn downward. Here is when Rafiq is missed: He could modulate the empathy and ask my harsh questions with a softer tone in a native tongue. I so want to give him my compassion. I will myself to look at his face. "May we come in?"

He opens the door wide, and we step through to a dark anteroom and then to a big sunny kitchen and a door that leads to a balcony and presumably an inner courtyard. "I'm so sorry to bring you such sad news," I say.

"You did not bring the sorrow into my house," he says. "My neighbors heard first and visited me this morning."

Mr. Hamid is a very nice man. Even in his grief he plies us with tea. Then he goes to a shelf in the sitting room and brings back the waterproof box. I know it is waterproof only because of the shiny way the paper is lit up in the light. It might not be waterproof up to six feet but if that box got caught in the rain, it wouldn't melt into an indistinguishable heap of cardboard. He pulls out a few photos of the children and then of his niece on her wedding day. The photo captured for eternity the gorgeous light and the couple's quiet yet confident gaze into the camera. "I am so sorry," I say again. "I want to give you a chance to remember her, and to tell the world about her so that she is not forgotten."

Mr. Hamid offers me a photograph of the husband and wife with the two children. It is not the Kmart photo that you see in American households, but rather the four of them outside, perhaps at a museum or in a botanical garden, clearly part of a family group outing, enjoying themselves. "Please take this one," he says. "I want people to know they were happy." The groom was from Afghanistan, there was a connection between the families that extended two generations. "They were a good match and they cared for one another."

Tears in the back of my eyes, I look at Mr. Hamid anyway and let him see me. Jean asks him what he knew about the family's presence in the city at the time of the bombing.

"My niece's husband was being called home; he is the son of someone important in government. He had big plans to modernize Afghanistan."

The trip to the café was part of a little vacation before they were to pack up and relocate to Kabul—it was to be a two-year posting, he says. "Then my niece wanted to return here and live near me. So I wouldn't be alone."

My parents call again. I had spoken to Hughes, and he said I should go home, perhaps as soon as the next set of stories about the bombings have been filed, even if it was only for a short time. He seemed to know more than he was saying, and I suspected that Dad had called him and told him something about my mother that I did not know.

It is a puzzle of time. It is a puzzle that needs to be cracked before I return home and see my mother. The bombings were all coordinated so they seemed intentional, purposefully planned. Hughes moves up the deadline. I am on the phone speaking with some ministry official's assistant about additional security for the people because of all the chaos the bombings had brought when Rafiq taps me on the shoulder and mouths, "Your parents are on the phone."

I shake my head slightly and write on a piece of paper: "Tell them I'll call them right back." Rafiq goes away and a moment later he returns and says, aloud, "No, your father, he wishes to speak to you."

I hold up my finger, then ask the assistant for some statistics he had on file about the number of dead in the province to the north, and he says he will call me right back with those numbers. "I'm happy to stay on the line. My colleague will wait for me."

He agrees.

Rafiq and I exchange positions. I go over to his desk, pick up the phone, and say, "Hello, Dad, I'm sorry to keep you waiting."

But it is my mother who answers. "Hello, darling, are you living your best life?" She coughs mightily, and it is a sound I have come to recognize: bronchitis. Or maybe walking pneumonia. That is the tell for Mom, when she breathes like a sickly accordion.

I smile sheepishly into the receiver and try to push away her infirmity. "Oh, you tricked me very well this time, Mom."

Mom laughs and coughs some more.

Dad gets on the line. "Hello, Elena, can you please come home today?"

This time Mom doesn't object.

I hear Rafiq speak into the telephone and watch his hands fly over the paper, the pen striking the white sheet and the numbers and categories magically appearing. "I have to finish this story, but I will come back by Tuesday." I hear Adam talking in the background.

Dad grunts. "If it gets worse, we're going to the hospital."

"I promise I'll be on my way soon."

Mom says, "Wonderful, darling," and for a second I don't know who she's speaking to.

After deadline, Rafiq and I talk. "Why don't you come back with me? Your paperwork is still in order, and we can do what we need to do in America and then you can return and pick up Zahra or she can join you there."

He says, "I will speak with her." We nod at each other. He adds, "I'll let Hughes know that I'm coming."

There is yet another bombing, and everyone is strangely calm. It is as though we are all poised to see what will happen next. It is as though we are all holding our breath, collectively. This is the true terrorism, a paralyzing fear. Still, I pack my bags. I decide to take everything with me even though I know I'll be back the following Tuesday. I decide not to leave anything in the hotel or in my room but just to check out and start afresh when I return in a week.

In the morning I rise and call the airport, and they say that my afternoon flight is still on time, that I am scheduled to depart as it is stated on my paper ticket. I will leave in the afternoon and, through the magic of international air travel and time zones, arrive in New York in the afternoon. I'll miss the party for Virginia, but I'll call her when I get back and make plans to see her tomorrow or the next day. In my hand, I hold Rafiq's ticket; it is sturdy and printed on thick paper. I look at my watch and finish zipping up the suitcase and go downstairs with luggage in tow. Check-out is easy and I exit through the revolving doors. Zahra and Rafiq arrive just as I push my bags through the door. Zahra greets me and says "I am your chauffeur today" in a perfect French accent. "I will drive you to the airport and I will see you hopefully in a week or two."

I smile, remember she'd told me that she attended university in France. "Merci."

We reach the airport, and from outside, there is no hint that anything is wrong. Another placid morning turned into a placid afternoon: The heat waves shimmer, and the planes are at the gates, waiting to take on new passengers and take to the skies. The guard looks us over and is stern as he says that there will be no drop-off at the departure terminal, that Zahra must park. Rafiq starts to complain that our bags are heavy but the guard barks at him and says he doesn't have to let us into the airport at all if we're going to have that kind of attitude. We apologize, and the guard points to the place where Zahra must park.

"What's going on?" I ask. "Rafiq, did you hear anything?"

He shrugs. "Nothing."

We grab our bags and walk into the terminal.

Chaos.

Cacophony of voices.

We catch the tail end of an announcement, and then the message is repeated. Something has happened in New York a short time ago, that a pair of airplanes have crashed into the World Trade Centers. All flights bound for New York have been canceled, all flights bound for other parts of America have been suspended and delayed indefinitely. Zahra gasps. Rafiq's mouth hangs open for a long moment before he closes it shut and his lips become a single compressed line. I wave my American passport to whomever tries to stop me and say I must speak with someone at the airline. The line is long and there are angry American ex-pats in front of me, frightened, who do not want to remain in the region in light of this unfolding incident. The ticket agent is a young man with disheveled hair. "Go home," the ticket agent says.

"I am trying," I say.

"No." He points to Zahra and Rafiq. "You go home." He turns to me, and I see a tiny mole above his upper lip. "You, we will find someplace you can remain at the airport, and we will find the next flight for you."

I point to Rafiq. "He has a ticket to go home too, he has business there."

The ticket agent shakes his head. "Our government has called us . . . and will not allow anyone to travel outside of this country, holding a . . . local . . . passport. Only you will be allowed to go home."

Zahra starts to say something, and the ticket agent interrupts. "The police are rounding up people who are trying to leave. Go home."

Zahra's eyes are wild and darting every which way. "Rafiq," she says, "you must come back with me. We must either go home together or we must leave this place together."

I look at Zahra. "You have no clothes. None of your belongings are with you."

She produces her passport from her bag. "This is everything I need."

Zahra is a girl after my own heart. Like me, she takes her passport with her wherever she goes.

"You need your things," Rafiq says.

"I will have someone bring them," she says vigorously, pointing her finger at me. "But we must leave here. It is not safe for you, and it is not safe for us to be here. Rafiq has helped you and I have helped you."

I turn back to the ticket agent who is at once speaking to a balding white man and telling the crowd all around us to calm down. "We must leave as soon as possible. All of us."

Once again, he reiterates his position that he has a seat for me whenever the airport opens again, whenever the flights are unfrozen, and he reiterates his position to Rafiq and Zahra again: Go home. He says, "I have one seat left on a flight for Spain and from there I can get you to London tomorrow. Do you want it?"

There is a complaint in the air. Someone behind me says, his voice loud and midwestern and male, "Hey, that's not fair! I asked you a while ago . . ."

The ticket agent is young and scared, there is fear written like wrinkles all over his face, the way his face muscles move independently of his mouth. He singles out Zahra and points to me. "Do not be seen with her." His hands tremble.

"What do you think?" I ask. "Will we leave tonight?"

"One may go tonight," he says. "The others, not for days." He shows me the sliding door where most of the ex-pats are waiting, huddled together in a large lounge that is already overcrowded.

Zahra grabs me by the hand. "Please," she says. "You cannot leave, you cannot leave us here with no help, please help us."

"Days," I repeat to the ticket agent. The faces of Mom and Dad briefly appear before my eyes, my own voice promising my brother and my parents that I'll be home echoes in my ears. I feel dizzy. "Do you have a working phone?"

"Only internally," he says. "We can receive calls, but we cannot place calls outside. All the lines are busy."

"Please," Rafiq says this time. He grasps my hand. "I will give you anything you want. Anything."

I think of Ford, how he yeses people to death and then does what he wants. I could leave right now for Spain, find Seb, find a way home. But even this plane isn't leaving for five hours at the earliest. I could help Zahra and Rafiq and then head home. I can still make it to Mom. With all the bravado I can muster I tell the ticket agent I will return soon, to hold my seat. "Okay. Zahra, you must find me a place where I can use the phone."

She nods, wipes tears and the perspiration from her face.

The three of us wade through the ex-pats that have formed a circle around us, a mob event, and walk back to the car with the baggage.

The guard looks us over. "You're not staying?"

"No," we say in unison. Then I add, "This flight has been canceled for today. We will come back."

"I cannot save you this parking space," he says, and he turns away.

"We will make different arrangements," Rafiq says, more to Zahra than to anyone else.

The guard lets us go. The short drive back to town is tense. Rafiq turns on the radio and there is a report in Arabic about the incident in New York, and now in Washington and now another plane that crashed in Pennsylvania, a plane that was on its way to the White House. He turns the knob and on a different station, the BBC announcer reports the same information in English. The BBC announcer holds obvious dismay in his voice, like an accent: There's been a horrible act of terrorism in New York and Washington, D.C., on this day, September 11, 2001. Thousands of people may have been killed and injured, that the Towers have fallen, that a plane has flown into the Pentagon, and more have been killed and injured; that a plane destined for the White House has crash-landed in Pennsylvania but there are no survivors. I gasp. I look at my watch and do the math: It is still early in the day in New York. There is a good chance people had not yet arrived for work.

"Let's go to the Americans," I say. "Let's go to the American embassy."

When we get there, I realize that Zahra and Rafiq do not live that far from the embassy. I tell Zahra that we will wait in the car until she comes back with her clothes. We do not wait long, as Zahra has packed lightly. "I will get more clothes," she says, showing a small bag with some essentials. We walk to the wrought-iron gate. I show my American passport and say that Rafiq is my translator and that he has the paperwork, and that Zahra is his spouse.

The guard is young. "You and your translator can go in but not his wife."

"No, they are married," I say. "They have equal rights because they are one unit." I think of Ford, and I think of Sebastian and how none of us were ever one unit, how we were each a fraction, a portion of the pie competing for control. The marine lets us in, albeit reluctantly. They scan our luggage, and I argue with one embassy official then another for the next hour, two hours, three hours. Someone brings us tea. Another half an hour. Other families have arrived with problems that are not dissimilar to ours, with people that they love who do not hold American passports or green cards but who have been promised safe passage. I check my watch and realize that if I don't leave right now, I will miss my flight to Spain. An embassy official announces that everything has been halted out of the region, until at least tomorrow. Mom's face flashes before my eyes. I tell Zahra to get through to the airport, and somehow, she does. I get transferred to the ticket agent. "Do you remember me?" I ask loudly.

"Which one are you?" he asks in return. "The businesswoman or the journalist?"

"Keppler," I say, and I add the name of my newspaper, grateful for the first time for my American-sounding name.

He pauses and I can hear him doing something, moving papers around. "Come now, or the other woman gets your seat."

I look at Zahra, her eyes wild, and Rafiq, his face pinched. "I'll try," I say. "Is the flight really taking off?"

"There is a chance," he says.

The embassy official appears on the threshold and waves at us to follow him.

"Goodbye," I say aloud.

I do not leave. We are there, until the long night has stretched through the hours to an uneasy dawn. The air is uneasy. The people are uneasy. At times calm, but that is only because of the night. When the sun comes alive and sets the sky on fire, there is more shouting and lying and arguing. The next day finally someone at the embassy allows us to use the phone. I call Dad but his cell phone is not working. I call the house phone and leave a message on the answering machine that I've been delayed because of the Towers falling, that all the flights are canceled but I am trying to get home. I try to reach Ford, but he does not answer in any of his usual places. I try to call Sebastian, and it rings busy repeatedly. I finally reach Hughes and tell him the situation, and he says they may have a flight tomorrow. "You and Rafiq can get on it, and Zahra can remain in the embassy." His voice sounds scratchy, and he keeps clearing his throat.

I say, "Sorry, I cannot leave her alone. Zahra must either go with us or both stay behind." That is what the government has said.

"Let me see what I can do." He coughs. "I will call the lawyers."

We have made a commitment to Rafiq. He has done a service for this news organization, and we have made them a promise and I am going to keep that promise if possible. I shudder. I hang up the phone after I thank him and I turn to Rafiq and Zahra. "We are going to help you. We will do the best we can."

Rafiq nods and accepts this.

Zahra's eyes grow wild again, darting this way and that; she shouts about her father's recent death and how her sister's potential suitor had backed out of the agreement since there was no longer a man heading Zahra's household. "I have to consider my family," she says. "No, not the best of *your* ability. Only until we are safe and free."

We wait another few hours and finally the embassy person says he thinks he might be able to get them into Jordan as embassy employees who are being transferred, and then from there, they can go where the newspaper has made arrangements. But this ruse does not work. Another day goes by, and the American embassy has agreed to grant some kind of temporary protection order: not exactly a green card or a visa or a passport but something so that Zahra and Rafiq have proper documentation; they will remain in [--------]. It is not perfect but it is a small miracle. It is sufficient.

I call again, a round robin of calling my parents and Seb and Ford. I try calling the hospital where Mom has her appointment coming up. No answers and a dissonance of busy signals. I try the airport: A seat has opened and a flight to Frankfurt with a connection to Amsterdam and then America. Hughes calls and assures Rafiq and Zahra that they will have work and they will have this paperwork. "One day when it is safe, they will come to America," he says. "Rita, your husband and your parents got a message to me, and I let them know you're okay. Fly safe."

Five

[SEPTEMBER 2001] — ON SEPTEMBER 15, A SIKH BUSINESSMAN IS shot and killed outside his Arizona roadside gas station as he tends to his flowers. A white American will later be convicted of this murder, and he will justify it by saying Balbir Singh Sodhi's beard and turban made him believe that the gas station owner in Mesa was a terrorist and somehow connected to the events that had shocked the United States and, indeed, the world, four days before.

Earlier on that day of September 15, Sodhi had donated the contents of his wallet to help the families of the 9/11 victims. (But none of us will know that for years to come. All the stories mention the flowerbeds, but none say what kinds of flowers he was growing.)

The chaos in the newsroom must have been unbelievable.

It must have been.

But I am not there that day, or the day before or the next or the day after.

I arrive late to the United States—my connections across Europe are imprecise, the hours falling away and my voice growing hoarse as I plead with every airline attendant I can find, first in Frankfurt, where the stern associate says he has a seat to Amsterdam that will leave in an hour. Everyone is talking about the Towers falling in hushed tones, but it is the same information that I'd heard hours earlier on the car radio when I was hitching a ride from [--------] to the airport in Egypt. I found myself holding my breath, counting to a hundred in French, then Bengali—then counting by tens to a thousand in English.

At Schiphol the air is less tense than in Frankfurt. I try the first attendant, who directs me to one person on the other side of the terminal, and then another person halfway the distance back. By this time, I'm run-walking. I eye the bank of phones near the cafés and news kiosks but then, along with everyone else, find myself glued to the TV monitors: the planes running into the Towers and then the Towers falling and then another vicious circle as the planes fly into the Towers again and the Towers fall again. Then a pair of headshots: Johanna and Margot have been yanked off a plane. Trying to exit Damascus. Their whereabouts are unknown. My mouth falls open and I swallow air and cough violently as the anchor says a group has already claimed responsibility and is seeking the return of their imprisoned comrades. I close my eyes and open them again, but their smiling faces are still on the screen.

I run from the monitors to the nearest uniformed employee and break through the line, thirty people deep. I stumble through handbags and feet, brush up against a myriad of suitcases and their tiny wheels. There are protests rising from the line, but I ignore them and elbow my way to the fore. I say to the casually dressed man in the front, "I have to interrupt you."

"What makes you so special?" he asks, his eyebrows knitting together, his voice gruff, a sheen of perspiration on his face.

His voice booms in my ear though I know he wasn't especially loud.

I want to curl into a ball on Ford's long-ago couch. I think of him for an instant and then remember he's following the baseball teams around, he's in Chicago. Instead, I point to the monitor behind us. "My friends might have been killed," I say loudly, and the line falls silent. I look at the brunette attendant, JULIA written on her tag, and I too fall silent. I pull out my press badge and hand it over. Without a word, she begins to type into the screen in front of her, her lips smashed together in concentration. Several minutes go by, and she looks up from her screen and says triumphantly, "There's a flight in two hours." A murmur goes through the line, and I thank her, then thank the man whose place I took. After

I leave Julia and the counter, boarding pass in hand, the crowd parts for me, and a few hands touch my back and wish me good luck. Their touch feels strange, as if I'm a bird just out of my captor's grasp. There are announcements overhead in Dutch, English, French, German, Spanish, about a departing flight to Madrid. The woman's voice is smooth and impersonal.

I return to the phone banks. I try Sebastian's numbers. Office. I get no answer at the first number, not even a receptionist. I call the second number, presumably his apartment, and a woman answers on the third ring. "Hello?"

I look at the receiver. Did I dial his office by mistake? Another message about another flight sounds and drowns out whatever she has said.

"Who's calling, please? Hello?" First Spanish. Then in an English spoken with a lilting accent.

Who is this woman? Why is she answering Seb's phone? "Never mind," I say. I hang up and call my brother and there is no answer. I try the hospital where Mom works, and it rings busy again and again. I try my parents' home number in Westchester County and leave another message on the machine. "My flight leaves in two hours. I'll be there soon," I say with false confidence.

I call Virginia and get her machine as well. "Chicken butt," I say. "You're it. I'm stuck at the airport," and I read off the number of the phone to the right of me. "Call me!"

Finally, I try Hughes, again. A group of students dressed in their university's bright yellow attire walk by me, their heads down and some leaning against each other. I gulp. I think of Mom at the bus stop in Kolkata when I was eleven. Same shade.

Hughes picks up after the first ring.

"Did you hear?" I ask.

"How did you hear?" His voice is tremulous, a dam on the brink of collapse.

I didn't realize that he knew Johanna or Margot well enough to be on the verge of tears. "It's all over cable news," I say, trying to remain calm, trying not to think about the fear Johanna and

Margo must be feeling, the moment armed men came onto their commercial aircraft and removed them forcibly off the plane and took them, trying not to give in to the urge to go back to Julia and change my ticket and rush toward Damascus, trying to push back the numbness in my hands, the tingling in my feet. "They even managed to get headshots. Who gave them to the network, anyway? Do you have any more news? Have they been released?"

"Rich has Mike Barrett on . . ." Hughes exhales audibly. "Why do they need two headshots?"

I stop. "Wait, who are you talking about?"

He clears his throat. "You go first."

"Johanna Becker and Margot Durand."

He says nothing.

"Your turn, Hughes."

He coughs. "Virginia."

Then neither of us speaks. On his end I hear nothing but his breathing, audible. On my end the airport is alive, people run-walking to their flights, people crowded at the help stations, people queued up by their gates, waiting to board. More neutral voices telling the time and announcing arrivals and departures. I blink rapidly. "Virginia who?" and then a second later: "My Virginia? Virginia Lawson?"

Hughes doesn't reply.

"She doesn't work anywhere near there . . ." I start to say but then remember her job interview. September 11. A hand goes to my mouth for a moment. "Are you sure she kept the appointment? Are you sure it was Tuesday morning?"

Hughes exhales again. "I'm not sure of anything. But she's not answering her phone." He groans. "I have Sam on it."

Sam is one of the editorial assistants, and he's a miracle worker. He can find out anything. In fact, Sam's family knows Mom. They had met at the emergency room two years ago. Sam's sister's water broke six weeks before her baby's due date and Mom had delivered a boy. "Okay," I say, a bit of relief warming me. "I'm boarding in an hour."

I call back Virginia's phone. "Chicken butt, Sam is looking for you. And so is Hughes. Forget me, call the newsroom."

I go past the monitors from before and keep walking, past the sparsely populated cafés and sandwich shops, the even more sparsely populated candy store. Through the glass, I see the bins of peppermints and butterscotch ovals, and I want to cry. All look ghostly in this loud white overhead light. I walk all the way to my gate where there is another cluster of people watching the group of monitors. I stop next to the university students I'd seen earlier and look up to see them loop the coverage, from the Twin Towers to Johanna and Margot. This time I'm able to hear what the anchor is saying: "A group of men dressed like soldiers forced the plane to open its doors on the tarmac, struck the flight attendant, and forced the two journalists . . ."

I shiver with cold again. I look down: My hands cannot stop trembling. Then I cannot hear anything at all when I look back up at the screen: our photograph, lunch at the movie set, our smiles oversized on our faces, Rafiq's wave frozen forever. There is a long silence in my head, and then all the noises of the airport, the automated voices, the crowds, come rushing forward. Cacophony.

The student next to me looks over and studies me. Big brown eyes and an oversized yellow hoodie. "Is that you?"

I nod, unable to speak.

The flight attendant uses the mic and announces boarding, and I cannot walk fast enough toward her.

I arrive at another ghostly airport; there are more men with clothing labeled SECURITY and airport attendants than passengers. JFK. No one looks at each other, everyone wears the same pallor and fatigue and shock. The automated voices announcing the local time and the arriving flights echo. The first person to speak to me is the customs agent as I hand over all my documents. She is a broad woman with a scowl, beady eyes, tall hair, enough eyeshadow to paint all my fingers and toes aquamarine. I hope she doesn't ask me a million questions. And my wish is granted. She looks over everything twice and then hands back all my paperwork and my passport. "Welcome home," she says, her voice very high and squeaky.

I manage a small smile, say, "Thank you."

I catch a cab through the queue after I'm told the trains are not yet running. It is clear the older gentleman does not want to drive me all the way to the hospital when he hears the address. "Are you sick?" he asks.

"My mother is," I say, simply.

He has no answer. He locks his brown eyes with mine in the rearview, says, "I'm sorry." The rest of the ride is quiet. At some point, I look out the window and see the New York skyline and I gasp: The Twin Towers are absent, the Towers are gone forever. My throat closes in, and I cough. Although I know it intellectually and have seen the video countless times, it is unnerving to see it with my own eyes. I go completely still, my eyes burning. After we pass the skyline, I close my eyes and keep them closed until we reach the inland highway, and then I take stock of what I see: It remains the same as I remember it. The two gaping atrocities are behind me. Virginia's name thrums in my veins, and I pray that Sam has found her alive and unharmed.

I arrive at the hospital, thank the driver profusely, and rush into the emergency room. I find the attendant and explain that my mother is both a doctor and a patient. The young woman looks at me with pity and sends me to the sixth floor, to the cancer ward. I step off the elevator and ask a hollow-eyed nurse about Dr. Das, and I'm met with a blank stare. "Mrs. Keppler?" I say, trying again.

"She was in Room 621 . . ." the nurse says, and I rush away before she finishes her sentence.

Down the hall and to the left. I stop at the door, slightly ajar, take a deep breath, enter the room. It is empty. The bed is stripped down, and all the equipment is unhooked. The air is super cool inside this room, as if no one had been here for at least the past hour. "Rita," a familiar voice says behind me.

I turn around and run to Adam, his big arms envelop me in a

monster hug. He smells of laundry detergent and pressed-clean clothes. I lean back for a moment. "Brother, am I too late?" I ask, already knowing the answer.

He draws me close again and hugs me harder. "She left us this morning," he whispers. "I'm so sorry."

I feel the tears coming, the avalanche of tears that I know I must shed. But they are stuck in the spaces between my throat and my eyes, between my head and my heart. I missed her by a few hours. I would never hear her voice again. I could have arrived sooner—if only I hadn't stopped to help Zahra and Rafiq, if only I had caught that first flight out of Cairo to Spain. I would have been here, holding her hand, sitting on the edge of her bed, saying goodbye. I step back and see the grief and fatigue in the smudges under Adam's eyes.

A doctor walks into the room and greets Adam. He extends his hand to me. "Miss Keppler? I wanted to express my condolences to you as well. Your mother was a great lady, and she spoke of you often."

The doctor is wearing scrubs, but Adam supplies his name since his tag isn't showing. "Dr. Nichols, thank you for everything."

I echo my thanks to Dr. Nichols as well.

A code blue sounds overhead. "Take care of your dad, okay?" he says, then runs out of the room.

I look around again. "Where is Dad? Where is everything?" I know people must have come by with cards at least, if not flowers. And where are Mom's clothes, her shoes, her watch, her toothbrush?

Adam sighs. "He's . . . on a schedule."

I draw breaths, hiccup-cough, and Adam claps me on the back three times until I stop and can breathe again. "Where?"

"At the funeral home," he says, and his tinny voice belies his tall athletic frame. "He's already marshaling . . ."

I exhale. "How's he been?"

Adam hesitates. "He's different now than he was yesterday."

We leave the hospital arm in arm, and only when we are in his car, Tracy Chapman's "Fast Car" on the radio on low, the sun shining through the windshield and warming my waist and the top of my jeans, do I start to shake uncontrollably, my teeth chatter. Adam doesn't drive. He leans over and wipes away the stray tears on my face. "She said your name, Rita. Mom said *your* name before she died."

I expect Dad's hug to be perfunctory, not what a parent does for a child but rather something that is out of obligation. Something to check off the to-do list: "When the prodigal daughter returns, extend a cursory embrace." Surprisingly, he kisses my cheek and holds me close for a long moment.

Adam is here and so is the funeral home director. The home is spacious and tasteful, it can accommodate a big crowd if necessary. Dad hesitates for a moment after he lets go. "I got your messages," he says, so softly.

I want to say something, anything, but all I can think about is Rafiq's and Zahra's pinched faces, their terror and their defenselessness, how they begged me to stay. Mom always says part of the Hippocratic oath, "First do no harm." Mom *had* always said. My mouth falls open at the past tense as I silently correct myself. I stare at Dad, try to say something, but my throat is paralyzed.

Dad looks behind me and offers Adam a smile.

Then the haggling begins, negotiating the details of Mom's funeral.

First Mom's proposed attire into the afterlife. Dad pulls out her garment bag and unzips it, revealing, among other things, an electric-blue pantsuit and pearls. He holds it up and says, "How about this one? She looks so smart in this outfit."

Adam glances at me and I shake my head. "I don't know, Dad," he says. "She's not going on a business trip."

Dad sucks in his cheeks. "I want something appropriate and befitting her position."

What is he thinking? Next he will say she should wear her doctor's coat and sport a stethoscope like a necklace. That blue outfit makes her look like a politician running for reelection. "I want something she loved to wear, that illustrates who she is." My voice booms to the point that the windowpanes hum briefly.

"Calm down," Dad says piercingly in return. He walks to the other side of the room, opens a bottle of water on the counter next to a large arrangement of lilies. He takes a swig from the bottle, then pours the rest into the vase.

Adam sits down in the nearest chair and covers his face with his veiny hands.

I rummage through the rest of the outfits and find the silk violet-colored sari I once saw her wear to an awards banquet. She was so happy that evening, all smiles and jokes and carefree laughter. I look under the carefully folded garment and find the matching petticoat and blouse and sigh in relief. "This one," I say.

Adam lowers his hands and votes. "Yes."

Dad looks away but remains silent.

The undertaker is a tall man with clear-framed glasses that elongate his round brown face. He opens the door near Dad, and his wife walks in, sees me holding up the outfit, and asks me if I know how to put on a sari.

Luckily, I do. (Mom insisted I learn before leaving for college: "How will you wear my good saris if you don't know what to do?" she asked almost rhetorically, and I laughed and agreed.) The woman's name is Anne, and she asks me to follow her. In the next room, Mom grows cold and colder still on a table. Anne takes the sari from me as I stare into the face of my mother. She has circles like tree rings under her eyes and her arms are dry and ashy, her hair is limp and she is shrunken, her skin hangs like flaps over her narrow bones. She is in the clothes she must have worn to the hospital: black slacks and a loose gray sweater tunic. There are dark spots on her face and neck. And yet, she is the most beautiful woman in the world. This is no fairy tale. It does not appear that she is sleeping, that she will momentarily awaken.

Anne says, "We will give her a makeover." Her husky voice is calm. "We can match her makeup with her outfit."

I nod. I see Mom before me but can only think of her as she was when I was eleven. Young and self-possessed, parting a dark crowd in her yellow sari. She is not my first dead body; in fact, she was with me when I saw my first dead body. We four were all together. Still, the shock settles around me like a second skin. After a long while, I let go of her hand, fold it neatly on her chest. I look at Anne and croak out a quick tutorial on how to fold a sari. The two of us dress her in the blouse and petticoat, pleat the silk in tandem, drape one end over her shoulder. Anne's brown eyes are wet when we finish, and my heart feels as though it is encased in cement.

Anne leads me to another room, the formal parlor, sofas everywhere and the walls an understated ecru. Dad and Adam have each found their own loveseat, and I find one across from them so I can see them both at the same time. The undertaker and his wife withdraw after apologizing for the jam-packed chairs and sofas in the room we are in: "We are embarking on an Eastern service later today and the religious leaders have insisted everyone sit on the floor."

Dad does not look me in the eye, not since that first hug when I entered the funeral home. "I know this is delicate," he says, his eyes mostly on Adam, and yet his voice carries to the both of us. "Let's bury her in the family plot."

My brother's mouth falls open. "What plot?"

I now lock eyes with Dad, stormy seas in their depths, but neither of us looks away. Although she was a Hindu woman by birth, Mom had not formally practiced, to the best of my knowledge, for many years. Practicing or not, I know in my soul that Mom wouldn't want to be buried but cremated, like her parents had been, her ashes spread in the Ganges. "In New York?"

He slowly shakes his head. "No, it's in a little town in Wisconsin—that's where all of the Kepplers are buried." He sneezes, but neither Adam nor I offer the standard "God bless you." Dad is capitalizing; he retrieves a handkerchief from his pocket and blows his nose. "That way I can be close to her when my time comes."

My brother's shoulders droop, and he begins to weep.

I glare. I remember the funerals I attended in India, in Kolkata. "Practicing Hindu or not, we have an obligation to her," I say. "We should be cutting our hair and arranging for a purohit and following the rituals of fasting, for starters."

Dad gets up and sits down next to my brother, puts his arm around Adam's shoulder. "Son, I know . . ."

"No, Dad," Adam says. "You have to let her go." He looks at me. "We have to let her go."

Dad hugs my brother harder. "I have to keep the family together."

What family? I want to scream. What a family. I am happy in that moment that my brother still has a father and devastated that I feel as if I have lost both parents. This carousel ride goes on for almost an hour: Dad trying to modulate his voice and Adam weeping intermittently, and me walking a jagged route through the maze of furniture and ending up where I started. At some point, I find tears on my face, tears that I wipe away with the backs of my hands, but I don't remember when I cried.

Then Dad says, "Let's table it for today." He gets up, repockets his soiled handkerchief, nods at us, and abruptly leaves.

Seb and his parents show up and rent a time-share near my parents' home. At first Adam says we should stay with Dad, through the funeral at least, but Seb insists that Adam and I stay at the rented house with them. "You need some sleep," Seb says, kissing my cheek, then putting his hand on Adam's shoulder. Seb had asked Dad after dinner, but Dad declined, said that he wanted to stay with the neighbors down the street. The rented kitchen is beige and well-lit and utterly bland—it could be a kitchen on a movie set, there is nothing distinguishing about it. Adam agrees to stay the night. It is the evening before the funeral, and while we make plans to stay up late and talk, he passes out on the couch in the living room just fifty feet from the guest room where his dark-gray suit has been hung in the closet. Seb's mother puts a blanket over him, and I say thank you and goodnight, unable to say more. I trudge up the wide staircase to Seb's room. After he turns off the light, Seb wraps his arms around me, and we snuggle on top of the sea-green comforter, in our sweaters and street clothes, as if we are on a narrow cot instead of this plush queen-sized bed. We say nothing, and I sink into him, my muscles relax. My eyelids close just as dawn breaks through the picture window. A short time later, Adam calls up to us and we are startled awake.

In the end, Dad wins. We have a funeral and Mom is not cremated, but in an open casket for everyone to see, her face beautifully made up, her batik sari pleated just so.

Seb and his parents, as well as Hughes and his wife, Charlotte, have been helpful during the formulaic, nondenominational, vaguely Christian funeral service. They are somber and quiet, say the appropriate things, are gentle and kind. Everyone is dressed in black or dark gray except for me. I had found a midnight-blue silk sari hanging in my closet, a matching blouse and petticoat pressed and neatly hanging beside it. No doubt Mom had left it there. Charlotte brings me coffee and holds my hand when the funeral director talks about the casket choices and again when Dad's voice becomes boisterous upon seeing some of the neighbors. Many of the doctors from the hospital are present during the service, including Dr. Nichols, who stands up and says a few words about Mom's generous spirit and her love for her family.

Afterward Dad hosts a catered cold-plate buffet service at the house. All the things that have made their home a hoarder's paradise are mysteriously gone, no doubt shoved into some room upstairs or out in the garage. The cats are gone too. I manage to enter their bedroom, and everything is strewn about as it normally is, as if she'd gone to work and would return shortly. The anti-hoarding unit had not made it to the master bedroom.

Dad finds me at the doorway looking in and says stridently,

"Let's sort through everything later. Let's not keep everyone waiting."

Who did this? I want to ask him. Who made these arrangements? Instead, I nod, take his hand and lead him downstairs. His palm is cool and dry. He makes eye contact and squeezes my hand just before we enter the living room. Then he lets go.

A charcuterie board and cucumber sandwiches, cold noodles coated with a forest-green pesto. None of the foods Mom counted among her favorites. Those closest to me all present well and make small talk and refill glasses. For the most part, Dad is with his neighbors in the living room and then outside on the front lawn. My brother and I sit in the living room for the first hour and tolerate it as much as we can. We look at each other when the invisible alarm sounds, and we go outside on the wooden deck and then down the steps into the woods. "Let's walk," Adam says. I can tell that Sebastian and his parents are looking at me, but no one stops us, no one questions us.

My brother and I are silent except for the birds and the trees, we are silent except for a pair of jet fighters overhead doing their now-daily sweep and the cars negotiating the freeway at a distance.

"I owe you an apology," Adam says after a while.

"For what?" I'm thinking quickly back to the past three times we had communicated since his wife left him. Truth be told I love his wife, and it took the pressure off me, his being married to Jennifer and them living thirty-five minutes away at the converted farmhouse. I had heard everything about Dad's schoolboy crush on Jennifer, and how she loved to garden with Mom, that they were thinking about apple trees, something that would take some time to come up but something that could bear fruit for years to come. I had heard all about Adam and Jennifer's elopement and the big surprise party afterward: I had met her once when I was rushing through town. Mom had made what seemed like a vat of chicken biryani and there were hardly any leftovers.

"I know things are hard between you and Seb, and I haven't called," he says.

A pair of birds answer his sentence with a plaintive, repetitive chirp.

I had called him when Jennifer left. She had strenuously objected to the potential job transfer to Arizona and, in the end, departed unceremoniously one day, didn't even pack anything except for her clothes and the quilt her grandmother had sewn for her in college that she'd kept in a keepsake trunk in the guest bedroom. "She didn't even take the trunk or the rest of the stuff in it, she just grabbed her patchwork and took off," my brother had said. We'd admired the special quilt, which incorporated pieces of what she wore when she was young: T-shirts, nightgowns, bathing suits. A visual encyclopedia of the past. "I don't know what happened. But none of it makes sense, and none of it feels real." In the end my brother didn't take the job offer and he still lost his wife. And shortly thereafter, Mom is dead.

"Don't sweat it," I say now. "We have bigger things to worry about. Like where Mom is going to be residing for eternity."

He grunts and then stops on the path. "You've been back there, haven't you?"

I don't have to stop and explain or question. I am eleven again and he is fifteen. We are back in India. "In proximity," I say. "I had been talking to Mom about it. I really wanted to take her . . ."

He starts walking again, his pace brisk, and it takes a moment to catch up and keep pace. "Not now, but soon," he says. "We need to . . . need to . . ."

"Remember," I fill in.

Dad leaves with Mom's casket, presumably for Wisconsin. He says she will be buried at the cemetery in his hometown of East Cambridge, the church on the corner of North Pleasant Street, across from a Piggly Wiggly. "It's tradition," he says, his hands warming over the mug of black coffee, the kitchen lights off in his house, the mood of the world around us as overcast as the morning sky outside. It is early and already Dad has stubble on his cheeks. "I'm telling you where she'll be so you can visit her." My brother and I offer to go with him, more than once, more than five times, but he never answers us.

After he puts his empty mug in the sink, he reaches into his pocket and retrieves a small velvet box. "Your mother asked me to give this to you," he says, his voice toneless. My hands shake when I see her opal ring resting snugly. She wore that ring every day since I can remember. "Thank you, Dad," I say, wanting to hug him. But he has already turned away. "She was saving it, a gift for you when she became a grandmother."

The coffee swirls like a tornado in my stomach. Adam frowns, and lines appear at the corners of his mouth.

Then a car arrives in the driveway, a long sleek white limousine. Dad says, "See you soon," as if he is going on a joyride.

We are alone.

I voice what I've been thinking the past few days: "I am an orphan." I release the words, but I do not feel better.

Adam shakes his head and his face sags in sorrow. "No, you're not. I'm not. We're not."

"What was that exit?" I say, more forcefully than I intend. "How could he leave with her, and not take us? How could he leave?"

Adam winces. "Everyone grieves differently, Rita."

I cry, the avalanche smothering us both. No matter what happens in the nebulous future, this is the point of delineation, the first moment we are truly alone in the world.

I call every conceivable number and ask about Virginia, but it is chaos, and no one can help me, no one has the answers to my questions. I have unearthed her mother's number, and in Danielle's voice is an echo of our worst fears. Still, we comfort each other with the one big fact: No one has a definitive answer. This gives us hope. Virginia's still missing and it's far better to be in that column than the column next to it: confirmed dead. I promise to call Danielle again and hang up, drained.

Sebastian comes downstairs, leans across the wooden table and with his outstretched hand takes my fingers and touches my wedding band. "I think we should stay another couple of days. I don't want to leave like this."

The air inside the rented house is stifling as well as outside where the unexpected heat is causing the flowerbeds to shrivel. We hear his mother talking vociferously upstairs and his father's murmuring assent. I will all the muscles in my face to remain motionless. "I already called the airline," I say as quietly as I can. "My flight is in four hours." That is not true. I am not scheduled to leave anywhere, but Hughes is expecting me later in the day. Just an informal chat, he'd said.

Adam and I call Dad's cell phone but it rings and rings, then goes to a rapidly busy signal. My brother leaves for Chicago, some kind of work assignment for his architectural firm. My husband and his parents leave the rental and return to their lives. I know his parents are heading back to California, but I am not clear if Sebastian is heading back there with them or returning to Spain. I'm certain he told me, but I can't remember the details.

I have an appointment with Hughes. On the way I stop by Virginia's apartment. It is my dream to find her there, curled up on her sofa, watching old Hitchcock movies ("*Rear Window* is the bomb," I can hear her say), lounging in her striped forest-green pajamas. I am already playing in my head what I'm going to say to her when she reappears: part relief, part chastisement, all love.

The super recognizes me: "Rita, right?"

I tell him everything I know: that she'd had a job interview on that Tuesday morning, that she never made it home, that she was believed to be heading to the Towers. The super's face grows long and haggard with every sentence I utter.

We march up the narrow flight of stairs and he lets me in. I cannot cross the threshold. I look into her apartment, and it is like looking into a life-sized diorama of a life: her framed diploma, the posters of Broadway shows on the walls, the tasteful leather couch and mahogany coffee table, the vacuumed carpet. I look back at the super. "John," I say, drawing his name out of the stagnant air. "Can I come back later?"

Without a word, he closes the door and locks it, hands me the spare key. I follow him down the stairs and say goodbye and move in a fog out the door and onto the street. I walk toward the taxi stand, but at the last minute I stop, then decide to keep walking. My mind tries to take in what I saw when Hanan pops into my head. How Rafiq and I combed through her rooms and rescued her cat. By contrast, Virginia's apartment is a scene from a movie, something to be viewed but not physically disturbed. Hanan and Virginia are both missing, and the world has moved on.

I enter the building and show my badge, take the elevator. An instrumental version of "Oye Como Va" plays as the elevator climbs. I step out but do not proceed. I can't help it. I stop to observe, as if I am doing a story, as if my observations are going to make it into print. There is an air of tension, muskiness and humidity, as if the air-conditioning had broken down and everyone is soaked to the skin in their own unease. I see people I recognize, acquaintances from school and from other newspapers where we had worked together, and yet my feet root on the black-and-white checkered tile. I count the number of fluorescent bars overhead that are flickering (four), and the number of men wearing white shirts (fourteen), and the number of phones ringing (eleven). This newsroom resembles what's depicted in the movies: organized clutter. It is a grid of cubicles and gray desks, swivel chairs and desktop computers, and newspapers stacked in empty spaces. Some of the reporters are organized and their cubicles are tidy; the reference books are neatly arranged, and their desk calendar is open to the correct month. Others are messy, and stacks of papers and manila folders and old newspapers lean against the cubicle walls. The grid is bounded by the editors' offices, glass on one side and windows on the other, and coveted doors that can be shut—for privacy. I know people are looking at me, but I don't want to look at them. Finally, my feet move, and I walk past my own empty desk down two clusters and to the left and find myself staring at Virginia's tidy desk and cubicle; nothing out of place, just like her apartment. She had thumbtacked a photo of us, arms around each other, in our caps and gowns on graduation day, our matching white dresses, our matching white flats. Many years before. We look so young, we are both grinning broadly. I can hear her voice: "We're twinning—well, along with everyone else who's graduating," she had said. "Ten years from now, we'll forget about everyone else and talk about how we dressed alike." She was right. It has been longer than a decade, and yet in the moment now, I can't remember anything but our dresses and her need to capture a moment on film, and how she begged her mother to take the photo.

Hughes comes over to stand by me. He puts his arm around me, and I lean in. He smells like cigarettes and aftershave. (I thought he had quit smoking.) I squeeze him in return, and we release each other.

He says, quietly, "Can we talk in my office?"

I don't trust myself to speak, so I nod. Gray streaks at his temple and in his short beard. Now more than ever, he and Rich resemble each other, like brothers.

As I pass by a colleague's desk I see on the screen a photo of John Parker Nelson, head of the think tank where Virginia was going for an interview. ("You know me: I'm hyperpunctual . . ." Her voice trails in my ear.) I look down at the desk and see a thick file folder: The newspaper is preparing his obituary.

Hughes asks me to close the door and offers me a seat. The silence in his office is deafening. I cannot hear myself think. I almost put my hands to my ears, but the heaviness dissipates when he clears his throat. "I talked it over with Rich," he says slowly, eyes down. "I'm going to keep you here for now."

I shake my head. "I need to go back! I promised Rafiq that I'd be right . . ." My knees begin to shake.

"Rafiq and Zahra are going to be okay." Hughes offers an update: Because of their fluency in several languages, including English and French, Rafiq and Zahra have been offered steady employment. "I give you my word." He picks up a pen and signs a form on his desk. The managing editors had convened and wanted to have some of their reporters shift their focus and remain stateside. "We are leaving that spot—the job you were doing—open for now." He lifts the pen off the desk and twirls it with his fingers. "Michael Reyn is heading to France and will keep an eye out."

This is Hughes's way of saying that Michael Reyn has my job. "I have to go back," I repeat, trying so hard to not beg, to not sound so desperate. I put my hands on my knees to stop them knocking.

Hughes stares at me and shakes his head slowly. "You're not in any shape to go back . . ."

I swallow. I want to say something, anything. I want to cry. Instead, I watch Hughes's eyes fill.

He breaks down like an old car on a lonely stretch of country road. "I can't lose you too . . ." he sobs.

I want to add my sobs, but I find myself comforting him, and my unshed tears feel like a stack of stones lodged behind my eyes.

I leave Hughes's office and duck into the nearest bathroom. It is surprisingly empty, and I am relieved. Hughes wanted to give me a few more days off but I demurred, said it would be better for me to get back to work. I pull myself together, breathe deeply a few times, wash my hands, and walk back toward the elevators. I know this feeling inside my body: It holds the same weight I've carried with me since I was eleven years old in India. Mom's voice rolls through my skull: "First do no harm." I push the button, and moments later the doors slide open and there he is. Ford. In a sports jacket and jeans, hair combed. I step inside, and the doors close behind me. I step into his open arms.

"Several little birds told me you were in the building," he says into my hair. "I'm so sorry about your mother, honey."

I allow myself to relax a little in his embrace and reply, "Thank you." So he had received my message on his answering machine.

Then he pushes the button and the elevator halts. "What are your plans? Do you need somewhere to stay?"

I step back from him and look into his eyes, the blue cloudy with worry. Sebastian is at least a thousand miles away by now. I want something from Ford, but I don't know what.

He kisses me on the forehead.

I push the start button and reply, "I'm heading to Arizona on Wednesday, there's an arraignment and some kind of hearing."

The doors open and we step out together. "I know a place we can have a drink . . ."

Rafiq's face pops into my head, then Zahra's. I must try to reach them. I believe Hughes has a magic wand that can make all their troubles disappear but I don't know that he's in any shape to use it. By helping them, it's clear that my troubles did not disappear. I lost the most important opportunity: the chance to talk to my mother. "I can't drink right now . . . but I'll cheerfully eat something." That's not exactly true. My stomach is in knots. I probably can't eat, but I can sit next to him at a restaurant and watch him eat. He nods and squeezes my hand for a moment. Then we are outside the building, walking apart, two colleagues from work going out for a meal.

Four days after my trip to Arizona, there are reports that a Gujarati-American man outside a New Jersey convenience store was killed. I take the tunnel, interview witnesses. I get quotes from law enforcement reluctant to answer my questions even after they inspect my credentials; and details from the victim's family, astonished to see me. This gentleman had come to the country a few years after I was born, married, and had kids and a nice job as an engineer. He happened to be in the convenience store that evening buying snacks and an energy drink. His assailant knew where the camera was in the store and had avoided revealing his face. The shooter casually walked in, raised his gun at the one brown-skinned customer in line, and discharged his weapon. Balbir Singh Sodhi's murder on September 15 was just the start of violence against people like me whom the public deem enemies because of the color of their skin. Still, I have one shield: On the telephone

I identify myself as Rita and no one knows they are speaking to a woman of color. In person, the newspaper's name figures prominently on my press badge, which I wear on a dull chain around my neck. So far, those victims' families I've interviewed appear to be mesmerized by the ID and relieved to see me. The representatives of law enforcement are not as enamored.

Not two days go by when an elderly Sikh man is killed outside his home in Tennessee while walking his dog. He died at the hospital as doctors tried to stem the blood loss the bullet wound created. A week later, a pair of Indian-American schoolkids are stoned at a local playground by some neighborhood nannies in northern California. It seems that one of the children's nannies at the park where the kids were playing said she knew someone who knew someone who knew someone who lived in New York, and that person may have been killed in the South Tower. That is enough for one six-year-old to nearly lose an eye and her four-year-old brother's teeth to be chipped and two fingers broken like twigs. I fly to California on a plane that's nearly empty and spend the entire flight staring out the window at the fields of clouds. I miss Mom every minute of this assignment. I cannot think of anyone to talk to about these events. I cannot find appropriate words to write this story; every other word I want to type is an expletive no newspaper will print. My lede (ultimately): "A brother and sister each spent hours on neighboring operating tables at Daly City Memorial Hospital Tuesday after they were allegedly stoned by their playmates' caregivers at a local park. Their purported crimes? Their brown skin and names that reflect their South Asian heritage."

Soon I'm on the sixth murder (and spending all my downtime eating salted caramel gelato out of the container and watching *Wheel of Fortune*). In Chicago a man of Lebanese origin is targeted outside his gas station, then a day later a Pakistani-American man and father of four is killed at his Dallas convenience store. On cable news, human rights groups and local religious leaders, especially in the South, are asking people to stop wearing ethnic clothing: no more niqab, hijab, burka, dupatta, chador. No more salwar kameez or sari, no more kurta tops, no more singing Bollywood numbers aloud or talking in any language except English. Just until the emotions settle, the leaders say. There is victim shaming even in these earnest requests.

Twice I've picked up the phone and dialed Mom's office number at the hospital only to hang up when an unfamiliar man answers.

Hughes tallies the dead. So do some government officials and a law professor who writes a guest opinion column for the paper. Now seventeen people of South Asian or Middle Eastern descent, all hyphenated Americans, have been killed since 9/11. All the purported assailants are white men. The cable news coverage around the country is predominantly in favor of giving the public the troubled sad histories of the assailants. Mental illness and distress from 9/11 are given as justification for these murders. The coverage is unrelenting, around the clock. I, just like other reporters from newspapers across the country, try to write long stories about the lives that were senselessly taken.

The law professor is helpful, and I interview him for another number story: sixty-five reported instances of Brown people who are accosted and assaulted, screamed at and spit on, outside their houses and places of worship. Their businesses are vandalized or set on fire. There are public service announcements from Elton John, Paula Abdul, and others, talking about tolerance and love, expounding on the idea that no matter what, we cannot harm people or rush to judgment based on the color of one's skin. I'm not sure who listens. This is the United States, a nation that still has not reckoned with its own history. Media watchdogs and liberal think tanks collect data too, and I find myself reading as many of their reports as I can find, some published as guest columns for my newspaper, some discussed on weekend talk shows on the public broadcast system. The experts say one consequence of the terrorist attacks is relaxation of some standards. Up to this point, despite the preponderance of cable news, when something went into the newspaper it was generally accepted that whatever you put in the newspaper had to be right for at least a day. But after the Towers fell and the planes crashed, media watchdogs were concerned that news coverage was aligning more and more with what the police forces and government officials stated. Single-source stories. Narratives provided by law enforcement are regurgitated. As if law enforcement has the undisputed facts. The police and the federal government officials are being treated with more and more deference. It feels like there are a thousand pundits on TV, on morning talk shows, on the big stations in the evenings just after a news summary is given. I know it's just a handful of longtime print reporters who go on TV in the evenings and on Sunday mornings, who insert their opinions and analysis of the news. But I can see in the faces of the ordinary people at the airport who watch that almost always these analyses are accepted as facts. On both liberal and conservative channels. How I miss Mom and Dad, how I miss their salient discussions while watching the evening news when I was much younger. I am floating in dismay as I watch the news.

Other things are happening too: My former colleagues in Florida and Illinois are losing their jobs, along with a lot of small-town reporters across the county. There are many brief stories of local newspapers around the country going out of business and shuttering their doors. One pundit said a local paper cannot compete with a twenty-four-hour news cycle.

There are other kinds of stories appearing in the big papers and on TV too, about media giants merging with each other, about federal regulations that check monopolies becoming relaxed or eliminated. Two stories this month on companies that already own a lion's share of the print media in big cities like Dallas and Atlanta buying up their competition, in radio or TV.

With fewer reporters on the job, there's less competition, fewer eyes on local officials, more likelihood that reporters will have tough times accessing information. Another pair of stories: Quietly, state and federal governments have enacted legislation that civics classes are no longer required in public high schools. The public is no longer required to learn the Bill of Rights or the preamble to the Constitution. The consequences are plain and simple: An electorate that doesn't know the rules won't complain when their rights as citizens and residents are taken from them.

It could have been me. That's the tiny thought that thrums through all the stories: But for an accident of birth or a red light, or my friend begging Dad to let me stay at the party five more minutes, I would have been the participant in the thing that I ultimately was called to bear witness.

I was born second, so I was too young in 1977 to be behind the wheel and I didn't die at the hands of the drunk driver like Dad's boss's sons did. I missed my segregated school bus, so I wasn't on it when it exploded in Birmingham in 1971. Dad drove me to school another morning, albeit grudgingly, so I missed being targeted by a killer trolling Brown and Black girls walking to school. There were so many church bombings back then, and so many burning crosses left in the front yards at night. We were not immune, especially when we lived in Alabama and Tennessee. In the daytime, there were mutterings loud enough to hear, and pointed looks and women putting on gloves so they wouldn't touch the same grocery carts Mom or I did. More often than not we were not asked to leave because my mother would open her mouth and her British-Indian accent would dispel whatever assumptions the store manager had. At night there were crosses burning in our front yard or in the front yard of the one Black family (originally from Liberia) who lived down the street. The policemen always came late and in a pair. The younger one inevitably said something in sympathy, but the older one typically retorted, "Well, if they don't like it, they can always move."

I was old enough to remember that they didn't know what to do with my brother and me. We were in a white school but in a separate classroom with the children of foreign dignitaries. Then we were bused to a Black school and for a moment they lumped us all together in remedial English. I was old enough to see the National Guard line the streets when they finally integrated the schools in Knoxville (years after the rest of the country had), and I remember Mary Alice Schafer's daughter Susannah crying when I got an A on my math test and she got a B—and she accused me of cheating. I remember Dad coming to school that day and the vice principal arguing with Mary Alice. Mary Alice, all five feet eight of her, pointed her finger at Dad and called him a name and threatened to tell the police he was violating about four different miscegenation laws.

I was old enough to remember when Jackie Kennedy got married to the shipping magnate a few years after her husband, the president, had been assassinated, how Mom crossed her arms as she tucked her feet under the sofa cushion and said, "Good. She deserves a little happiness." I was old enough to remember the Olympic athletes pumping their black-gloved fists into the air. I was old enough to remember Nixon's speech and his victory sign before riding Air Force One for the last time, and President Ford's pardon a year later. I was old enough to remember people in the streets of America protesting the war in Vietnam and burning their draft notices in open-mouthed metal cans. I was old enough to remember all the maxi dresses, and The Hustle, and the bras being burned, and the ERA proposals and rejections.

I was old enough to remember watching the moon landing, Neil Armstrong's first steps, and my brother's disbelief: "Mr. Howe says it's all a Hollywood movie."

For the only time I could remember, Dad turned his head and barked at him to shut up, that Mr. Howe was ignorant and a fool.

I was old enough to remember Jimmy Carter taking the oath of office, and I remember the long gas lines and the hostages in Iran and his loss a few years later. I remember the former president's voice cracking when he announced to a small group in Georgia that the Iranian government was releasing those embassy employees held hostage for 444 days.

[December 2001] — Now I'm old enough to witness my friends being released as hostages. After weeks and months of mounting darkness, a glimmer of light. Johanna and Margot have been released—for medical reasons. News reports say they have been flown to Germany for medical treatment because both women are gravely ill with undisclosed illnesses. Their parent news company issues a statement of gratitude. There are more holes in this story than in a block of Swiss cheese, and I call but can get no answers. I try Rafiq, but the number of the house where he and Zahra lived last fall has been disconnected. I slam down the phone and then try the hotel. Mr. Salim has resigned, someone tells me. No, they cannot help me, and what help could they give? Rafiq never stayed at the hotel as a guest. I try the embassy, but the line is very poor and they cannot hear me at all. I remember Johanna's husband's name, Dieter Becker, and try to look him up. There are thirty-seven D. Beckers in the latest directory I can get hold of, which is several years old, in Frankfurt. I try almost twenty, but none of them speak English and I give up. The cable channels put up their headshots again, as well as the photo of us all eating lunch.

Then the light is somewhat extinguished. Today I turn on the TV and see Johanna's husband on the screen, standing next to a doctor in front of the biggest hospital in Frankfurt. "Mrs. Becker has succumbed to her injuries," the doctor says. "She was readmitted to the intensive care unit last night and died this morning." I miss the couch and land on the floor, bend my knees and pull my legs close to me. I lock my hands around my knees and hold myself tight as the doctor thanks the staff and offers nothing more of substance. He doesn't list her injuries but says she suffered those injuries after being forced off the plane and held captive for months. He mentions Margot, only to say that Miss Durand's condition has improved but she has sustained significant injuries, and that she is expected to go home. I mute the TV and cry myself to sleep.

Six

[MARCH 2002] — A RARE LUNCH WITH COLLEAGUES, AND I MISS Virginia at the table cluttered with baskets of bread and butter, water glasses and mason jars with slender stalks of roses inside. It is an age-old question in an American newsroom: What is it that makes something "American"? Even now, in the wake of 9/11, the nation argues "One Nation under God" in our Pledge of Allegiance. How very American of us, the pundits say on TV talk shows. Also, the age-old arguments that I first heard in Florida as a cub reporter again rear their ugly heads: English only. In Florida there is constant political turnover, congressional representatives waving hello and goodbye every two years. In this cycle, the "English only" is a flame, hot to the touch but so bright that it is hard to turn away. The initiatives for bilingual education fall on a deaf electorate. Now, with so many dead and so many missing at the hands of terrorists, the public is turning insular.

I fall squarely on the side of more education, wanting to make America more educated, more part of its neighborhood. "Why shouldn't we have a mandatory second language?" I argue at the restaurant, members of the newspaper's editorial board present at the banquet-sized table. It is unusual, a lunch out with colleagues, an effort for the reporters to meet and mix with colleagues whom they typically don't see. In the past, I'd attended when the sports department was invited. Ford sat down next to me. I scarcely breathed when he casually put his arm around the back of my chair, and Virginia grinned at us from across the table. Just a few years ago, but today it seems miles away and in a previous lifetime. "We're in the Americas so we should all learn Spanish and learn to converse with our neighbors," I say now.

But the naysayers, all those white men who were of a certain age, they won't hear of it. They are the assistant city editors, copy editors, assistant managing editors. On the TV news side, I can imagine they are the men behind the scenes, assigning stories and airtime. "Everyone learns English, that's the standard language."

Then someone said something about how Benjamin Franklin had cast the deciding vote, long ago, about English. "We were one step away from German," this voice said from the other side of the table.

But most Americans don't know that. There's a lot of history as well as more recent events that have not been touched upon in either textbooks or newspapers: Tulsa and Wilmington massacres, the Trail of Tears, George Washington and Thomas Jefferson as slaveholders; the resurrection of the Ku Klux Klan in the early twentieth century all because Woodrow Wilson had screened *Birth of a Nation* in the White House. It feels like every week there's another set of Holocaust deniers being given airtime, or there are Americans telling reporters that Japanese-Americans were treated equitably and with respect, that the stories of internment were exaggerations. I know these histories only because my college history professors had insisted we read and learn the stories behind the headlines. "Why shouldn't Americans learn something else?" I say, citing my mother as an example, unsure whether any of my father's stories were true, and so I left him out. Mom had studied English and Sanskrit and Bengali and Hindi, all before the age of twelve. She had gone on to an English-speaking high school and had to prove fluency. "It'll only help."

But Rich isn't convinced and speaks inelegantly. "Help with what? We don't help. We observe."

"You only see what you want to see," I mutter under my breath. Luckily no one has heard me.

Rich's statement is both true and untrue. Journalists are not relief workers; we do not actively help. But our words do help. They bring awareness to a situation or public concern; they give the public information to make informed decisions. And I'm not the only one: I've seen many of my colleagues slip a twenty to someone whose need was dire and literally a matter of survival or extinction. In rural West Virginia, after a devastating fire. In Colorado, after a school shooting. Outside Kolkata, after a massive outbreak of cholera that took six members of a single family, I pulled out my wallet and handed over thousands of rupees, Gandhi's bespectacled face looking past me repeatedly, the equivalent of fifty dollars. No matter what I work on, no matter where I am, it all returns to India.

Before our brief visit to India: We were the Kepplers for a long time, the four of us: Karl, Chameli, Adam, and Elena. Adam and I Americans by birth. Mom a naturalized citizen after medical school and marriage. Dad, who said his family had emigrated from the Rhine area three generations ago, grew up in Wisconsin and had family who had gone into politics. For a long time, Dad spoke of his distant cousin who had been a count and a diplomat, and then later, he said their family was first cousins with the family of the Kepplers that produced the atmospheric scientist who oversaw the development of weather radar and the national storms laboratory. None of that proved true or accurate in the end.

Many a Saturday Dad had promised us that his parents, John and Eleanor, or his sister Stacy or his Uncle Joseph were coming to visit. At first Adam and I cleaned up our rooms, changed into nice clothes, played quietly around the house, waited all day. The first time I cried and begged Dad to call them and if they didn't answer to call the state troopers and the hospital because surely something had happened. Mom stood by silently and watched Dad, said nothing. Dad stood by the phone but didn't use it. "They'll be all right," he said. "They'll come when they can." His eyes were bright from what I thought were unshed tears and what he always insisted were stifled yawns. By the fourth promise of a visit, the beds were left unmade, the dishes soaking in the sink. Mom read a book on the couch, feet propped up on the coffee table, Adam and I on our bikes racing through the freckled side streets, sunlight dappling through the maple leaves.

"They'll never come," Adam said on that day, stopped at the

entrance to the park. "They're not even real." His voice was starting to change but in it I still recognized a child's disappointment.

More than anything in the world I wanted to know the truth.

Still, for a long time we were the Kepplers, with a father from the Midwest and a beautiful mother from India and two children, then all growing up in the suburbs of college towns: Montgomery, Birmingham, Gainesville, Tampa, Knoxville, Chattanooga, and a host of towns in between. Rented houses, two cars, a stay-at-home mom who used her M.D. to bake and sew. Dad used his M.D. not to practice medicine but to teach premed classes. After a couple of years, Dad would inevitably and quietly be asked to leave, the promise of tenure denied.

My parents had different approaches to each new city to which we were forced to move. My dad would ingratiate himself with the first five people who were even remotely polite to him, and soon there'd be coffee meetings and plans to organize and labor rights. It didn't matter where we went: Kentucky, Tennessee, Florida. There would soon be agitators at our doorstep, sign-making parties, talk of worker rights. If the town or college was especially small or conservative, he conversely would make himself the indentured servant of the person who hired him, and every time it would be "Mrs. Weathers, Dean Weathers's wife, really likes Indian food. She found a lovely curry dip recipe she'd love for you to bring when we go for dinner."

My mother's stare was priceless. I wish I could have bottled it and brought it out and sprinkled it later when I knew I would have to look at someone in that way. In an alternate universe, it would set the object of the stare on fire while simultaneously freezing him into a molten statue. "Who is Dean Weathers's wife?" my mom asked politely. "Is she Indian?"

"From New Hampshire, actually. Well, darling, please don't interrupt. I was having lunch with them . . ."

"At their home?" Mom inquired.

Dad's face imported a scowl. "No."

Mom exported a tiny, frigid smile. "At their country club?"

Dad's eyebrows squished together to form one big brow. "Darling, as I was saying . . . Now I've forgotten what I was saying . . ."

Mom examined her nails. "At the department?"

"Darling, it doesn't really matter where the conversation was taking place . . ."

"No?" She bit a corner of her nail. "Well?"

By this time, Dad would simultaneously melt and freeze under her gaze. "It wasn't lunch, exactly. It was a reception at the front of the business school, Dean Weathers and his wife were invited, and they extended the invitation to me. And Mrs. Weathers—darling, you're going to love Mrs. Weathers so much—she said the curry dip was an absolute favorite at her Junior League. This year they are considering lending their support to the illiterate. Perhaps you should consider lending your support . . ."

By this time Mom, who could not join the Junior League or even eat lunch with these ladies in public—not because segregation was still on the books but because no one seemed to remember that it was no longer the rule of the land—shifted in her seat, her eyes two tiny black holes sucking in the entire universe very slowly. "So, when are we going to dinner?"

"Darling, these things are so delicate," Dad said. "We didn't quite converge on a date . . ."

Mom smoothed her hair. "How lovely," she said, and she left the room before the sentence was even finished.

I later came to find that Mom's approach to making new friends was standard issue Bengali practice: The white pages in the phone book. "Every town has a Bengali," she said, flipping through the white pages. We have several chances in every town to find the "B-C-D-M-S League": Biswas, Banerjee, Chatterjee, Choudhury, Dasgupta, Malik, Mazumdar, Mukherjee, Sanyal, Sen. And sometimes, if *Y* is counted as a vowel, Roy. "The problem with Roy," she said, "is that some white families use it."

She'd had some unfortunate run-ins over the phone. Luckily, they were just phone mishaps, she said. She'd heard of the Indian boys who came over and saw signs for Aryan Brotherhood meetings and thought they were Indian cultural meetings. They'd barely made it out with their lives. "There are so many people like me," she said, "who came over and got a job and tried to make it in America."

If she meant putting up with Dad and having to make a curry dip that used milk and mayonnaise, then I probably would have returned to India. But there lies the chasm between Mom and me: I'm willing to go anywhere but I'm firmly rooted to the idea that I'm American. I would never emigrate from my home country. She's firmly rooted in the idea that she could never return to India, and although it'll always be her real home, she had to leave it to make progress.

Mom calls all the Bengali last names in the phone book. There are usually at least two because there are Bengalis everywhere, and soon she finds one at home. A quick conversation later, we are in the car; sometimes my brother joins us too, but never Dad after the time he insulted Mr. Biswanath in Birmingham. And soon after that we are having masala tea and spinach pakoras made with Bisquick because chickpea flour is damn hard to find and the nearest non-American store is seventy miles away.

And suddenly, Mom is herself again. Speaking rapid Bangla and talking about Puja, though we never did celebrate at home. Dad comments each time she lights a candle or puts a battery-operated votive in front of her picture of Durga, the one cut out from a calendar that some cousin sent her one year.

Suddenly Mom has color in her cheeks, and she is alert and making jokes. Everyone presents well, and it is true that we have a great family photo that Mom keeps in her wallet and the Indians are always so impressed. She's wearing a sari, and I'm wearing a kameez, and the boys are looking so handsome in their tucked-in shirts and slacks. Everyone is usually so impressed that she's a medical doctor, and they look at her so strangely when she says she doesn't practice.

India: the one moment that changed the trajectory of my life, and all the questions that came after, and how almost none of those questions have ever been answered. In the summer of my eleventh year, Dad, Mom, Adam, and I went to India—to Kolkata, specifically—on the pretext of my distant uncle's wedding. Mom said it was high time to go home, even if it was for a few weeks, and what better occasion than the start of her favorite cousin's new life with his new bride.

Dad did not want to go and offered to send Mom alone, or with me, a mother-daughter trip. But Mom said no, that she wanted to introduce her husband and children to her family. Dad grudgingly agreed but complained bitterly about the expense, the time away, the heat, and the potential for illnesses such as dysentery and cholera and hepatitis.

We arrived in the middle of the night after a series of long flights, first from Chattanooga to Atlanta, then from Atlanta to New York, then from New York to Frankfurt, and then Frankfurt to Bombay. From there we were transported to the domestic terminal, queued up for the last Kolkata flight, and arrived close to midnight. Dad and my brother complained incessantly the entire time: about their fatigue, about the quality of the airline food, about the length of time it was taking to reach our destination. But not me. Mom called me her ideal travel companion. I looked out the window and took in everything as much as I could. I ate everything put in front of me, from the hard rolls and frozen pats of butter to the purported chicken swimming in tomato sauce and the tidy squares of pudding with a single slice of fruit on top.

I had flown once before with my parents, back when Dad was employed at a big college in Tampa. We had money and were able to fly to Colorado for some conference Dad was speaking at while my brother was away at soccer camp.

But this was flying at a whole new level. I squeezed Mom's hand and said this was a good idea. I had a thousand questions about the events taking place and the people we would meet, and our banter in Bengali was soft and low, the murmur of a running brook. Between our conversation and the drone from the airplane engines and the bad movies that were being randomly shown on the pull-down screen, my brother finally fell asleep on our snoring dad.

Dad insisted on a hotel, so we holed up the first day at a decent place by the airport until we could wake up. Mom's family had arranged for us to stay in the same building as her parents, at an unoccupied but furnished flat. Her parents were away at a cousin's house while their flat was being refurbished, and we were to see them soon. A few days before the wedding, my uncle had arranged a trip to the Calcutta Zoo. We were to eat lunch with cousins at the family home, then hop in a cab at the bus depot in Baguiati to meet him there. "You can do it, Didi?" he asked Mom, who answered confidently that she could manage.

Lunch was simple but delicious, and the cousins showed off eating with forks while Adam and I showed off eating with our hands. The cousins were more than happy to call us a taxi. But it was Dad who said we should walk off the lunch. We were on the Foira Bhavan side of Baguiati, Mom pointed out. The road was wide enough to accommodate the buses that rumbled by every so often, overladen with humans. A Kali mandir was around the corner, and incense was in the air. But the smell from the competing open sewers and the fly-infested mud left me feeling queasy. Adam and Dad were walking stiffly in their slacks and pullover half-sleeve shirts. I could tell from Dad's dismayed face that he wished he had said yes to the taxi. I was dressed in a salwar kameez that had sunflowers embroidered on the hem, and Mom was in a matching yellow sari. "This is where your great-uncle has worked as a homeopathic doctor for decades," she said. The lines to his clinic snaked over the lawn and onto the street every morning. "We're sure to see him at the wedding, he's busy now."

Mom leaned in and whispered that she was excited for her parents to finally meet Adam and me. Mom's parents were arriving later that day and we had to get back before dark.

Near the minibus stop, there was a taxicab stand. Suddenly a hundred men milled about as we walked, then waited, to catch a ride to the Calcutta Zoo. A chorus of voices registered, an orchestra of anger rising. Some competed for the loudest voice while others clearly delineated themselves with raised fists and swinging arms. Their heads looked up and around, their eyes became hot black stones, and anger brewed in the early afternoon sun. The breeze was nothing but a dust storm waiting to be born.

Dad did not understand what was happening but, like me, felt the air change and the mood shift. "Let's go back," he said.

My brother instantly agreed.

It was as though someone had flipped a switch. The density of the men milling about transformed into a mob. The bodies crowded together and pushed up against one another. Mom cocked her head and listened to their words, and I followed suit. A truck—they called it a lorry—had struck an old man on an oxcart. The man was fatally injured, and the oxen were bleeding profusely and would have to be put down.

Justice was swift. The truck driver was taken out of the cab and had no time to plead his case. "Please!" he shouted, an intermingling of Bengali and English. "No! Please!" Adam and I looked around at the faces of the determined men, lips rounded into blood-red Os, hands raised as if halting traffic. Some of these men fashioned a noose. A few women, standing on the margins of the bus depot, pleaded for the man's life, pleaded to wait for the police, pleaded for calm.

Mom stepped into the crowd, her yellow sari a beacon. I tried to follow, but Dad grabbed my brother and held him close, and he took me by the arm and hoisted me above his head so I was sitting on his shoulders, safely above the crowd. From there, I had an unobstructed view.

The mob descended on a construction crane and hoisted its driver away to safety. Within seconds, the mob placed the noose on the construction crane's arm, dropped the man's head inside the noose, and stepped away. The driver's neck broke. He dangled, dead.

I gasped.

Dad's grip on my right leg tightened.

No one said help was on the way.

No one spoke English except the driver, who was now lifeless.

Soon Mom was engulfed by the men of the mob, the yellow center of a dark flower, and still I saw her, her mouth opened, eyes ablaze, shoving the men back as they laid hands on her. "I'm a doctor! I'm a doctor!" she said again and again, her Bengali loud and unrelenting, pushing forward until she was practically underneath the crane and the hanged man. She screamed at them, the men of the mob, the men who were underneath celebrating this man's death. Finally the police arrived, and the man was cut down.

The crowd dispersed immediately, and the women in the vicinity all hurried toward my mother and the murdered man. I poked Dad on the head and screamed, "We have to help her!"

Mom checked his lifeless body and looked up at us, tears running down the length of her cheeks and dripping onto her collared yellow blouse. My brother's face twisted away from the body and nuzzled Dad's neck. I stared at Mom and begged Dad to let me down. At first he said no, but Mom nodded, and he put me down in front of her and the dead man. I looked past her and watched the men who'd done this run away, disappear into the alleys and side streets. "Why? Why? Why?" I thought I spoke aloud. My mouth formed the words, but no sound came out.

Mom told the police what she observed, and Dad and Adam stood like statues with movable necks, nodding in agreement when Mom said something about the crowd and the murdered man. No one asked me anything.

One of the women commented in Bengali that my innocence was taken at such a young age. Mom stared at me long and hard, and she refused to look at Dad.

Dad looked at Mom for the longest time, and then he looked over at me.

Mom and Dad asked my brother and me if we were okay. My brother was able to smooth over his face muscles by pretending to yawn, and then he nodded. I scowled, wanting to run after the men and ask them why they'd done it, but I focused my gaze on the straps of my sandals and nodded quickly.

The minibus came, and although it said LADIES ONLY (an informal admission that coed public buses were often unsafe for women, another informal admission that a culture's honor rested with its women and there was little or no chance of being molested on a segregated bus), the driver took one look at Mom and let Dad and Adam board the front of the bus. Later, at the zoo, the Bengal tigers pacing in their pens despite the heat, Dad said, "We have to put this behind us."

But none of us ever did.

The rest of the India trip was a blur, a stack of photographs that were out of focus. I remember the joy of meeting my grandparents, their terms of endearment, their elegance and charm, and the glamor of the wedding, the rows and rows of guests eating their dinner on banana leaves and drinking cha from clay-pot cups, the food that smelled heavenly even though I did not eat. Often, I remember our departure: Mom's arms around her parents, refusing to let go.

After India: We returned to America, changed. The chaos that followed threw our sensitive, high-strung family into turmoil. On the outside we were normal: a mom, a dad, a son, a daughter. Two things changed: Adam begged for boarding school and my mother acquiesced without even consulting Dad. Then Mom went back to work as an emergency room doctor. Dad became the trailing spouse, the house husband for a while. Although I didn't know the term at the time, once I finally learned it, in the context of a Michael Keaton movie where the husband stayed at home to watch the family, I applied the term literally. Dad was husband and father to whatever rented house we lived in—fixing the leaking faucet in the bathroom or changing out light bulbs with a special stick for the light fixtures that were too high to reach by standing atop a chair. It all seemed okay, but then he froze, then he lost interest in even maintaining his dignity.

Of course, the pakoras at strangers' houses and the cha and the conversation went out the window when Mom went back to work.

Mom had no more time to show off photos from her wallet or make Bangla jokes or find someone to reminisce about Kolkata or India. Those days were long over, but after she went back to work the color returned to her cheeks in a different way. Her eyes carried a wariness, but her body was more composed. Never did she raise her voice, except once, when she begged to go back to work just after she went into remission for the first time. Dad on the other hand kept playing the same slot machines with the same strategy.

Then Dad got a DUI one night, and shortly thereafter Mom got an offer to work at a hospital in New York—not the city, but north of Manhattan. So we moved and started over. My brother changed boarding schools, from the one that was a two-hour drive from our house in the South to a school that was a train ride to Connecticut. In Westchester County, I played the Why game every morning before school and every afternoon that I hitched a ride home with the Swansons. Mrs. Swanson worked in the principal's office, and her youngest son, Tommy, was a grade younger than me and wore thick glasses and was always buried in some sci-fi fantasy book that involved planetary adventures and flying sea creatures. I hitched because Mrs. Swanson didn't want me to cross the highway on foot by myself; I hitched because Dad refused to participate in a carpool. The questions rotated but were asked nonetheless: Why can't I go to a friend's house? Why can't I play sports? Why can't I go to the library? Why can't you pick me up after school?

At some point after India, for a good three years, maybe even four, Dad stopped looking forward: to the nebulous future, to the immediate future, to the next hour. He stopped bathing, he stopped shaving, he stopped changing his clothes. His at-home uniform was these paint-stained navy sweats and an old Minnesota Vikings sweatshirt someone had given him as a gag gift the year their team beat the Vikings in the playoffs. He began each sentence with "When I was your age, I . . ." and "Back in the day . . ." "When I was your age, I could go outside and play unsupervised. When I was your age, I didn't get piano lessons. I played clarinet in high school and that was good enough, and then I was part of the band and I walked home with my instrument, even when it was raining. When I was your age, I was respectful to my parents, and I listened to everything they told me. I accepted their view of the world."

And yet I still had not met his parents.

I attempted to involve Mom, when our shadows sailed past each other in the hallway or the foyer in the early morning or late evening, like ships.

Mom would purse her lips like a sultry silver screen star and take off her shoes and slide out of her sweater and hang her bag on the pegs of the coatrack. Then she would smile. "I can't be in charge of this," she said every time. "I only have a few hours before I go back. You'll have to find a solution with your dad."

Mom would wander into the kitchen, pulling out a container of plain yogurt and a cucumber from the fridge along with tamarind paste. She'd take out the puffed rice from the cupboard and make some quick version of chaat, offering me a bite before going to her bedroom to nap. I tried many times to interrupt this food-preparation routine, but Mom always held up a finger, as if to indicate she would be available in the future, a short time from this present. But Mom simply ate and put her dirty dishes in the sink and walked away.

Soon I began making plans on my own. There were days that Mrs. Swanson still gave me a ride, but most of the time I made myself indispensable to the very pregnant math teacher who was about to go on maternity leave and needed help with the photo copier and cleaning the chalkboards. Mrs. Brady was only too happy to drop me off on the other side of the highway about a block from my street. "Well, I'm not supposed to take students in my personal car," she said, her cheeks flushed and her stomach distended under the red print dress. To me she looked like the young girl version of Santa Claus, merry and bright. "But it's my last month, and they can't fire me." She winked and I winked back.

Mrs. Brady's belly grew and grew, and the days became shorter and shorter, and still she insisted on driving me home. "It won't take but a minute," she said one Friday, as the first drops of rain landed squarely on her plump apple cheeks.

"You don't have to," I said. But Mrs. Brady waved me off and said it was all right.

There came the day when the rain was quite heavy, and Mrs. Brady's car slid into a ditch. She stopped the car and cried, held her stomach and cried some more. "I can do it," I said to her, and I got out of my side of the car as she slid slowly and painfully into my seat. I took the wheel and put my foot on the brake. My math teacher had a strong grip even then, and she righted the wheel and told me to put my foot on the gas. I did, and I felt the same queasiness I felt when Dad made me sit through the automatic car wash, how it appeared the car was moving forward, but really the car was standing still and the oversized brushes were bustling back and forth. Still, I managed to get us out of the ditch and drive awkwardly through the downpour to her driveway.

I dropped her off a few minutes later, right in front of the leaf-laden sidewalk, and she thanked me and walked inside to her house. Soaked to the bone, I hurried down the street and went inside my house.

Mom and Dad didn't appear to notice. There was no inquiry, and anyway, Dad had moved on by this point from his do-nothing phase to being actively out in the afternoons. He wasn't there that rainy day, and when he did come home, he was perfectly dry except for his hair, which looked trimmed and shampooed. He was surprisingly kind as he tousled my soaked hair and said "What's shakin', bacon?" before he wandered down the hall toward the kitchen.

Mom came home much later that evening—it was later than she had ever been. "Giant pileup on the highway," she said. "Every room was taken."

I spent the weekend fretting that Mrs. Brady had been on the highway, that she was part of the pileup. I slept fitfully all three nights and was only able to close my eyes after midnight on Sunday with the promise I made to myself that Mrs. Brady would be waiting for me the next day.

On Monday I practically ran into math class, and a young woman with long blond hair braided down the length of her back like Rapunzel was sitting in Mrs. Brady's seat. Her name was Miss Townsend, and her southern drawl was so languid it took her an extra five minutes to get through the attendance sheet. "What were y'all working on, on Friday?" Miss Townsend asked.

"Why don't you call her and ask?" I blurted out.

Miss Townsend's smile faltered. "Oh, she's not available."

My hand went to my head. It was as though there was an ant farm in my hair. I felt the unsettled breakfast in my stomach making a case for regurgitation and beginning to climb up my throat. "I need to go to the bathroom," I said.

Miss Townsend, though young, knew the look on my face—no doubt greenish and panicky—was genuine and excused me. Instead of the girls' bathroom diagonally across from math 102, I ran down one hallway, turned left, and ran down another hallway, the pass sweaty in my clenched fist. I arrived at the office and burst in the door. "Is Mrs. Brady dead?" I asked the three secretaries who had stopped their chitchat and were staring at me in obvious astonishment.

I didn't know the names of the two older ladies, but Mrs. Benson, who sometimes had lunch duty in the cafeteria, answered, "It's a boy. Seven pounds, four ounces."

I remember that as I walked back to class my ears felt like conch shells, my heartbeat so loud it drowned out everything else; for a short while I heard nothing but my own heart pumping—not the sound of the school bell ringing, nor the students talking as they poured out of the classrooms, and not the words Miss Townsend said as she tapped me on the shoulder, ostensibly to see if I was all right.

Seven

[SEPTEMBER 2002] — I WATCH THE ATTENDANT SUCCESSFULLY lock the door from the inside. And isn't this the metaphor I've been searching for the past year? I have locked the door from the inside: ignoring Seb and Ford, ignoring Adam, not allowing myself the smallest respite to mourn Mom or even consider what has happened to Virginia. I am trudging forward on the outside, assignment after assignment, a good soldier, stoic, writing declarative sentences. As I feel the airplane begin its initial roll to the takeoff position on the runway, I can only think of Johanna. Killed for doing her job. How she would have bartered away anything to feel her last flight soar into the sky. Margot is now a fashion photographer; I have seen her work splashed in glossy magazines. Everyone, including me, remains surprised that Margot continues to work even if it is at the periphery of her former life.

The plane rolls to a stop on the tarmac.

The flight attendant is nervous as she addresses us with a "one moment" in English, then Spanish. It is a domestic flight for this leg, but the plane and crew are part of a Continental flight from Mexico. She adjusts the red silk scarf loosely tied around her collar three times. She stands facing me, six rows ahead, her eyes firmly glued toward the window. I follow her gaze and out my window see the bulletproof German black sedan speeding toward the plane. It is night outside. I wonder how many minutes before the flight attendant is forced to walk up to me in 16A and ask me to grab my things and deplane. We are in America, and it is more than a year after 9/11 and everything has changed as it appears to remain the same.

I think of Zahra and Rafiq now, at the airport, their desperation. Johanna and Margot. How I wish the rules of the embassy and consulate applied to the inside of a domestic flight. When did I first have this feeling of fear? I pinpoint the moment a writer became the focal point of the Iranian government in 1989; and a fatwa was issued.

But now it's 2002: The car stops next to the airplane. No one gets out, no one goes in. Five minutes tick by in this way and there is no sound coming from the passengers. Not a single complaint, not even the sound of a passenger shifting in his or her seat. I am rigid, frozen in place. There is no one in 16B, but the woman in 16C is soaked through her headscarf; tears of sweat are running from her forehead to her chin and beading her upper lip. I wonder who she is. She is brave to wear a headscarf. Finally, the car speeds off back toward the terminal.

Finally, the captain comes on the speaker: "We are cleared for takeoff."

The passenger next to me exhales audibly as I continue to sip the air-conditioned air and will myself to not move until we are safely in the sky.

I land in New Mexico. I'm there for one reason but end up reporting on another: I see the police log, and there is a report of a Punjabi man, Mr. Bhatia, who has died of unknown causes on a park bench. I remember why the name sounded familiar: It is the name of the aid worker I interviewed in Delhi, the one who witnessed the destruction of the Buddhas of Bamiyan. In between covering the other story I'm there for, I reach out to law enforcement for the police report and to the funeral home for family contacts.

This Mr. Bhatia is older, in Albuquerque; he'd lost his job and his home, and also lost his grip on reality. The way the police tell it, Mr. Bhatia and his wife and son were evicted. They moved into a shelter, where Mr. Bhatia left his family three nights ago. Hunger getting the upper hand over him, he simply lay down on a bench by a Rio Grande vista lookout one day, covered himself up with the discarded newspaper from a metal trashcan, and died.

His obituary was no doubt going to be hard to write. He was an accomplished man on paper, highly educated, far from his native home in Punjab. He had made some poor choices and trusted the wrong people. He lost his savings and his home. His family in India wept on the telephone. I couldn't find any trace of his wife except that she had taken their son and disappeared from the shelter. The photo the police detective had provided came from an album that was somehow locked in a police evidence unit. Someone had thought to log it for a reason that wasn't clear to me. I had a photo of him. He wasn't smiling. But he had a look of confidence about him. His eyes were clear and his glasses had polished metal frames.

I talked to the detective, Jacobs, and after I spoke with him a couple of times, he knew the drill. When I don't have any easy answers, I emulate award-winning *Miami Herald* crime reporter Edna Buchanan and get all the details that might provide a portrait of the person lost: What was in Mr. Bhatia's pocket? A watch with an inscription. TIME IS FOREVER AND SO ARE YOU. Was there a date? Yes, July 1, 1994. And what else in his pocket? Well, the pockets were part of trousers that were tailored at Lloyd's, he answered. He may have been homeless, but he was wearing very comfortable shoes. What will happen to his things once his community holds a funeral for him? Given to the poor, I suppose.

My lede: "The inscription on Rakesh Bhatia's pocket watch, 'Time is forever and so are you,' will be the mantra his family in India will remember him by. Bhatia, 49, was found dead near the Rio Grande two days ago, a watch in his tailored trousers pocket, and expensive loafers on his feet. His family in the Punjab province couldn't believe the news and expressed concern for his wife and son, who have disappeared from the shelter where they were residing earlier this week."

Back in New York, the super is kind and helps me with all the empty boxes. The two boxes with cleaning supplies and packing tape, markers and labels, and garbage bags inside. "The moving van is coming tomorrow," I say to John.

His face crumples a bit more and he nods. "The family called me."

We briefly talk about the memorial service the family held—which neither of us attended. I was out of town on a serial murder trial in Florida, and John had not been invited. I assumed Hughes and Rich attended, but neither had bothered to tell me anything.

Then I'm left alone in the apartment, one that I know well though it is not my own. Virginia's mother had been so appreciative: "We just can't do it," Danielle said. "I'm eternally grateful that you can."

I am to sort and throw out things from the bathroom, kitchen, bedroom, and then box up what I can: books, clothes, music, art. Whatever I can't get to, the movers will finish packing tomorrow and take everything back to northern Maryland. All the things that made up Virginia's life will return to the "farm."

I open the blinds and the light from the sky fills the room in slants. There is a bit of dust, but the rooms are clean. I step away from the answering machine and go to the bathroom instead, a good place to start. I throw out her toothbrush and blush, her palette of eyeshadow, her dental floss. I know her mother doesn't want that extra roll of toilet paper, so I throw it out too, along with the half-used bottles of shampoo and mouthwash. The strangest thing I find is in Virginia's medicine cabinet: a pink packet with birth control pills inside. The last time she took them was September 10. I think back to the last phone call. Not even a hint there was a man. I thought she had broken up with Chris—or was it Christophe?—the previous June. I study the packet, shaped like a seashell, and notice half the pills in this cycle are gone. I toss it into the trash as well, along with the vitamins and the eye drops that get rid of redness and the feminine products. Then I leave the bathroom and head straight for the kitchen. I box up the pots and pans, and the stainless steel colander. I box up the spices and the unopened blue box of elbow macaroni and throw out the orange juice and the butter and the yogurt whose expiration date was ages ago. Then I head toward the answering machine.

I press the button and wait for the tape to rewind, look around, and make a mental note to box up the contents of the bookcase next to the couch, and take down the photos and art pieces in the tiny hallway that leads from the living room area past the bathroom to the bedroom. The first message is from Hughes: "Good luck tomorrow, kiddo. Call me when you're done." My back is rigid, and I can't feel my face or my toes. It's as though I'm wading through an arctic circle hanging off an ice floe. Another message from someone named Sheila: "Ms. Lawson, good news. We located your account, and the balance on your student loan has been forgiven. Call me back at your earliest convenience, and I'll go over the details with you." Then my voice comes on, twice: "Chicken butt," I hear myself say, the second time. "Sam is looking for you." My legs buckle and I'm on the carpet. I gasp for air as if someone had come and kicked me in the stomach, hard, twice. The machine stops and the voice says it's the end of new messages and gives me the option to delete. I scramble up toward the machine and, on my knees, press the SAVE button. The machine is still emitting a red light that flashes twice and then stops, and flashes twice again. I hit the SAVE button twice and the disembodied voice says, "To listen to saved messages, enter pin." Maybe the mystery man who was the reason Virginia was on birth control left a message. I try her birth year, her birth month and day, I try the year of graduation, I try the most common passwords, 1-2-3-4 and 4-3-2-1. Nothing works. Then I remember Virginia and her lack of interest in choosing anything difficult when it comes to pin numbers and passwords. I press 0-0-0-0 and the voice says, "Please wait." Finally, the tape rewinds and I hear the voice of Virginia's little sister, Claire, singing to her, must have been her birthday.

I stop the tape and carefully unplug the machine and put it in a box and make a note to tell Danielle that Virginia had saved her sister's message. Then I pack up the bookcase, slide Virginia's college trivia contest prizes into my backpack (a few poetry books), wrap up the desk lamp and put it in a box. I enter the bedroom, open the blinds: The bed is neatly made, the walk-in closet door is ajar, and I peek inside and cannot bring myself to disturb Virginia's dresses and work attire, the bridesmaid dress encased in plastic at the end of the rack. I will leave that for the movers. I look through her dresser drawers and box the underwear and pajamas, then rummage through the nightstands. On the left is a bunch of papers with phone numbers on them, utility bills marked paid, a couple of photographs of Christophe and her from two years before when they went to New Orleans for his sister's wedding. On the right is a flashlight and extra batteries and a screwdriver, a wrench, a couple of picture-hanging kits, a bright green tape measure, a ballpoint pen. I cry then, at Virginia's *MacGyver* drawer, and remember our Wednesday evenings watching TV.

After my sobs subside, I take deep breaths and draw the blinds down. I leave a note for the movers and take one last long look. I cannot solve the mystery. I do not know who she was dating last September nor where to start looking. I want to commiserate with her boyfriend. I want to talk to someone, and Hughes is out of the question.

The players are the same no matter the location and the year. A seemingly infinite series of sequences, of missing people and arrests, of accusations, of distant drought and famine, of punishments meted out, of arms deals and starvation, of disease and greed. I feel I am looping through one long week after the next, hopping from one incident to another and from one scandal to the next. Months arrive and depart. Hughes and Rich are in lockstep, sending me out in America, locally or across the country.

One day Hughes calls in sick. The computers on our floor are sick too, and several of us are asked to go upstairs and work out of sports. I return from my interview with the family of a murdered girl to see Rich taking over an empty desk in the middle of the room. He spots me and calls me over. Rich slides over the requirements, in written form. He avoids eye contact.

I scan the sheet. "Really? Five inches?"

Rich picks up his coffee cup but doesn't drink. "Well, if you write something super compelling, I could maybe get you an extra three inches."

Nearby, the sports guys laugh about some dunk during the pro-basketball game. I hear Ford's voice in the mix but don't trust myself to look. I try to catch Rich's eye. "The fact that this teenager, LaTonya Watkins, was kidnapped and raped and murdered is not super compelling?"

Rich stares. "Stop." Coffee sloshes out of his cup as he returns it to his desk. "You know that's not what I'm saying. What I'm saying is that you're competing with the euthanasia trial."

Yes, everything this week has competed with the rich businessman who married twice and killed both of his terminally ill wives with prescription pills. The public's need to know is insatiable.

I inhale. "If it's super compelling you'll put it on the front page?" The euthanasia trial has been riding 1A. LaTonya Watkins is at best going to be buried somewhere in the metro section.

Rich takes a paper towel from his neighbor's desk and wipes off coffee from the blank tabletop calendar. "If you can make it short and impactful I'll put it on the front."

I pause. "I have your word on that?"

Rich scoffs. "When have I lied to you?"

I resist rolling my eyes. "Lie? Never. Overpromise? Day before yesterday." It is always déjà vu with Rich. Two nights ago, an apartment building arson. Fancy building close to the Met. Rich liked my story and promised to put it on the front page. Almost everyone got out with some smoke inhalation. Except for a mother and son. Luckily, the little boy and his mother were still alive, expected to fully recover from their burns. There was a dramatic revelation in the euthanasia story, something about a bribery allegation, and my arson story went from 1A to 11C in metro.

Rich turns away.

I return to my desk, the breath in my mouth hot. I flip through both notepads and stop on the uncle's comments about LaTonya's future. I look up the start date of the HBCU where she had been accepted for the fall.

The lede practically writes itself: "On the night she was murdered, LaTonya Watkins was just 45 days away from attending her dream school, Spelman College, and pursuing her ambition of becoming a doctor."

After deadline, I take the sheet of Rich's typed instructions and fold and refold the sides into tiny triangles. I try to make an origami flower from memory but settle for the sailboat that Seb taught me to build using a paper menu from a Venice trattoria during our honeymoon. Rich's instructions about the story length act as sail numbers across the mainsail. Then I crush my origami boat into a ball. On the second try the ball rims the trashcan and goes in. I allow myself to look over at the sports department. Ford has already left for the evening game, but two of his colleagues are riveted by what is happening on the big-screen TV. I sigh. If only the public cared about dead Black girls the way it cares about professional basketball.

One night, I run into Ford outside the newspaper's glass entrance, and on his arm is a woman I know only as a popular weekend anchor for a cable station.

We greet each other casually, as if we see each other every day. Ford does not formally introduce me, and the woman blushes the color of the rouge on her cheeks after he says goodnight and my name.

They go inside, his hand on the small of her back, stride toward the elevators. I catch a cab and tell the driver to take me to the Met instead of home. I pay for a ticket and wander around, dazed. I enter the Egypt section and circle the Temple of Dendur, stare out the floor-to-ceiling glass wall. Nothing comforts me.

I am too lost in my thoughts. I make the mistake of complaining to Sebastian on the phone, about the work and the heavy load, about the long hours, about the lack of appreciation from Rich.

The next evening, Sebastian stands before me in our tiny apartment, wine in hand. I quickly find some glasses, and we retire to our bedroom. Hours later, we are out of the shower and in our pajamas, padding around the kitchen, trolling for something to eat.

"I found crackers," he says. He closes the cabinet, and the door thuds shut.

I open the fridge. "I found brie."

We take the snacks to the couch in front of the TV and sit close enough to share.

He grabs the remote and channel surfs. He pauses at a documentary about the famine that has spread in the Horn of Africa, a consequence of drought and two years of failed crops. Up to 38 million could be affected.

The heart-wrenching photos of emaciated children and their distended bellies make my mouth dry. The crackers now taste like cardboard. I put down the food and pick up the newspaper. There's a story on A4, not a big one, but some mention of the famine. No byline. Reuters. "I'm so tired," I say aloud.

Seb puts his hand on mine. "Why don't you quit? Find something else to do?"

I look at his hand, then his face. "What?"

"You're so stressed," he says. "You don't need this."

I take my hand away, walk back into the kitchen, and pick up my glass of wine. "You don't get to decide!" I drain the glass, find the bottle and pour generously.

"Look what it's doing to you," he says.

Ford, I think. If Ford were free then I'd get through it somehow, watch TV reruns on his couch, wade through somehow to the other side. "I can't let go," I say.

Use your imagination, kiddo. That's what Ford had said time and again. We had made plans to meet up, to talk, just before Seb and I were headed to Italy. I waited for an hour at the coffee shop. I wandered around the neighborhood, found a pillow at the flea market, one with the purported Mark Twain quote on it: "You cannot depend on your eyes when your imagination is out of focus." Of course, I took the train and ended up at his apartment, let myself in. I used the last of the duct tape, all shiny and sticky and silverfish gray, and blotted out the words so that it looked like a poem, an erasure poem. "Cannot depend on you." I left it on his couch, a parting gift before I married Sebastian.

What was I looking for except something to fill the silence? Or something to create patterns out of the sea of chaos and cacophony? Wasn't that my job, to find meaning? Who gets to tell the truth? And if you're not part of the accepted establishment, what does that look like?

It is true the first story I wrote for the local newspaper was about caring for Christmas poinsettias in an unusually cold time of year, unusual in that it was bright and sunny and cold instead of sleety and gray and cold. I had interviewed a nursery owner, Mr. Owens, and he'd given his perspective, how to care for them, how long they'd last, what to do if you wanted to condition the plant and try to extend its life—but it was Mr. Anand, owner on Forty-Seventh and Graham, who turned out to the diamond in the rough. His store was drafty, so the heat was cranked up and the poinsettias, he said, were drying up and becoming brittle. He was of Indian origin, but Punjabi, and apparently all our grandparents had gone to the same school of thought. He took ice cubes and sprinkled sugar on top before putting them in the soil of the poinsettias. Overnight the leaves relaxed and softened, and the droopy, dried-out qualities disappeared. I always remember Mr. Anand for answering all my questions on deadline, and for congratulating someone like me, a brown-skinned woman, for landing a job at a competitive newspaper that had many journalism students vying for the position.

In appreciation for the story, Mr. Owens had sent a Christmas bloom for me to the bureau. Stuart and Chelsea were the bureau chiefs, and they clamped down hard the moment the deliveryman placed it gingerly on my shared desk. "What did you promise him?" Stuart asked, as if I had exchanged sexual favors to get a quote on poinsettias. All five feet four of him stood over me as I sat down.

I stared at the big plant and its gaily wrapped base with silver and green tinfoil glistening under the fluorescent bars. "That I'd get the facts right," I said, parroting what Professor Monroe had told us in class, under the subject heading "What to Say When Being Harassed by Someone in the Newsroom." I knew that reporters were not permitted to keep gifts, but the threshold amount was fifteen dollars. I couldn't believe the poinsettia cost that much.

"We're not a PR firm," Chelsea barked, her acute blue eyes narrowing, her lips forming an expression of dislike. She walked over as well. She was even shorter than Stuart but wore amazing black platform shoes that elongated her wire-hanger frame.

I picked up the plant and looked around and saw Mary H. at the corner desk just by the door to the break room. I remembered suddenly that she was a Christmas baby, some sixty years before. I excused myself and walked over to Mary at her desk. She was typing some horrid wedding announcement for the weekend edition. "Happy birthday," I said. "A little early." I put down the poinsettia on her pristine desk.

Mary's eyes filled. "For me?"

I think of Mary almost every week now, every time I must write up a short piece about yet another local newspaper closing. Mary lost her job almost six months ago, during the final round of personnel cuts before the newspaper shut down. There was talk of reviving it, just as a two-man place where the paper would be filled with wire reports. If that scenario materialized, no one would be going to city council meetings and holding the elected officials' feet to the flame, no one would be asking tough questions of the local communities when something went wrong. Corruption would abound.

"Yes, ma'am," I said, and I hugged her after she leapt into my arms. From the corner of my eye, I watched Chelsea cross her arms but clomp back to the cluster of editors' desks. Stuart mumbled something and turned away.

"Any tips?" Mary asked when she sat down again.

"Ice cubes and granulated sugar," I said. "Mr. Anand swears by it."

My parents were the best news junkies. Even before the India trip, we crowded around the TV in the den, watching Walter Cronkite, our dinner plates on our laps. Once Adam left for boarding school, Dad purchased a tiny black and white for the kitchen. No matter who was home at dinnertime, our plates were on the table and our eyes were firmly fixed on this once-a-day ritual. I don't know why Mom and Dad were surprised when I declared my major, as it was their news-watching ritual that hooked me. That and the India trip.

The years looped into a perpetual déjà vu of assassinations in Egypt and Pakistan, airplane hijackings and accidents, Israeli annexations of Palestinian lands, bombings on the Lebanon border, bombings on the China-India border, hurricanes, tornadoes, earthquakes. The last several years before 9/11 were fraught: Rodney King's beating at the hands of police captured on film and replayed twenty thousand times; the Oklahoma City bombing, and the Columbine school shooting. More stories done about the L.A. police officers, McVeigh and the school shooters, than those who had suffered, those who had perished.

Even then, what did it mean to be news junkies? Voraciously reading the morning paper, watching network TV for half an hour in the evening, giving our brains time to absorb, think, question. These days, the onslaught of news is relentless, unceasing. Cable channels regurgitate all twenty-four hours. The public has become numb. I miss Mom even more.

II

Eight

[DECEMBER 2002] — I RECEIVE THE NOTIFICATION IN THE MAIL, regular post. It is almost junk mail, so I almost throw it away before I have the chance to look carefully. It is addressed to Elena Keppler, and my name appears to be handwritten. A high-worth, high-network realty agency with offices all around the world is showing a rather updated view of the outside of the Keppler family home: new shutters, black or maybe midnight blue, sporting a new coat of pale gray paint, a new roof with the shingles a darker shade of gray, all very tasteful. Mom would have approved. From the photos of the interior, I wouldn't have known that it is our family home. It is white on white on white: white walls, white parquet floors in the kitchen and blond wooden floors in the TV room, thick white carpeting, white windowsills, gauzy white curtains. Someone has staged it, presumably the people selling the house, because I can't see my dad doing anything like this. There are oversized white couches with a white ottoman serving as the coffee table, a white dining room set with plush chairs, and a giant white chandelier with crystals hanging like frozen rain above the foyer. It is a scene out of a movie about being lost in a snowstorm. The asking price is very high, but then it is a bigger house in an increasingly pricey neighborhood with a good school district not too far away from the city.

The phone rings. My brother says, "Did you check your mail?"

I say, "I was waiting for your call."

We both sigh in unison and then chuckle.

"He called me, you know, out of the blue a few days ago," my brother says. "Said he was going fishing with some friends. Wasn't too specific. I did get it out of him that he's somewhere in Wisconsin or Minnesota right now, with old friends he considers family?"

The invisible question mark hangs in the air. Strangely, there is no hurt or confusion in my brother's voice. Strangely, there is no hurt or confusion in my heart. Just curiosity coursing through my veins. From Adam's tone, I gather that he feels similarly.

"You should be a reporter," I say. "That's more than I've been able to get out of him." I relay my unsuccessful call with Dad, also a few days ago. I had called the home number and he answered but said he was just heading out. He did not mention that he was putting the house on the market. The reason for my call was that one of Mom's friends had seen him at a restaurant with a tall blond woman about his age. They were laughing it up at the bar and then sat in the picture window at the restaurant for their meal, and that's how Mom's neighbor knew. I asked him if he'd gone out to dinner recently, that one of my old teachers had seen him at the pasta place. He laughed and said, "I've been eating out a lot lately. I can't remember which night she may have seen me."

I knew this trick. But I didn't fall for the bait, didn't tell him which neighbor, didn't give him a description of the woman with whom he'd been seen. I said nothing. Usually I pose questions to which I already know the answer. Just to gauge the climate and temperature of the situation at hand, just to check the veracity of the person before me telling the story. Dad should know that about me. Dad should know a lot of things about me by now. What I had said to the neighbor was my standard diplomatic response: "He has so many friends. I'm so glad that he is taking some time for himself and having a good time."

"You're a good daughter," the neighbor had said.

I relayed this last bit to my brother, and I could hear the laugh in his voice when he said, "She's right."

I was most certainly not the good daughter and, unfortunately, that was not the first neighbor to call. Dad had been seen with a redhead a couple of weeks before coming out of a grocery store with a bottle of wine, covered in a brown paper bag, and a clear plastic bag that held a baguette and some cheese. It was clearly a date. Every time Ford and I broke up, there he would be the next minute with another girl on his arm. When an entire week would go by with no new girl, I knew the heartfelt apology was coming. "I don't know about that," I say to my brother now. "I feel like I should go investigate."

Hughes owes me a few days off. The first day is a Monday, and Sebastian happened to be coming through town on his way to deliver some lecture in Chicago. "Why don't you come with me?" he asks. His tone isn't unkind, but I see the frustration on his face, the way his lips curl. I check his fingernails, and it looks like he's been chewing on them like a little boy.

"I want to go see Mom's grave," I say in response. I suffer when I say that; my stomach drops and my throat closes. I recount cleaning out Virginia's apartment. Short sentences. When I am done, I close my eyes for a second and the unshed tears burn.

Sebastian holds out his hand, and I take it and squeeze. "Can you wait three days? I could come with you after I deliver the paper at the Thursday session."

I shake my head no. I explain as evenly as I can that Dad was vague about where Mom was buried and that it might take me a while to find her. His head snaps back as if he recalled a memory, and something clicked. "Now I think I understand what he was saying." Sebastian says he overheard Dad on the phone the last time he was there at the house, post-funeral. He says, "I didn't understand at first. No, I mean, I understood what he said. I just didn't know what it meant." Seb releases my hand, and both of his hands fly up like captive birds tethered to the ground by string.

"He said he intended to keep the matter private and to keep her among his next of kin, one way or another. Bury her close by," Sebastian says, taking my hand again. "Because she was *his* wife, after all."

Sebastian's comments make my skin itch, and I want to drop everything and run to the nearest airport. Instead, I squeeze his hand. "Lucky my brother and I aren't family and don't have any right to know."

Sebastian grunts in response and squeezes back.

I agree to accompany him to Chicago.

In Chicago, we have a nice dinner at that tower with the revolving restaurant. I put on a black dress and makeup. Sebastian says I look beautiful. I didn't think that restaurant would be open considering the Twin Towers, but it seems in the last six months not much has changed. People have returned to their normal routine outside of New York and D.C. and western Pennsylvania. Seb and I talk about how the population has moved past their arguments over "One Nation under God" in the Pledge of Allegiance, and the collective fervor is the fears about security and safety, reports of anthrax seemingly everywhere, stories every week splashed across all kinds of news outlets. Whatever unity had brought us all together on September 11 is already cracking. More and more stories we are reading and watching have a deferential tone toward the police. In the beginning, there was nonstop 9/11 coverage night and day; now the tenor and tone are different. I am frustrated by this slide in news standards, in the rise of double standards.

Sebastian squeezes my hand. "This is why I'm grateful I live in Europe," he says, his voice so quiet that the people at the next table's banter almost drowns him out.

This is the voice that reminds me when we first met. Sebastian and I started out as friends playing the pinball machines at the arcade next to the bar where all the reporters hung out after deadline. He was there with our mutual friend Beth, who went to school with him and her husband but worked with me since our Florida days. Virginia was out of town. I wasn't drinking that much then—on the periphery of my breakup with Ford. I was finally out of Florida for good and spending more and more time in New York near the lecherous crowd, as I called them, the friends of Ford. I was giving them a wide berth at the venue that night, but I didn't want to be alone.

Sebastian was tall and handsome, with longish hair that nearly reached his shoulders.

It was a bright and loud game, the machine had slot-machine sounds and canned victory music that played a second too long. I think he let me win. I told him so after, and he smiled easily.

Later I learned he had let me win, after we had hung out a couple of evenings like an old married couple watching TV and eating pasta he made, after we had kissed, after we had spent the entire night talking in the apartment that he kept in New York, the apartment that I moved into when we eloped.

"I've been looking at you for so long," he says, refilling my soda, "and I finally had a chance to hang out with you."

That first night Sebastian came over with a club soda in his hand. "What are you having?" I asked.

He smiled and said, "I have to drive in about an hour, so I'm pretending to drink today."

I said, "That's brilliant. I'm going to pretend with you."

We played our pinball game. Then we had a three-hour conversation punctuated by a lengthy tangent on microfinancing women in South Asian nations such as Bangladesh and Myanmar and Vietnam. At some point he looked at his watch and shrugged, then asked me another question. We talked about the power of working women in rural areas, how their incomes improved the lives of their families and their villages. Then we landed on how the tech boom in India had created this huge middle class that the government was prepared for but only in a limited sense. The government knew there would be more people driving new cars and that the infrastructure would have to be revamped and that factories would need to make more fridges and more material goods. But the government had not prepared for other signs of affluence.

"I think that everyone underestimated that eating meat is an emblem of wealth. Suddenly, four hundred million people who have been generationally vegetarian demanded meat. This caused a huge strain on the whole system," I said.

"Between the people and the crops, there's not much wiggle room," he replied in agreement.

I fell in love quickly. Here was a guy after my own heart, who wanted to talk about India.

The next morning in Chicago, I kiss Sebastian goodbye and take a short flight to Madison alone and rent a car. The air outside is quite cold. There'd been snow on the ground, but it has melted. There are some patches of ice. I remember what Dad said about the cemetery and the supermarket. My heart leaps at the sight of the Piggly Wiggly sign. I park in the half-full lot and walk across the street. My heart races. I will see my mother's name soon. The cemetery stretches across a field and down a slope. I start closest to the entrance. Tens of names, ordinary American names. I find no one's name I recognize. No Kesslers or Kepplers, whatever family my father said had been buried there for generations. Dad had described the cemetery and the grocery store perfectly. But there is no sign of Mom. There are no new graves on this side of the cemetery, and the headstones are at least forty years old. Someone had visited and left little sprigs of plastic roses, pink and white, in front of all the markers. Recently, I assume, because I can't imagine the flowers remaining in place during a snowstorm or hard rain.

I pull out a notepad and pen from my satchel and begin to note the clusters of families: some Shultzes, a few Robertses, one Deutsch. My white pen falls out of my hand and disappears into the ground.

A familiar voice says, "No Kepplers. But at the bottom of the slope, a whole bunch of people with the last name Chess and Chessler." I look up to my brother's face, flushed and red despite the cold. He looks worn out, as if he's been crying.

I clutch the notepad as I hug him. "How long have you been here?"

"An hour," he says, then shrugs. "I wanted to surprise you."

I laugh and he joins in. We laugh and laugh, the joke on us, a lifelong punch line in the making that leaves us with only questions and riddles, no answers, until all that is left are hiccups and the start of sobs. I wipe away my tears with my hands, retrieve my pen by kicking the ground with the points of my shoes, and then we walk briskly up and down the lines of headstones. Sure enough, a cluster of Chess and Chessler family members, but none are new. There was a Karl Chessler with a K, the way Dad spells it. But this Karl died sixty-six years ago, a few days after birth. An Elena Chessler is buried nearby and appears to be baby Karl's mother—she died shortly after giving birth. The way the names are chiseled and curled, it was done with a flourish, and those Ss could have been Ps from a distance. I feel nothing when I see my given name, Elena, on the headstone. Dad's mother, the grandmother I'm supposedly named for, a woman I never met. In this moment, I know I have left everything behind. I left it the minute Mom left the earth. Virginia's voice pops into my head, her college-days voice: "Mama's baby, Daddy's a maybe." But this is a puzzle that needs to be solved and then put away forever.

Then I find my brother's name: Adam. The last name is Chess, not Chessler. He's a young man, about twenty-seven, around Elena's age at death. Her husband? Brother-in-law? Were we Chesslers? Dad had failed to tell us our real names. Dad had played a game: two truths and a lie. There is a smattering of headstones, even older, of children who bear the Chess or Chessler name. I turn to my brother and find him staring off into the distance. The air is colder now than when we started this treasure hunt, and my lungs ache. "Who are we?"

Adam sighs. "I forgot to tell you about the other good news." His hands rise up like goalposts briefly. A neighbor had saved some keepsakes and photos from the pile that was heaped at the mouth of our family home driveway for the junkman to haul away.

"Apparently, it was quick. Ten guys showed up with two trucks and everything was gone in an hour."

[February 2003] — It is Sebastian's fortieth birthday. He is scheduled to remain in town, and we are having dinner with his parents, who are also going to be in town. There are drinks at this famous pub, followed by dinner at an even more famous Italian restaurant, and then dessert at our tiny apartment.

Sebastian said he would be busy on calls until five o'clock. I know he's not expecting me until five-thirty. I check my watch and leave work early. I go by the corner bakery, pick up the tiered coffee-chocolate cake he loves, and swing by the grocery store and buy a couple of pints of butter pecan and vanilla ice cream. I am surprisingly happy. Sebastian and I have been in New York, overlapping, for almost three months now. We have a seesaw of playfulness: Every day I forgive his procrastinations about taking out the garbage or calling Con-Ed to dispute a charge on our latest bill; and he forgives my tardiness as I'm notoriously late for everything that is not work related.

I'm very proud of myself—it is 3:45 and I'm at the big front door of the building. The doorman looks at me and says hello but there is no smile in his voice, on his lips. I am at the elevator at 3:47. I'm at my front door at 3:52, fumbling with the key as I precariously balance the cake with the ice cream. But as I go to unlock the door, it swings open and there is Sebastian dressed only in an oversized gray bath towel, kissing goodbye his old girlfriend Layla, who is fully dressed.

I cannot believe what messages the eyes are sending to my brain and back again. I want to do or say something, but then Elena Keppler the reporter kicks in, that grinning sophisticate. "How lovely. Aren't you a pretty picture?" I hear myself say. "I hope I haven't interrupted."

Layla and Sebastian spring apart, and Sebastian's face is a mask of frozen fear. The apartment is dead silent except for my voice. Layla's eyes go wide and she tries to flee, but I stand in the doorway and hand her two pints of ice cream. "Our in-laws are coming over tonight," I say with the brisk efficiency of a military sergeant. I look at her and the word *our* is not lost on her as she blushes. "This place must be in shipshape. Since you seem to know this place well, I will trust you to find the fridge and act accordingly." I pull my keys out of the lock and shut the door and secure the dead bolt. I turn back and hand the cake to Sebastian. Layla turns tail and heads toward the kitchen.

Elena is in high gear now. "I think the nice dessert plates are still in a box in storage, somewhere in New Jersey," I say. "But your parents gave us those green dessert plates, remember? For our second wedding anniversary? They're in the cabinet." I give him a little push on his back. I want to punch him in the kidneys but then a second later the urge dissipates, and I'm relieved I didn't hit him. "You may want to put on shorts, at least."

I turn back toward the couch and find an imprint of their bodies on the cushion. Clearly, they had just consummated their feelings right there. I take the pillows and rake them over the velour and then fluff them up—stifling the urge to scream. I turn back to the coffee table and see Chinese takeout cartons and two pairs of chopsticks. I peer into the boxes: remnants of shrimp in black bean sauce, twice-cooked pork. I stare intently. Who is Sebastian? I thought he was allergic to shellfish. I thought he stopped eating pork after our friend Paolo's documentary on animal cruelty aired in Tribeca and moved Sebastian to tears.

I gasp but have enough control to not slap my hand over my own mouth. *Ford* is allergic to shellfish. Sebastian is allergic to strawberries and eggplant. Sebastian was moved to tears at Paolo's documentary, but he consoled himself with a Cuban sandwich from his favorite deli.

A part of me is beyond enraged, the part that thought things were finally going well between us. That we had fallen into the steady rhythm of two people living under the same roof and adjusting to the rivers and valleys of domestic life. But maybe this was all a ruse. Maybe, like me, Sebastian could not release the past. After all, Layla had been his true love. His first true love. Out of the corner of my vision, I see Layla and Sebastian beginning to set the table. "Seb, can you start the coffee?" My voice rings out, a little louder than I had intended. I take the takeout boxes and close them, gather the chopsticks, and put them at the edge of the coffee table where I know at least one of the two people who ate from them would see and hopefully walk them to the garbage can or the fridge.

I see Layla wince.

I don't have to read her lips to know that she is dying to leave. Her manicured hands are empty, so I guess she put the ice cream away.

"Not now," he growls. "I'll start it when we come back for dessert."

My in-laws are nothing if not hyperpunctual. They are supposed to meet us at the bar, but I know them: I think they're probably going to surprise us and come to the apartment beforehand so we can go out as a family. As if on cue, my mother-in-law calls. "Call from . . ." the automated voice announces.

"It's your mother," I say blithely, though I would have paid handsomely for the situation to be reversed and for my mother to be calling. "I think you should get it."

Sebastian shakes his head. "I'll call her back."

"Nonsense," I say, and I walk over to the end table and pick up the phone. "Good afternoon," I say.

"Who is this?" My mother-in-law sounds anxious, confused.

Layla stares at me, and her mouth hangs open.

Sebastian takes a step toward me, clutching his towel. I almost answer "Elena, Ford's wife," but I don't. Instead, I feel the world spin. There is a wall of fire on my face, and then, mercifully, the world goes black and the phone clatters to the ground. The last thing I see is Seb leaning over me mouthing my name.

The apartment is in an uproar when I awake on the velour couch where Seb and Layla had recently been intimate. There is a cool compress on my forehead, and it smells vaguely of lemon-scented dish soap. Layla and Seb are shouting at each other and at Seb's parents, who are shouting back at them and then shouting at each other. A thick net of blame and embarrassment hangs in the air. They move from the dining room, set with green dessert plates and the birthday cake, to the kitchen around the corner and out of my sight. I listen for a moment and recognize Layla's voice: She had been the one to answer the phone in Sebastian's apartment just after 9/11, when my mother was still alive and I was trying to get home. I rise carefully and move to the right, where the bedroom is. I close the door gingerly and find my travel bag, my work satchel, an extra pair of shoes, and quickly toss whatever I can into my luggage. I remember my keys; on the ring was the key to Virginia's apartment. I had cleaned out the apartment, but I had held on to the key. I think of Virginia, all the times she had come over to this apartment when Seb and I were first married, how we sat side by side on the couch and gossiped and giggled. She has changed columns in the state of New York, from MISSING to PRESUMED DECEASED. I cannot think of the word *dead* and pair it with Virginia. I try not to gag; I try not to cough. I try not to weep.

I sigh, avoid looking in the mirror hanging above the chest of drawers, take one more look around, notice the mussed-up bedspread on our sleigh bed that I had carefully made earlier today. I sigh again, and a wave of nausea climbs up my throat. I crack the door and hear them yelling, and I tiptoe through the living room and to the front door. I turn back for one long look and catch Layla's eye. Her makeup looks runny, it is clear she has been crying. I raise my finger to my lips, and she nods imperceptibly. The door gently clicks shut behind me and I sigh again.

I have no trouble with the doorman at Ford's building, no trouble with the spare key he keeps above the doorframe, duct-taped on the very left. I have my baggage and most of my essential things. I check the bathroom and under the sink is my tiny duffel bag of toiletries, spare toothbrush, and makeup that I have always stashed at Ford's. Just in case. Ford is not home. I call the newsroom and then the sports desk. "Ford around?" I ask when someone answers.

"Hang on," and a series of clicks sound before he answers, very professionally.

"I hope you don't have any plans," I say.

He does not miss a beat. "I left the credit card in the cookie jar," he says, and I can hear the smile on his face. "Order dinner. Pick a movie. Open a bottle of wine. I'll be home at midnight."

The past six weeks have been circular. I go to work, I come back to Ford's apartment, I go to work. I look out the window and notice a pair of beagles go in and out of the building across the street. I notice their owner, a somber woman. Ford and I are careful with each other, and yet all of it is superficial: only small talk, only loud, funny commentary about comedians and movies. We drink a lot of wine; we don't talk earnestly about anything serious. I revert to old habits: sharing Ford's bed with him in it, spending more and more time under the duvet, wearing pajamas. It is at once familiar and still I am shocked at myself, at how quickly things shifted, how quickly I adapted and changed, how much like Dad I had become, disappearing. I call Adam before work one day, and I can tell Seb has talked to him. "Are you safe? I don't want you to lie to me so I'm not going to ask where you are."

"I'm fine," I say. For once, I'm showered and dressed. I have on a sweater and slacks, mascara, my hair is washed. "Just trying to get my bearings again."

Adam switches the subject a couple of times, then lands on his ex-wife. "We are trying again," he says, a smile as long as his shadow in his voice. "Jen called me and asked."

I had always liked her. "I'm happy you're happy," I say, and I mean it.

Neither of us talk about Dad, neither of us even know where to start.

I call Adam again.

"I just can't believe Dad would lie like that. It's as though he vanished into thin air." His voice is tired and scratchy, the edge of a razor.

I feel sorrow—not in my heart, like an attack, nor in my head, like a migraine, but in the marrow of my bones. Everything in my bones, from my elbows to my knees, aches. I know that Adam and I are vastly different, I know how much I can carry and how I've carried all that we shared since the time we were kids in India. I take a deep breath, stare not at the telephone but out the window, the streetlights twinkling the way I imagine the stars do in the night sky. "I'll ask Sam," I say to Adam. "He's a genius. He can find . . . almost anyone." I say "almost" because of Virginia. Hanan pops into my head for a moment, and I wonder if Sam could find her too. I haven't heard back from Rafiq and Zahra in ages either. Maybe I should draw up a to-find list for Sam, offer him a bribe.

Adam says, "Really?" and there is hope in his voice.

I haven't asked Sam, and I don't know if Sam has the time or inclination to help me on a personal matter. Still, I cannot tolerate the ache in my spine, nor the profound sadness in my brother's voice. He hasn't sounded this down about the family even when his wife left him. "No problem," I say. "I will ask him tomorrow."

The next day I stop by Sam's desk, but he is absent.

"Sick?" I ask Teddy, who sits in the cubicle next to Sam's.

"Dentist," Teddy says. "Root canal."

"Ouch," I say.

That evening, I call Adam and leave a message on his phone: "He wasn't at work today. I'll try him tomorrow."

But the next day I'm sent to eastern Pennsylvania. A doctor has euthanized her sick husband. The state charged her with second degree murder, and the police had cuffed her at the hospital in front of the residents. She was being held in the county jail, pending arraignment.

The arraignment is a circus, and the judge is the ringleader in a black robe, hammering the gavel and trying to restore some silence to the proceeding. Everyone is talking over one another, and the spectators in the gallery are also shouting, and chanting. Posters materialize and there are people screaming for justice for the dead husband, and there are others shouting for the doctor to be released.

I expect a relatively young woman. I am surprised at the wrinkles on her cheeks and the crow's-feet around her eyes. I'm surprised by the spots on her veiny hands. I look over the cable news reporter's shoulder and see a photo of the husband. He is frail, the clothes hanging off his body as if he were nothing more than a stick figure.

Tonight, after I filed my story but before I check out of the hotel to head back to the city, I call in to the newsroom. "Sam there?" I keep my tone light.

The voice answers, "You're in luck, he's about to leave."

A series of clicks and a brief, horrible instrumental version of "Hotel California," and then Sam's voice cheerfully answering.

I greet him and tell him what I want. I mention Adam.

"I was so sorry to hear about your mom," he says. "We remember her in our prayers every night."

I feel my eyes well. "My brother really needs to speak . . ." The words catch in my throat. I cough, unexpectedly. I remember Mom telling me that Sam's sister—Janet? Jane? Janice!—had written her a thank-you note, sent a photo of the baby Mom safely delivered. "I . . . I really need to speak with our dad." I explain that if Sam locates the cemetery where Mom is buried, that will narrow the gap and Adam and I would take it from there.

Sam sneezes, then excuses himself. "I'm slammed right now," he says. "But I can tackle it this weekend, when I'm not at work."

I exhale audibly, and I hear Sam laugh. "Good enough," I say. "What can I do for you in exchange?"

Sam chuckles again. "I was going to call you, believe it or not. My sister is having a shower for baby number two. She's really craving Indian food."

I smile into the receiver. "I can help with that."

"Friday," Sam says. "Sorry for the short notice."

I feel physically fine until one morning I don't. Ford is on the road again. I don't know when he'll be back; I think he told me, but

I can't recall. It was casual the way we left it before he departed. "Stay as long as you need," he'd said last week, handing me a cup of extra-hot coffee and the day's newspaper. He eyed his watch, then we kissed goodbye. A long, lingering kiss that caught me off guard, in fact. It seemed he didn't want to leave, but then when his arms stopped encircling me, he turned and walked out of the apartment without a backward glance. Later that morning, I felt sick to my stomach.

Today I wake up, rush into the bathroom, and throw up. I go by the pharmacy and come home and throw up again. The two blue lines appear on the white plastic test stick in Ford's bathroom. Two parallel blue lines. Ford. Sebastian. Ford. Sebastian. I run out to the kitchen; I reach for the cordless phone out of instinct. But then I put the receiver down on the side table, sit on the couch and put my hands behind my head, lean back, think of everything and nothing and anything, a collision of images of Sebastian and Ford, of my wedding day and our Italian honeymoon, of seeing Sebastian and Layla in New York, of Ford and me at the beachside café sharing French fries and beer, of Sebastian and me on the gondola, of Ford coming home drunk in Florida, of Ford's kiss goodbye just a few days ago, of Sebastian holding me tightly through the night before Mom's funeral. My mother's question "Are you living your best life?" echoes inside me.

The phone rings and I pick up without thinking. "Yes, hello?" I ask.

A woman chuckles, then draws a breath as if stemming a tide of anguish.

I freeze.

"Oh my god, I knew it, I knew it," she says. "You're Ford's wife. Right?"

I open my mouth to agree but close it and say nothing. I hang up the phone and turn on the answering machine. The phone rings again and the machine catches the call. "This is Erica, again. Can you pick up the phone? Please. Can I talk to you? Please. He said he was separated, and that you had moved out. My number is . . ."

I leave the room, closing and opening my mouth as if I'm a strange fish trying to breathe.

I get ready for work. I spy the velvet box and put on my mother's ring. When I arrive, I catch Hughes's eye. "Do you have a minute?" I ask, projecting warmth though everything inside me is opaque and dimming by the second.

"For you, yes," he says.

I follow him back to his office and close the door. "I'm ready to go back."

Nine

[APRIL 2003] — ONCE I LEAVE NEW YORK CITY AND ENTER THE world of transit and travel, everything converges into a game of finding patterns among the seas of impermanence. I have convinced Hughes that I'm ready to venture overseas again and I have convinced myself that this move back to [--------] is just the antidote to my personal chaos. I cannot wait to be on a different continent, away from America, away from Ford and Sebastian. I notice the things that have changed: The smiles have been replaced with steely eyes and a palpable air of wariness. Security is tighter than skin. My documents are inspected at every turn. When I say the city of my destination, my documents are inspected again. Burly agents with guns ask me to step out of the line for a long moment, then I am released once my press credentials are produced. I am torn. I'm only too willing to acquiesce to their demands. I am almost as equally willing to scream at them: I didn't see you do this when McVeigh blew up the federal building in Oklahoma City in 1995 and killed all those kids! I didn't see you stop every white man with a history of fringe and a propensity toward extremism trying to join a racist militia! Instead, I let the anger wash through me. I keep my mind focused on my goal: to return to the war. I offer a nod, a soft phrase. "No problem."

I remember that day in Oklahoma City, the photos of the federal building up in smoke. I remember how everyone, including the national media, first said: Oh it's a terrorist from the Middle East, it's got to be. I remember how I'd lost my cool for two minutes and responded to the reporters who congregated around the TV watching cable news and spouting their opinions, including the now super-lauded Mike Barrett, who played basketball in college and had an aura of stardom over him.

"Do you think for one second those extremists know where Oklahoma is?" I stepped away from the group of reporters. "They know New York, San Francisco, Los Angeles, maybe Miami, maybe Chicago, maybe the Statue of Liberty, maybe the Grand Canyon." I waved my hand over the body of the United States on a world map tacked to the wall. The rest of the country was blank to them. "Why would they choose a place they never heard of?"

The men all looked away, then after a long moment carried on as if I hadn't spoken at all. The one female assistant city editor, Sandra, mild mannered and wearing a dressy black pantsuit, nodded and said, "Good point." And then McVeigh was caught and everyone—reporters and government officials alike—started talking about the rise of domestic terror, the rise of the white militia, Confederates and neo-Nazis. Sandra came through a couple of years later as well, when Mother Teresa died the week after Princess Diana. The higher-ups had assigned all of us to call Catholic organizations as well as the various archdioceses to get information and reactions. "What about Indian cultural groups?" I asked. "They lost someone too."

Once again, the mostly white men in the newsroom looked up from the desks and computer screens and stared as if I'd just vomited by the city desk.

"She was Mother Teresa of Calcutta," I said, "for more than half a century."

Sandra nodded. "Good point," she echoed, then asked me to gather the phone numbers and make the calls. Two of my quotes made it into the next day's paper, and another two made it into the Sunday paper longread.

I fall into familiar habits. There are three women named Nadia on this return trip. The first is the ticket agent, her airline uniform snug, as if it were stitched to her body, her nametag high on her blouse; her makeup providing a sheen of dew on her oval face. She is blond but more brass than gold, and I remember what Virginia once said, when she was in her post-breakup strawberry blond phase back in school: how the best blonds are really brunette underneath. This Nadia recognizes me as she stamps the boarding pass and checks the passport photo. She asks politely, "Another tour abroad?" I smile and say yes, remember to thank her though my sudden urge is to throw up in the trashcan that hides under the table and board the airplane free of my recent nausea and exhaustion. I keep smiling as I remember that neither Ford nor Sebastian nor Adam nor Dad knows where I am and where I'm headed.

The second Nadia comes eight hours later, after the flight lands in Schiphol Airport. It is night but the terminal is bustling with travelers, and the restaurants are filled with couples and small bands of military personnel. By the looks of their uniforms and insignia, they are NATO peacekeepers. I wonder why they are not flying out of the nearby military base and then notice their stacked duffel bags, their other luggage. They are on leave. The war has spread as America enters its fourth week of incursion into Iraq, searching for weapons of mass destruction. The United Nations has issued several statements in the past week warning that the drought and civil strife in several North African nations will lead to unprecedented famine and a refugee crisis that the world has never seen before. Mostly I see on the TV monitors videos of Iraq being bombed, with maybe a thirty-second mention of famine. All around the world, there are protests denouncing the Iraqi invasion; those are getting some airtime. I watch on the TV monitors, listen to regurgitated promises to find and eliminate weapons of mass destruction. There are longtime newspaper reporters in America and the U.K., and in the region where I'm heading, voicing their skepticism, citing their local sources, saying the claims of a cache of superweapons is simply not true. But most news outlets continue recycling their footage of Iraq's destruction.

The second Nadia is older, with thick shoulder-length hair the color of topsoil and a tiny gap between her two front teeth like Madonna. She wears a cardigan that matches the blue of her eyes. Her work badge hangs like a locket around her neck. She apologizes after she announces that my flight has been delayed and offers me a pass to the lounge usually reserved for business and first class. "I believe there is a shower," this Nadia whispers, and I am conscious then of the faint odor of vomit lingering on my clothes. I had spent as much time drinking ginger ale and eating tiny pretzels on the airplane as I had expelling both in the rear lavatory. I manage a smile, and this Nadia points like a game show hostess toward the sliding doors. The lounge is nearly empty, and I have the bathroom all to myself. The soap smells of orange and mint, and the steam from the hot water refreshes my nondescript slacks and blouse, my unremarkable heather-gray sweater that I only use on the road. There is a meager sampling of food in the buffet area, some cold cuts, a platter of cheese. I aim for the bread and ask the waiter for some hot tea.

I spy a basket of fruit on the far counter, red apples and greenish bananas, and take one of each. The banana is surprisingly ripe and sweet, and my stomach settles almost immediately. After, I find an empty couch and use my bag as a pillow and my sweater as a blanket and I fall into a dreamless state. The second Nadia wakes me, hours later. "Your flight is finally ready to board," she says, her voice low and cordial. I thank her and sit up. The lounge is half full, mostly businessmen, some trying to hide their smiles. I scan the faces and the result is a blur of strangers. I'm grateful I do not know any of them. I use my fingers to comb out my hair.

I see a handsome man, distinguished, bald but in a purposeful way, well dressed in a seasoned traveler sort of way, black jumpsuit but with athletic shine, walking with a cane but not really needing to; the limp is so slight it doesn't slow down his gait. I almost walk past him at the airport terminal just where the security check-in starts and he says, "Why, hello, I never thought I'd see you again."

I know that voice. It is a voice that reminds me of the newsroom, drowned children, *Hogan's Heroes,* Ford. It is Derrick Anderson's voice. I look over him again and see the old blue eyes, still bright and alert and curious. We are years and miles away from Florida. "Why, hello yourself," I say. It is true. I thought Derrick had overdosed on Mountain Dew and Snickers bars by now. I thought Derrick had overdosed on his own misogyny by now.

"Surprised to see me, right?" A smile dances around his face.

"Indeed," I say, because that's what I say now when I'm surprised. It's a throwaway word, like *interesting* and *wow.* It is like "ici" in French class when the Madame called roll in high school. But it doesn't denote emotion. It doesn't say this is how I feel about the news. Because all of that is unnecessary. I've been conditioned and trained to avoid emotion and opinion. "Are you well?"

Dutifully, he pulls out his wallet and opens the billfold, shows me the photo of his wife and daughter. I do not recognize his spouse.

"They're beautiful," I say, noticing the Disney castle in the background, the same smile on mother and child.

"Best thing I ever did was leave the news business," he says.

"Indeed," I say again, then point to the intercom system as my flight is called, final boarding.

Derrick offers me his card. He is now a public relations consultant, part of a big house based in New York. I thank him, say, "Good to see you again," though it really isn't and though it floods me with old memories of Angela Mason and the tongue-lashing and gender-shaming he gave her and how she transferred to features a short time later and away from his supervision. I think of Ford, the day we nursed soft drinks in paper cups and watched the sunset from the pier. Someone had come up to us to thank Ford for an article he had written about a disabled athlete and how that man had said the same phrase when leaving us: "Good to see you again," as if they were old friends.

Then I board the airplane.

The next leg is relatively short, and the flight is completely full. The man seated at the aisle looks me over more than once. Recognition flickers in his eyes, but he cannot place me. Even in color, newsprint is not becoming. My pixilated photograph renders me homogenous, another face staring at the war, another body standing in between the war and the American public. I turn and stare out the window, will him and my nausea to leave me alone. As the wheels touch down the city is bathed in golden light, and the sky is clear. For a moment, I wonder why I've returned, what the necessity is. This is not a country riddled with war; from this angle and light, this is a beautiful destination, the start of an adventure, a region infused with living history.

Customs is long, unsurprising, and there is a car awaiting me as I exit the frosted doors. It is not Rafiq, and I am somehow both relieved and disappointed. I had pictured Rafiq as the first familiar face I would see at the war. I had pictured that everything would have remained the same. The new driver introduces himself as Malik, tries to make conversation, but after I study his face, I feign a couple of yawns and coughs and he quickly turns his attention back to the afternoon traffic, not quite rush hour by American standards, but congested.

I arrive at the hotel and my heart leaps at the sight of the dilapidated awning on the side portico, the maroon fading in the desert sun into the color of dried blood. I recognize the song in my heart: I'm happy to be back here. I pay Malik, apologize for my fatigue, and take my things inside to the front desk. The interior lobby is still quite grand, with a chandelier beaming amber light, and polished floors and an array of ponds and papyrus and tiny bridges in the open courtyard. Two years since I last set foot here, and everything inside this lobby remains the same—except for the people. The third Nadia wears a dark suit and eye shadow the color of a new bruise. "Welcome," she says. "Name?"

I thank her and hand over my documents. Nadia does not gawk. She lingers at the computer for a long time. The gray light from the screen makes her tanned skin appear ashen, as if she is bathed in fluorescent bulbs. Her brown eyes look up. "Welcome back," Nadia says. "Your usual room is open."

My heart leaps again. It is on the third and highest floor. A tiny sitting area adjacent to a picture window and a minifridge next to a good worktable. I remember Rafiq and Mr. Salim and my colleagues from years ago. Other reporters hate having a window because of the shelling. But I am happy to return to the ways things were before September 11. I have missed the view, the landscape laid out before me. I know when I see that interior stairwell again I will grip the railing like an old friend.

"Shukran," I say.

"Afwan," this Nadia replies, her brassy nametag glinting.

I wake to a recognizable sound. Together the street vendors play an asynchronous octave of a distant xylophone. Each vendor—whether they hawk dates or bananas or sugarcane juice, wind-up toys or socks or salty snacks—has a different bell and produces a different chime. In concert, it is the start of a tune that is at once familiar and mournful. I'm happy to hear it again, and the music makes me want to weep. Two years have passed and I have changed. I awake as the vendors cross the streets below and greet each other, sit up quickly as the adhan is delivered via loudspeaker for the first time. I climb out of bed and stumble to the window. The diffuse light at the horizon's hem gains speed and intensity and brightens the visible world. I stretch my arm over my head and realize I am nausea-free for the first time in days, but my throat is dry and scratchy when I swallow. Fine time for a shitty sore throat. I look around for my bottle of water. I remember this time of day in New Mexico the year before, the high school marching band practicing the theme to *Star Wars* as the roosters chortled and the dogs snarled. I was there to cover the 150th anniversary of the founding of a conservatory of music, and some locals had used the opportunity to steal some artifacts from a nearby museum.

It is still early, and I know Hughes will not call for another several hours. I call down to the front desk and a man's voice answers pleasantly, identifying himself as Mr. Awad. "Yes, Miss Das, how may I help you this morning?"

I begin to answer and realize midway through that he spoke

Arabic and I translated with only a small pause. I'm relieved that my rudimentary Arabic language skill has somewhat returned and ask about breakfast.

"We are almost finished remodeling the dining station." His reply comes hurriedly. "Tell me what you'd like, and I'll have it prepared and sent to your room."

After a breakfast of garlicky ful medames and bread and a hard-boiled egg and mint tea, I rest for half an hour. The alarm sounds on the nightstand just as I enter a dream where I made a different choice two years ago and was able to see my mother's face one last time, alive. I opt for a longish shower. The soap smells of lime and sugar, and the water is surprisingly steamy. I dress in more nondescript clothes and throw a silk scarf over my shoulders just in case I'm asked to cover my hair. I realize with chagrin that I have left the abaya that Rafiq and his mother gave me long ago at my apartment in New York. For a second I wonder if Seb has put it away or thrown it in the trash. The telephone rings, and I answer. Mr. Awad's greeting is cheerful, and he informs me in English that Rafiq, "your friend," has called and should arrive shortly.

I cover the receiver with my hand while I exhale as if I'm smoking a delicious and forbidden cigarette. I was surprised that Rafiq had not met me at the airport yesterday, but his appearance soon will save me the pain of trying to find him. I calculate that his reappearance (granted of his own free will) is not coincidence: He still knows people, keeps tabs on activity at the airport. This is not uncommon: My concierge in Kolkata had friends at the airport too. Then: "Can you please ring me when he arrives? I'll meet him in the lobby."

I take off my watch and try to reset the time, but the dial is tiny and my fingers are slick and feel abnormally fat. Finally, I nudge the dial to the correct hour. I toss the watch into my satchel and look at the alarm clock. Still morning here, which means Hughes is snoring back in New York. I reorganize my small bag, test the pens against the cover of a magazine, flip through a pad of paper, fold the list of contacts into a square, find the notes I'd taken in Hughes's office. He wanted a follow-up to a wire story about the skirmishes to the north, and a numbers story about the famine in North Africa and the waves of people fleeing the region. Then he said that I should focus on what I do best: putting faces on the big picture problems, humanizing the consequences of abstract philosophical and political debates, providing a bit of analysis in my war reporting. I have no idea yet where to pinpoint my focus. I have no idea of anything except that the conflict is still a fever in this country, in this part of the world so far away from America. It is a fever that has not broken much in the past sixty years—what, twice?

The telephone rings once more. "Your friend has arrived."

I toss my room key into the unzipped pocket where the watch lies, and there is a faint click when the two items touch.

Although I'm alone in the elevator, it stops at every floor, a bell sounds, and the doors open. The ride down to the lobby leaves me winded and a bit dizzy. My heart beats loudly as I exit into the lobby. It is empty except for a very thin man. A very thin, well-dressed man. I almost walk past him. But then I stop. It is Rafiq. He is clean-shaven now and wears black-rimmed glasses. His suit smells new, it is pressed. It is the first time I've seen him in a tie and a chalk-white workshirt.

"Rita," he says softly.

My eyes readjust. Whatever I felt or knew or hated about him melts in the moment, and we embrace. I see him and the clock rewinds two years, and my mother is alive again, Virginia is a phone call away, Johanna is in Damascus. He leans back and kisses me on both cheeks, and I smell the lime and sugar of the hotel soap on his skin.

"You haven't changed," he says.

I smile. "You've changed enough for the both of us."

He laughs and his teeth glint. "Is their dining room fixed yet?"

I shake my head. I want to know why he's asking me a question he already knows the answer to. I want to know why he's a guest at this hotel for foreign journalists—but I smile and bite the inside of my cheek to keep from questioning him.

"Then we will have to go out for our morning coffee," he says, and he takes my hand in his. "My car is outside."

From the corner of my eye, I spy a clerk exiting the staff office, probably Mr. Awad. I squeeze Rafiq's hand and drop it. "I'll meet you outside."

I head toward the public restroom sign as Rafiq exits through the revolving door. I veer sharply and stand in front of the check-in counter. "Did you call my room to let me know my friend was here?" I ask in Arabic as evenly as I can, as if I am asking about the laundry service or housekeeping hours.

"Yes," Mr. Awad says, his eyes round like his face, his potbelly out of place with his skinny frame, his voice clipped.

"Why didn't you tell me he lives here?" It is all I can do to not raise my voice, not wag my finger.

"He maintains a room here, yes," Mr. Awad says, then switches to English, "but . . . he was not sleeping here this morning."

"He was not in the hotel last night?" I ask in English.

Mr. Awad nods. "He returned this morning."

I thank him, attempt to inject warmth into my voice. Outside, the air smells of breakfast and car exhaust, and there are more people moving about than could be seen from my window three stories up. Even the parking lot is bustling with motorists and women in headscarves hurrying into the hotel or the next-door building—the old conference center, presumably—late for work. I walk a short distance to what I guess is Rafiq's car. It is the same type of car as before. It appears to be a French model, but it is shiny with newness, and upon closer inspection, I see that the car was manufactured in a neighboring nation-state.

Rafiq carefully removes his suit top and lays it on the backseat. He rolls up his shirtsleeves and gets behind the steering wheel. "I know a place," he says and then laughs. That phrase is quintessential Rafiq. He never let me down. Well, that's not true. It's because of him, my last day before 9/11, that I missed seeing my mother.

But I can forgive him for a fleeting moment. After all, I had convinced Hughes to send me back to this place, to Rafiq.

I join Rafiq's laughter, and we continue to giggle like schoolchildren as he shifts the gears and putters out of the lot and onto the crowded street.

Rafiq drives me into the beating heart of the city. We drive in silence past where the government operates. I don't know why Rafiq is silent, but I know him well enough to know he has questions he does not yet have the courage to ask. For my part, I want to grill him on everything, on Zahra. I want to get updates on the orphanage I wrote about two years ago, the fledgling school for the blind, the medicine shortage after the last outbreak of cholera, and what the status is on the local tax hike for taxi drivers I'd read about over the wire last week. I want to incorporate at least one of the five topics I feel don't get enough attention: child marriage, female circumcision, family planning, female education, vaccinations.

But I look over Rafiq's thin, drawn face and hold my tongue between my teeth and look at everything we drive by, the dust-laden streets, the markets, and the fancy glass buildings mirroring an impossibly blue sky. We drive past the city center north toward the most fashionable part of town, past all the shops and European-style commerce centers, to an area where, in my absence, new houses and neighborhoods have sprung up, wide buildings with flower-laden verandas, and miniparks with gazebos and pergolas with winter roses and jasmine creeping along. I recall the story I read two weeks before, about the birth of neighborhoods like these, for the foreigners who are stationed in [--------].

Rafiq says, "Watch now, we'll talk later," then honks at the car ahead of him for nearly colliding with another vehicle. I think of all the stories I want to tell, how each of this myriad comes from the same roots of displacement and war, famine, and disease, how the climate is shifting but the governments are not shifting alongside it.

I remember my portable tape recorder and take it out of my bag. I show it to him and lean into the back, put it on the seat next to his suit top.

"Shukran," he says.

He drives a bit more and we come to a gently walled area and a pair of iron gates with a giant flowered arch. Rafiq stops when the guard raises his hand. On his clothing, just above the pocket, his name is printed in block letters: HAMID.

"I'm here to take my friend to lunch," Rafiq says when he hands over our documents. Birds call to each other in the midmorning sun, and the traffic we have left behind is the distant cymbal rolling off the distant sea.

Mr. Hamid sports a healthy physique, and he smiles at me. "Open the trunk, please."

I try to return the smile but fail. After a few moments, the guard waves us through. I stare as the car climbs the tree-lined road toward the top of a giant hill. I insist we stop at the peak. We have entered a city within the city. There is a vista point, a panoramic view of this gated community. In the distance is the city where both my hotel and the war reside.

Rafiq smiles as my mouth drops open. It is an eternal spring here. In this small city within, the young travel in trios, wearing the latest fashions. Old couples stroll hand in hand, the wife stopping as her husband pauses to tie his shoelaces. In gratitude, he carries her purse, slings it over his shoulder. I remember Sebastian carrying my bag on the Amalfi Coast once, as we transferred from the first hotel to the second. It was on the same day we visited a beachside restaurant and received a small cooking lesson: Seb's tarte tasted infinitely better than mine, his attention to the smallest details made his dessert look sublime. But that was eons ago, time stamped as the distant past.

This older couple take turns around a square with its heavy European influence, a mock-up of old-century architecture where kings entertained their guests. It's a life-sized Monopoly board:

hotels, a museum, a bank, shops, small cafés where they froth milk in a stainless steel canister for cappuccinos.

"The French have paid for this?" I ask.

"Mais oui," he replies. "And the Italians, the Spanish, the Dutch, the Portuguese."

The avenues are lined with jacaranda and cypress, and the smell of figs hangs in the air. There are statues of famous forefathers (never the mothers), pointing toward their own achievements, pontificating on the state of their eternal stares. There are some women, green-colored with a faint smell of metal emanating from them, at the base of tall fountains, fountains that are dry as bone.

There are others, like me, with guides who cart them around. There is no evidence here of the homeless or the poor, the smell of garbage or manufacturing or the desalination plant to make use of the sea that is not too close. We return to the car and drive on into the square where I watched the old couple. Rafiq parks and guides me to a building with wide glass doors and a covered entrance. "Let's go inside," he suggests.

A hotel. Much fancier than the one where I stay. The lobby is warm and inviting and full of people. The café opposite the front desk is doing brisk business. It sports a green sign with yellow lettering: OASIS. The customers are drinking coffee and eating flaky pastries, and their chatter melts into a collective sound of contentment. One waiter spots Rafiq and removes the RESERVED sign from one of three empty tables and motions for us to come forward.

We are seated, and the waiter drops tall green menus into our laps. The restaurant workers need not have bothered. There, in Arabic, French, English, Italian, Dutch, Portuguese, are the simple offerings and the prices for coffee, tea, water, pastries, fruit. I order water and pastries, while Rafiq says he'll have coffee and fruit. We stare at each other. Finally, he says, "There is something different about you. A stillness."

I ignore him. "What is this place? Who lives here? Why do they know you?"

He shrugs. "My wife has won . . . what do you say? The lottery."

I smile at his lie. "Zahra would never go for a bourgeois place like this." I pause and remember Rafiq and Zahra in the days after 9/11, their eyes wide with anger and fear. Rafiq takes off his glasses, places them on the paper napkin on the table, retrieves a handkerchief from his pocket and polishes them with it. "She is well, thank you."

I look at him closely, remember the smell of hotel soap on his skin, plunge the knife. "Why do you live at the hotel when Zahra lives here? Have you divorced?"

He places his glasses on the bridge of his nose and pushes them closer to his eyes, then shakes his head. "She has secured work as a translator," he says. "It requires her to maintain an apartment here." His wrists swim in the loose fabric of his shirt cuff.

To me, Rafiq is practicing the one thing I hate above all in our line of work: the appearance of neutrality. Still, I haven't seen him in years. It's probably none of my business, except that he's my translator and partner here at the war, and I need to trust him. Perhaps he's forgotten who I am. I decide a reminder is in order. "She threw you out."

Rafiq smiles a little smile. "Let us eat, and then we will visit her."

I smile back as the grief floods me. I look at his face, and though it's changed, there is a look about him that reminds me of the past, of that mopey, lovestruck young man two years ago. A name pops into my head. "Do you know anything more about Hanan?"

Rafiq's smile falters. "It was one of her people who saw you at the airport yesterday."

Her people? Which "her"? What is happening? I notice the crow's-feet, the faint bags under his eyes. I thank the waiter for the bottled water but decline the ice and the spotty glass. With a flourish, the waiter places a small plate in front of Rafiq, a plate hardly the size of an old forty-five record my father used to play on the weekends—with a tiny tangerine and a pair of pygmy bananas. "Will that be enough?"

He nods and breaks open the bananas as if he is cracking open a loaf of bread.

Like most people, I take my cues from the women in my life. The mother is the first focal point for everyone. How she behaves with them. How she treats their sister or brother differently. How their grandmother treats their mother, what their sisters and aunts are like, the kaleidoscopic dynamic. It is a rare woman who makes no distinction. And then there are the friends in their lives, the girlfriends. Their dislike of rock and roll, their love of jazz, and the way coffee or gin and tonic smell on their breath after a long night. The way that they perform their rituals: their morning teas, their evening baths, the hidden midnight snacks, the lies they tell about their lovers, the unspoken lifelong crushes, the awkward friendships that dissipate after their school years are behind them. My mother, my compass, has been, ever since her death, a relic pointing to the past.

I stand at the pristine intersection between the hotel café and the parking lot where Rafiq has placed his car. The women on the sidewalk across the way walk in pairs and, from this distance, wear smiles and contentment on their faces. The sun glares overhead and casts skinny shadows along the walls of the building across the street. Rafiq joins me after using the telephone.

"Zahra will meet us at her—our home." He turns back toward the hotel and gestures with his hand.

I step back. "No," I say as gracefully as I can. "I have to get back. Hughes will be calling. I will see Zahra another time."

Rafiq pauses. "She's on deadline, Rita. You understand?"

I smile. "I do understand"—though I don't care—"but I cannot miss my call with Hughes." I don't give a damn about Hughes at this moment. Suddenly, I am tired of Rafiq. Suddenly, I'm wondering where I can get a new translator. I see Rafiq and all I can recall is the sequence of events that led me to miss saying goodbye to my mother. But my curiosity about Zahra is outweighed by my desire to get back to my room and lie down.

He checks his watch. "What if I promise to take you back in ten minutes?"

I check the watch I dropped into my bag, a cheap travel-hardy gift from Sebastian many years ago before we were married. Waterproof, plastic, and virtually indestructible. Three qualities I wish I now possessed. "Five," I say.

Rafiq nods and we turn back toward the hotel.

A few moments later we stand in front of the double elevator doors. Just as we enter, Zahra steps out, handbag in hand, wearing a black and white outfit and a pale pink headscarf. "Hello, Rita!" she exclaims, bubbly as ever, a grin of genuine pleasure on her face.

Rafiq beams like a proud father.

Hotel guests and staff move around us and enter the elevator. Bells sound and a telephone rings. I stand still inside Zahra's arms, breathing in her French perfume. I return Zahra's hug—how could I not?—and pretend I'm greeting Virginia after two long years. I let go and say, "Congratulations on the new job, Zahra. Such exciting news."

Zahra and Rafiq exchange a look, and Zahra's grin transforms into a pair of compressed lips. "I didn't realize Rafiq had spoiled the surprise."

"Oh, he didn't," I say. "He gave me just enough information to be dying of suspense."

We laugh together, and Rafiq's face relaxes.

Zahra says, "We can sit down for pastries, or we can go up to my suite and I'll order us lunch."

I shake my head. The Oasis Café has lost its luster. "I've got to go, I'm afraid," I say. "Why don't you walk us back to the car?" I attempt to remain in the moment, take in every detail of Zahra's face, try to glean invaluable information, try to be a cordial colleague, but all that swims in front of me are the memories of Hughes's breakdown in his office and my voice on Virginia's answering machine.

Stills of the funeral arrangements and the silk sari my mother wore before she was enclosed forever in her coffin. More stills of me walking in on Sebastian and Layla; then cleaning out Virginia's apartment, dropping her hard-won copies of Carolyn Forché's *The Country Between Us* and Lucille Clifton's *The Terrible Stories* into my bag.

"You've only just arrived," Zahra says. "You can't be on deadline yet."

I laugh inwardly at Zahra's forthright tone. For a second, I even admire it. That was how I used to be. "Hughes is Hughes. Must answer the phone when he calls." I grin. "Otherwise he gets nervous. And if there's one thing I despise, it's an editor on the international desk thousands of miles away who's nervous."

Zahra and Rafiq shrug at each other and the three of us move toward the lobby. Zahra explains she has secured employment as an official English and French translator and is getting steady work at the embassies in the city. This gated community had sprung up recently, and she was able to secure a furnished room on the top floor of its hotel because of her work connections. "My mother and sister are fine now; they moved to a small community not far from here."

I vaguely recall Zahra's sad story about her newly widowed mother, her yet unmarried sister.

Zahra clears her throat. "I want to thank you, Rita," she says as we step into the sunshine and make our way toward the street corner. "Your efforts those days in September helped us both." Rafiq nods in agreement and says he's translating for the wire service reporters who are all newer to the area, and for the time being he's been given a room at my hotel.

It all sounds above reproach, but as I look at them again I can see the chasm between them: the way Rafiq and Zahra hold each other at a distance, their vacuous expressions, an overcompensation in their laughter and hugs. They are definitely separated. This is terrain I know well. Sebastian. Ford. I attempt to keep my face neutral, pleasant even, as I say, "You're welcome." I manage it.

"Yes," Rafiq says as we wait for the light to change so we can cross the street. "Your intervention saved us." Yes, I had helped them on the days following 9/11, but I think my needling of Hughes over the first few months after I returned stateside forced him into action on their behalf.

Zahra puts her hand on my arm, and I'm surprised how cold it is and that she has had time to get a manicure. "I was so sorry to hear about your mother," she says. "Had she been ill for a long time?"

I dig my bitten nails into my palms, and the pain steadies me. We don't talk about the herd of elephants, as it were, of all the stories that are threaded together by blood and sorrow. Still, Zahra asks me as if our stories are independent and carry no weight with each other. For two years, when I think of Rafiq and Zahra, I have been seething and resentful, I have been an internal storm wreaking havoc and casting blame. Now in this moment, Zahra stands before me with love in her eyes and imprinted on her face. No matter what, Mom is still dead. I look into Zahra's eyes, and there is genuine concern staring back. The storm begins to recede. "A long time." I manage not to choke on my words. I manage not to vomit and create a scene. I manage to shuffle memories of the day I tried to go home and those fraught hours. Instead I remember Mom and her mantra, "First do no harm."

Zahra squeezes my hand.

Something in my chest loosens a little bit, and it is slightly easier to breathe. I squeeze back. My eyelids feel heavy as if I were trying to balance a coin over each eye.

We say our goodbyes, with promises of a longer visit next time. Another hug, another kiss on the cheek. To the outside eye, we are old friends parting. Rafiq drives me away, and in the side-view mirror Zahra's form grows smaller and smaller. After the checkpoint, I fall asleep immediately and miss all the opportunities to grill Rafiq, to view the war from a distance and as we reenter it, to gain context, and to prepare for my opening salvo with Hughes. In my dream, I am with Virginia again. We are in Central Park playing chess over the soft, itchy board of my checkered blanket. There is a red queen. There is a black bishop. So many pawns scattered between the cotton-wool boundaries with frayed edges. In my dream we pick sides, and I take red. They look bigger, meaner. Virginia yawns, then says, "You might win this time." I awaken to the car lurching to a stop just outside the hotel.

"We're here," he says. "Are you all right?"

"It must be jet lag," I answer, glad to tell him the truth about one thing, something, anything at all.

Ten

[APRIL 2003] — I THROW UP AGAIN. LUCKILY, I MAKE IT TO THE bathroom and curl around the toilet bowl and end with dry heaves. I smile, then frown, then smile. Sebastian. Ford. Sebastian. Ford. I am certain Hughes will bring me back to New York the minute he hears of this. I am lost in thought and almost miss the phone call.

Hughes delivers his usual preamble; it is meant to be funny. I haven't heard even a version of this since I've been back in the United States. Of course, I tune out completely as his Boston accent wafts over the line from halfway around the world.

"I don't have to tell you," he says, and I know we are at the beginning of the end where he jokes about his expectations for me, "but there is to be no fraternizing with a source, no nudity, and not one instance where there is a compromising photograph of you being circulated by some bum at the wire service on the weekends."

I laugh, though I know these lines by heart. "You're no fun, Hughes," I say. Of course, he doesn't know about the countdown clock growing in my womb. ("Mama's baby, daddy's a maybe," Virginia quips again in my head.) Hughes knows Ford only as an ex, and the last time he saw Sebastian was at Mom's funeral. In fact, I realize with some inner triumph that I have successfully compartmentalized every one of the men in my life. In fact, I have a secret that I can keep for many months. Except that damn Rafiq and his superhuman observation skills. I make a mental note to never throw up in front of him. As if I can will it. "I know the drill."

Hughes does not skip a beat. "You're my best girl," he says. "I know I don't have to say anything. I'm reverting to old habits."

Nausea creeps up my throat, and disappointment and self-loathing crack my chest like heartburn. It is not because I wish I could go back and change everything. It is because I stubbornly would never change a single moment that has passed, except for the moment when I put Zahra and Rafiq ahead of my mother—Zahra's screams inside the airport, her eyes wild, and Rafiq begging me, desperate, offering me anything and everything in the world, everything but the one thing I wanted. It echoes but the volume is lessening, the images are moving a bit farther away.

Ford's voice echoes inside: *You know what to do*. "What do you have for me?" I ask as lightly as I can. It is my first story back at the war. I typically pitch to Hughes with relative ease. Today is different. Hughes's decision to return me to the war was last minute. Rather, I asked Hughes last minute, and I didn't tell him the truth about me.

"Feral goats," comes Hughes's reply, accompanied by a chuckle. "It has become a national issue."

"Here?"

"A bevy of kids, really," Hughes says, chuckling at his own joke. Apparently, they'd made headway in the one golf course still open and chewed through the pipes that filter the water and drinking supply.

I know this is a national issue because important men still dress up like *Caddyshack* caricatures and play at least nine holes, often eighteen, at the golf course. Foreign heads of state are often entertained at the hotel, convention center, and mall adjacent to the golf course. In fact, I remember a story on the wire about a protest in the city, how valuable water was diverted to keep the grass green at the expense of the more vulnerable population, the poorer sections of town where orphanages had sprung up overnight. I jot down the information that he has.

"You need this by midnight?"

"Yes, please," he says. "Fifteen inches. Twenty tops."

I want to ask about Rafiq and Zahra. Clearly, they've negotiated themselves into good positions. But I don't believe their bullshit about having to live apart—my scalp itches when I think of what I sacrificed only to see them floundering. I don't want Rafiq distracted, again. The job is dangerous enough as it is. I don't want to alarm or alert Hughes that there has been a shift from the old days. I listen to Hughes cough and am reminded of seals barking by the water's edge. "You sound terrible."

Hughes laughs through his coughs. "Coffee went down the wrong pipe."

I'm not convinced. I'm an expert on sudden-onset pneumonia and the sound of an older person coughing out their lungs. Mom. "Suit yourself. But my relationship with bronchitis is ongoing and intimate."

Hughes grunts. "It really was coffee, Rita."

Outside the window, kites are flying from the rooftops in the distance. The children of the war are home from school. I pause, then dive against my better judgment. "I should go. Have to find Rafiq."

Hughes coughs again, this time a prolonged agony that echoes over the line. It is winter where Hughes lives, and a large storm front has been dumping sleet and snow onto much of the eastern seaboard. It is technically winter here as well. Because of the prolonged drought in the city and surrounding hillsides, the climate change in the entire region, there is no evidence of winter except for the chilly night air and sheen of dew on what's left of the gardens and city parks and the one golf course still open. "I talked to him already," he says after he catches his breath. "Rafiq promised to be free by the time we finished up."

I turn on the TV, change the channel to the BBC, and put it on mute. It has snowed so much in the United States that the blond talking head is speaking intently as the icy visage of New York loops behind her right shoulder. "Are you working from home today, Hughes?"

Hughes clears his throat. "Sadly, no." He clears his throat again. "However, the Chinese place around the corner is still doing business. I think Charlotte is doing takeout."

Charlotte is Hughes's assistant. She is twenty-seven, unmarried, and wears short skirts. I wonder what she is wearing today. Hughes is married to a nice woman I like and who also happens to be named Charlotte. His wife, Charlotte, brought me coffee at the funeral home almost two years ago and held my hand as the undertaker described the tiers of funeral services offered. Hughes is one of the smartest people I know, but he loves eye candy. "Hot soup," I suggest.

He chuckles. "Yes, Mom."

I smile into the receiver and project all the warmth into my voice: "I would hate to lose you, Hughes."

He laughs, coughs, laughs again. "You're not getting rid of me, Das," he says. "I promise I will cab it to the train." He coughs and coughs, even as he says goodbye.

It is never up to me whom the world chews up, whom the world spits out.

I check my work phone for messages and return Adam's call. He had made a short trip back to the old neighborhood, to pick up what the McAllisters had salvaged when Dad dropped the contents of our family history by the side of the road. "Did the neighbors do a good job?" My tone is not lost on my brother.

He laughs and says, "It's a bridge back to the Indian subcontinent." The neighbors had filled four boxes worth of framed photos and photo albums: some of Mom's parents and family in India; some of our baby items, a couple of silk saris, our report cards and transcripts all the way from when Lyndon Johnson was president to when Ronald Reagan took over after the Iran hostage crisis derailed Jimmy Carter; and some drawings Adam and I had done in grade school that Mom had framed and put in her office. Adam had done a black and white sketch of a helicopter flying over an urban landscape and I had finger-painted our family with thick paint and made Mom and Dad the same height and width, though Mom was dark and diminutive next to Dad and, in comparison, thin.

"Mrs. McAllister was very apologetic," Adam says. "Apparently there was more but the junk guys showed up a second time and hauled away everything else."

I sigh. "I call dibs on the art," I say.

"Yeah? What do you need it for?"

The baby's room, I want to say. But I cannot tell Adam now, I cannot tell anyone just yet. "It'll be worth a mint someday," I say. "I just want to get in on the action on the ground floor."

Sam calls. His voice is warm and bemused. "I've been waiting for you to come back to the newsroom," he says. "When they said 'out of town,' I thought you were in Florida or California."

I laugh. "Give me some good news, Sam."

He clears his throat and proclaims with triumph, "I found her!"

I want to shout from the rooftops. I want to reach through the telephone and hug Sam. I want to call my brother. My heart races. "Where is she?" I cannot control the glee in my voice.

"London, Wisconsin," he says. "There's been a name change." Apparently the town used to be called East Cambridge, Sam says, but the town changed its name a few years back. Mom's gravestone is in a cemetery across the street from a Piggly Wiggly, off North Pleasant Street. Sam relayed some more details, including the addresses for two Kepler families, spelled with just one p. This town is just a few miles from the one Adam and I had searched in.

"Are you coming back anytime soon?" he asks.

I shake my head, but of course Sam cannot see me. The constriction in my chest eases. Dad had told some truth, after all. "No," I say. "I'm going to recruit Adam."

Sam says, "Fair enough."

Rafiq is already waiting in the car just outside the entrance when I step into the lobby. In the glass roundabout, I find myself circling across from Margot, Johanna's longtime photographer. We stare at each other, reach out our hands and touch the glass that separates us. We stay inside the revolving door for another two rounds before Margot steps out onto the portico and I follow. "Mon ami," she says, her voice hoarse and low, her short blond hair covered loosely by a scarf, her arms all bone and sinew as we embrace.

For the first time in two years, I want to collapse. I did not think I would ever see Margot again, except maybe outside a Paris café or a magazine shoot somewhere along the Amalfi Coast near Positano. Gone is the full-bodied woman who was never without a cheeky grin. In her place is a pale imitation. After Damascus, after Johanna, Margot had taken time off and then moved to entertainment, lifestyles of the ultra-affluent. Instead of tears, I swallow hard, twice, and open my eyes to see Rafiq's face paling in the car as he recognizes Margot's unmistakable form. I close my eyes again and breathe in the butterscotch. As usual, Margot never goes anywhere without a handful of lozenges in her pocket: peppermint, butterscotch, café au lait. "Is there a fashion princess visiting the war?" I ask, my French hesitant.

Margot squeezes me tightly for a long second, then releases me, arranges the scarf more securely around her face. "It's fashion week," she says and smiles. "There are at least half a dozen self-proclaimed princesses. I believe the [--------] government has called for a ceasefire."

I smile in return, point toward Rafiq. "Maybe I can buy you some candy later today?"

She nods. "I leave the day after tomorrow." She looks past me toward Rafiq. "Be careful, mon ami. Everything only appears unchanged." She squeezes my hand and enters the glass booth. So many questions bubble to the top of my throat, yet I watch her go.

I get in the car and secure my seat belt. "Did you know Margot was here?"

Rafiq has changed out of the suit and wears pressed trousers and a blue workshirt. He shifts the gears out of park, and we creep forward onto the street. "She's leaving the day after tomorrow."

I sigh. "And you didn't think to tell me?"

Rafiq shrugs. "You were asleep."

I pound my hand against the dashboard and Rafiq's mouth

drops open. "Don't play with me." I spend the next several miles uninterrupted, weighing out loud the pros and cons of hiring a different interpreter or going without one altogether. What I don't say is how I've come back to the war to escape my American life, to unravel the knots, to lead a life of my own choosing before the inevitable change.

To Rafiq's credit, he drives with ease and confidence, seemingly unperturbed by my anger and threats. It is just another afternoon at the war, a sunny day, the battles raging out of our sight. I run out of words and take small sips of breath to calm my heart. We reach the golf course, and there is the day's assignment: Hughes was right. It is a bevy of kids eating the thick green grass, defecating everywhere, bleating blithely, no shepherds in sight. Government officials traverse toward us in golf carts while some workmen set up a podium and a bank of microphones by the ninth hole. Rafiq looks at his watch after he parks the car. "We're early," he says.

"Thank god," I reply, stepping out of the car. "Time to get to work."

Hours later, I return in silence to the hotel, leave Rafiq without saying goodbye, and take the elevator to the mezzanine and business center. It is empty, except for an attendant stocking several cases of water in the fridge. He offers me two chilled bottles, and I drink while I file my twenty-inch story filled with quips about the feral goats and the government golf course, the plan to corral the kids and send them to the mountains, the plan to divert more resources to the neighborhoods already burdened with prolonged electricity shortages and now a mushrooming water crisis. Of course, that last part came after the UPI reporter and I had cornered the government official, Mr. Hamsa, during the Q & A. Mr. Hamsa scowled but answered our questions.

I go downstairs to the lobby to interrogate the concierge. Where are the good cafés now? Where is the best newsstand? What happened to the tailor two blocks over? What happened to the family who sold fruit on the next corner? What happened to the father and son who ran the confectionery shop?

Most of the answers are similar, ranging from a simple shake of the head to "I don't know, Madam," and I am conscious that the last time I was in the region, I was a Miss and not a Madam. I have aged, or maybe it is my pregnancy, or the residual heat from my exchange with Rafiq. A man from the check-in desk walks to the concierge area and says, "There's a good newsstand close by, a short walk from here." His nametag says Mr. Haddad, and he offers to walk me out to the street. I accept, and he takes me past the guards and points down the street and in the direction of the museum, now closed. "The center has shifted," Mr. Haddad says, smiling a little. "Turn left after you cross the museum, and you will find everything you are seeking."

I thank him and walk away, careful to cover my head. This new center is apparently in a conservative part of the neighborhood, and I had not seen any woman walking with her head uncovered. The museum has been closed since the residents looted everything a while ago, after the world broke open when the Twin Towers fell. The museum windows are boarded up, and hopeful signs in Arabic and French claim it will reopen last year. I remember reading that the museums were looted by locals but that much of the art had been recovered. I feel my face pinching into a frown, and I wonder if anything will revert to the status quo of pre-9/11, whatever that "normal" meant. Indeed, after the museum there is a busy city street on the left, with cafés and shops and several newsstands. I spot the one I used to frequent, the one with a striped blue and white awning and yellow letters. But the man inside the booth is new.

The vendor looks me over and smiles. His Bengali is fast. There is rust in my mouth as I attempt to answer him. It has been a year and a half since I last spoke to my mother in her mother tongue, it has been more than two years since I last spoke to Mr. Biswas, my favorite concierge in Kolkata. It is at once strange and wonderful to hear Bengali. The vendor is not my old source who kept his eyes peeled on my behalf, a girl he pitied during the first days she witnessed the war.

This vendor is young and has an air of dissatisfaction about him. His eyes are black bullets loaded into a gun. His face is unlined, but his mouth is a pair of compressed lines that smiles as easily as it frowns. He tells me his name is Ahmed, calls me Didi, and says I have a typical Bengali face. I haven't heard anyone say those things to me in more than two years. My mind travels on memory's road past the edge of the horizon and on the other side of 9/11, when I lived in India and someone young called me the honorific term for older sister.

I seem to remind him of someone. He offers me the items I need without asking, the periodicals, the gum, the magazine that has published Margot's photographs. In the background someone is playing The Who's "Behind Blue Eyes," and a policeman walks by the square and shouts for someone to turn down the volume.

"Didi, you will ask me for what you need," Ahmed declares, his Bangla very *vous*-form, very polite.

"Of course," I reply, wondering what he wants.

He does not waste a second. "My family needs help," he says. "Maybe you could speak to the embassy and get them visas."

I stare, amazed at his boldness. "To America?"

"They won't let us go there," Ahmed says. "Even though my brother has always wanted to see the Grand Canyon."

I remember the Grand Canyon when I was eleven. That summer, our family vacationed there, my mother cranking the air-conditioning in our station wagon, my father pulling over to the side of the dust-blown road and handing the keys to my fifteen-year-old brother. "Good time as any to learn," Dad said. "There is no one here. You can't kill anyone." I remember Mom's protests, but Dad scoffed and rode shotgun. All afternoon my brother lurched from vista point to vista point in the heat, the sun a bare bulb dangling directly above us. Our dad practiced patience and kindness. That was the last summer all four of us had gone on vacation, the last time we crammed into a car together to sightsee. First a trip to the American West. And then we took our big vacation, a few weeks in India. That was the last trip there as a family unit too. The incident left an indelible stain, which colored my vision. "Where does your family want to go?" I ask the vendor now as his eyes dull.

"Here," he says, spreading his arms wide. [-------].

"Why do you want to get them visas to the war?" I look behind him to see if he's speaking for someone else. But he's alone.

"It is not a war to me," Ahmed says. "It is not *my* war," he says, correcting himself. "Here we will be cared for, and there is a school where my nephew and nieces can attend."

That is true. Girls and boys both attend school at the war. Despite the picture that some news outlets have painted in more rural areas, the norm in the urban centers is that many if not most girls attend school all the way through, attend university even. In the cities, many if not most finish and earn degrees. There are exceptions, but there are exceptions in the United States as well. "How can my embassy help?"

He flashes a smile, revealing uneven teeth. "They're American. They were born in the USA when my brother and his wife were in Oklahoma during their graduate studies."

"Oh, yes?" I am curious about the American-born children. This might make the start of a good story. "What did your brother and sister-in-law study?"

"Civil engineering," he replies. "They want to build villages and houses for poor people."

I study his face, how he chews the side of his lip, how the bags under his eyes accentuate his fatigue. "Why now? Why the rush?"

"If my nieces don't leave Bangladesh now, somebody in the family will see them married."

Ah. "Could I interview you?"

Ahmed smiles again. "What for, Didi?"

"Child marriage is everywhere," I say.

"Not in America," he says.

"Especially in America," I say. There is no federal mandate outlawing marriage between adults and minors, I tell him. Most of the states in the United States have antiquated rules allowing children as young as twelve in some cases to marry. "Everyone looks the other way."

"No, Didi, they point their fingers at the rest of the world."

I nod. "Indeed."

Margot's flight is postponed twice because of mechanical problems. She is due in France. Lyon, I believe. She is supposed to meet her older sister and then, together, they are supposed to visit their grandmother, who is on the cusp of ninety, had survived two world wars and the deaths of two of her five children and the death of her first grandson to illness. The grandmother is the last surviving matriarch in her extended, blended, divorced family. On the third departure attempt, I accompany Margot to the gate, the smell of roses heavy in the air. We look around and find no flowers or pop-up florist. A trio of women are spraying perfume from sample bottles onto their wrists at the duty-free shop—then waving their limbs about as if learning to dance interpretively. When the flight attendant puts the red CANCELED sign over the flight number on the departure board, Margo calls Camille while I call Rafiq. We head to the tarmac to identify Margot's luggage and retrieve it. The baggage handler says he just found out he'll be working tomorrow and that the flight should depart then. When Rafiq arrives, I put Margot's bags in the trunk of his car and ask him to go to our hotel.

His greeting to Margot is muted, as if he had slapped his own hand over his own mouth. Her smile in return is forced. I am extremely polite as I ask Rafiq to arrange with the front desk to extend Margot's room for another night. He agrees and leaves without saying another word.

"I told you that you couldn't leave without me replenishing your supply of candy," I say.

Margot laughs and her shoulders shake as if she is racked by sobs. She recalls the department store we used to frequent. It is a boxy two-story affair that holds everything in the world one could possibly want, including hard candies wrapped in cellophane. It is in a part of town that I have yet to be reacquainted with.

"Let's go," she says.

I hail a cab, happy to be free of a moody Rafiq. It is the weekend and there are people out and about shopping at the kiosks, walking through the entrance of the nearby park, and patronizing the many restaurants that have reopened. There are people smiling at one another, stopping to shake hands and kiss cheeks. It is an unusual moment in a series of sunny, nondescript days.

Margot notices too. "The ceasefire will end soon," she says.

Just then a convoy of open trucks carrying soldiers dressed in brown and drab olive passes us, heading the other way. I watch peripherally. After the last of the trucks has passed her window, I turn. The trucks head out of town, north toward the most active part of the war.

The taxi driver and I lock eyes when I turn back in my seat. Then I remember him: He drove me my first day back, from the airport to the hotel. On that day he was happier, more at ease.

"What is your interest?" he asks, his tongue thick in his mouth, heavy with anger. "Why are you here?"

"She's a journalist," Margot answers, her Arabic crisp, textbook.

"We are both journalists," I add. I almost ask for his name, then remember it: "Malik."

Margot and he grunt in unison. Malik locks eyes with me again, and then he breaks into a smile. "Airport pickup, yes?"

I nod, smile in return.

Malik says the trucks have been full since early yesterday morning. "They go out full, but they come back empty." He turns his full attention to the road.

I look at Margot. "It may be the shortest trip to the department store in the history of women."

Margo smiles. "How long does it take to buy peppermints?"

At the war, things are different. Until two years ago, there was the unmistakable sign of Western progress—or, as my mother would have said, "colonization": shopping malls under construction. Behemoths complete with escalators and skylights and food courts, multistoried, offering a bewildering display of Western and native costume, the latest fashion trends that most locals see only on state-controlled television as negative examples of "Western indulgence." Now the city is pocked with evidence of disagreement, of collision: Some public places are boarded up, others are featured in newspaper articles about looting. After the bombings late last year, there are buildings where half the apartment remains demolished, exposed to sun and wind. Detritus covers the pathways at the small parks and the far side of an elementary school. Margot points and explains in French, her voice a loud whisper. I think of the small towns in Ohio, Kentucky, and western Pennsylvania where the economy has been decimated. Houses boarded up, department stores cleaned out by looters and sitting dark and empty, the winding lines at the soup kitchens, the shelters.

Malik stops at the entrance to the store. Some pedestrian traffic goes in and out, but not the same quantity of customers as before. The wind blows briskly and the nation-state flag whips back and forth. I pay as Margot steps out of the taxi, and we head inside. Malik makes a motion that he'll wait for us, but then an older couple approaches him and he accepts the fare.

I point to the staircase in the middle of the department store's main floor. It is dark there. Last time I was in this place, there was a candy counter on the second floor, next to the children's clothing and toys and some kitchen goods, toaster ovens and other chrome and stainless steel and copper items such as kettles and frying pans. Margot walks ahead and reaches the bottom of the stairs and turns, her face contorted. "They're out of everything."

I reach the bottom of the stairwell and look up. The second floor is demolished. The staircase reaches nowhere; a black tarp covers the ceiling. A thick coat of dust carpets each of the steps. This bombing must have taken place just after I had left the city and the war. But then a gaunt young woman with a pair of children approaches us and replies to my unspoken questions. There is something so familiar about her, but I cannot place her—her face is beautiful but austere, and her hair is completely covered.

"Have you seen the martyrs' wall?" she asks.

I shake my head and Margot, somber, asks the young mother to show us. Behind the staircase, a wide white column shoots up to the presently nonexistent ceiling. There, taped side by side to form a square of sixteen faces, are photos of smiling young women, mostly mothers, and children.

Margot extends her hand to the woman. She takes it, squeezes, and then purposefully guides Margot's fingers to a photo of a boy, no older than nine, whose curly hair and toothy smile appears next to a woman who resembles the one standing next to us. I almost remember the woman in front of me just before she speaks. "My nephew, Omar, and my beloved sister, Farah."

We stare at each other. I want to barrage her with questions. I remember Omar's name; he took in a cat once it was discovered that Zahra was allergic. I remember Farah's face in the window of her parents' home. The ground shakes suddenly and a current of electricity flows through all the bodies in the room, all around us.

I frown.

Margot mouths the word, mostly to her herself: "Bomb."

I stand in awe as I remember what this feels like. That is the difference between the war here and the wars fought in America: the aftershock stemming from shelling and bombs going off. I mouth, "Close?"

Margot shakes her head and holds up one hand, five fingers: Five kilometers away.

I notice the date taped above the square of faces. It is not even four months old. "My condolences." My throat closes and the nausea begins at the center of my stomach. "Do you come here often, to visit them?" The building rumbles again.

"Every week," she says. "You know, I was going to accompany her that day, but these little ones fell ill, and I told her, 'Pick up some sweets for me and I'll pay for your candies the next time.'"

How well I know that feeling, a promise of the future shattered and irreplaceable.

I touch the woman's hand, and the familiar stranger grabs hold of my fingers like a child. Her name is at the very tip of my tongue.

Margot reaches into her pocket and takes out her last three butter mints, hands them to the woman and her two children.

I reach into my pocket and pull out a white business card, blank on one side and the phone number of the hotel hastily scrawled on the other, my name underneath. "May we speak later?"

The woman's eyes sparkle with unshed tears. "I knew it was you."

Margot and I exchange glances. I fall short of remembering anything concrete, just an impression that the last time I saw her, she was not wearing a headscarf, and she was not holding the hands of children. Then a flash: of Rafiq and I standing in her bedroom, a photo album on the floor; Zahra speaking with the uptight parents. "Hanan?"

The woman's eyes shine. "Rafiq said you would forget. Zahra said that people like you are only temporary friends. But I told them that you were different. Are you different?"

Margot puts her hand on my arm to caution me. Everything returns in a rush: the purported kidnapping off the street, her family's strange behavior, how her nephew Omar had adopted her cat Habibi when Zahra developed an allergy. Hanan wasn't kidnapped—that was certain—but whatever happened, this outcome did not work out for her. Somehow she blames me for what went wrong. Hanan takes the two girls and walks quickly to the exit, my business card still in one hand. She turns back to look, one time.

I do not know what to do exactly but I cannot let her go without at least trying to get some answers. "Wait!"

It is Margot who freezes for a moment. She then pulls out a small camera from her bag and turns around to photograph the martyr's wall. I squeeze her arm, then hurry toward Hanan, whose glare is steady. As I run toward them, I think about Hanan's parents and their strange behavior. "Where did you go?" I ask. "How did you return here? How long have you been back?"

The stare gives way to tears. Her face pinches into sadness.

"Will you help me return? Please? Will you help me?"

Her English is scratchy and raw to my ears.

Everything inside me screams to not get entangled again with her and Rafiq and Zahra. They cost me everything two years ago, they cost me saying goodbye to my mother. But my head nods and my hand takes hers as if my body were independent of my brain. I find myself asking Hanan to call me at the hotel when she is free.

Margot is visibly shaken by the encounter. Her hands tremble and her breath becomes shallow. She needs candy, something sweet to mask the bitter taste in her mouth. I have nothing in my pockets. We walk toward the exit, and when we are back outside, Hanan and the two girls are long gone but there are several taxis in the stand queuing up, waiting for customers. "Let's go back," I say to her. "I need a nap and you need a cold drink."

An older man with cloudy kind eyes drives the first cab in the queue.

I say the name of our hotel and he nods cheerfully.

Margot says, her voice uneven, "Mon ami, it is time for me to return to France."

All the things I wanted to say in the moment to reassure her are lost as soon as I see her eyes and the way they drift from one side of the road to the other. She looks for an exit plan, an escape. She's looking to run—from this country, from this region, from me. I'm very sorry we ever made this trip to the bombed-out mall.

"Tomorrow you will," I say.

"Please forgive me," she says, and she closes her eyes.

The driver looks at us via the rearview mirror. "Is she ill?"

"Very tired," I say. "Long day."

"Long week," Margot says, her Arabic faint. "Next time someone else will have to shoo . . . *photograph* the princesses."

I glance at her; grateful she changed the verb. Her eyes remain closed, the headscarf snug around her forehead and cheeks. "Better yet, you can photograph them strutting around Milan."

Margot laughs as she opens her eyes. "To think I gave up an assignment in Pompeii for this."

I smile and open my mouth, but no words tumble out.

Margot looks over at me. "But then I wouldn't have run into you."

I wink at her, ask the cab driver where the nearest sweet shop is.

"We're driving by the central stores now," he says, pointing to a string of squat, dilapidated buildings on my left, "but the best place is close to your hotel."

I squeeze her hand and ask, my voice barely above a whisper: "Why did you come back, Margot?"

Her grip is surprisingly strong. "I'm starting to forget her, you know." She exhales. "I do this job to honor Johanna, to show everyone I am not defeated."

Tears streak my chin and drip onto my blouse.

Several minutes later, we are back at the shopping area the concierge pointed me to the other day. "Can you walk?" I ask Margot. "Or shall I ask the gentleman to wait?"

Margot struggles with the seat belt. "The air will do me good."

I pay the driver and offer him our thanks. We set out toward my Bengali vendor, but then Margot spies another vendor with not one but four different types of hard candies, individually wrapped and bagged. "Look," she says, her voice childlike, high, excited.

I can't help but laugh. For a moment I consider that one day I will take a child to the store to buy candy. But even now that seems as remote as a trip to the moon. I dig my nails into my palm and force myself to return to the present with Margot.

"What'll you have, mademoiselle?"

"One of everything, please." Margot fumbles with her purse flap, the same color as her blouse, the strap discreetly cutting across the tunic.

"No, no," I say, putting my hand over hers. "My gift to you."

"I really do want one of everything," Margot says.

"And you shall really have it," I reply, then I tell the vendor what Margot wants. I buy an extra bag of the peppermints for myself; I had read somewhere it was good for the nausea. I can see my vendor through my peripheral vision, his frown visible even from a distance. "Excuse me," I say, pointing toward my vendor after handing over some cash for the candy.

Margot looks past me, appears satisfied, and turns her attention back to the green plastic basket of candies.

I walk quickly toward my new friend the vendor and make a big show of greeting him with an effusiveness I no longer carry inside my body.

"I have sweets, Didi," Ahmed says. He pulls out a tray that holds some hard candies wrapped in shiny foil, but already some of the fruit-colored pieces are leaking, and even from where I stand, I see the surface is sticky.

I scan for butterscotch and see none. Victory. "She's so picky," I say, praying suddenly that Margot does not wander over. I order two cold Sprites and the latest edition of the newspaper that came from London.

His face relaxes and he fills my order. Using stainless steel tongs, he carefully extracts a pair of straws from a box.

I ask him again about his family, and he tells me about missing his mother's birthday yesterday.

I cannot help myself. I begin to quiz the new vendor, and he is amenable and answers my questions. He tells me about his mother, who suffered at the hands of his father, but in the end, she took a micro loan from some nongovernmental agency in Bangladesh and started a textile business. First it was her and his sister embroidering T-shirts and blouses, some things to sell by hand at the airport or at the marketplace to tourists in Dhaka. Her workmanship was so good, the quality of her work so fine, they had more orders than they had hands to do the embroidery work. She was able to get a loan, he says.

"She's able to hire two more women, and now they have a little shop and don't have to sell on the street."

I find the paper money in my back pocket. "What will happen to her if your sister and family move here?"

He shakes his head. "She must come here and start over. She cannot be alone."

I wonder what has happened to his father. I see Margot walking toward us.

The vendor grins when I tell him to keep the change.

Eleven

[MAY 2003] — NOT ONE SCRAP OF FOOD, NOT ONE SCRAP OF PLAStic, not one scrap of fabric is wasted. Everything is repurposed. Even the plastic wrap that the bread comes in is quickly gathered and ironed flat. Someone produces a needle and thread, and the pieces are sewn together to create a makeshift flap for one of the tents that has become frayed. Rafiq explains that the tarps that have gone into states of disrepair are now often cut into strips and then braided together to be used as awnings, something to block out the sun and the heat of the day so that the children can go outside and play.

It has been two years since I've been here last. Nothing really has changed and yet everything has changed in the world: more famine, more conflict, more fires. Some Americans in America, those in the government, appear fearful yet angry—they voice their anger and theories on live television; American politicians are casting blame, and now American troops are embedded in Iraq. Another round of promises to locate and recover a stockpile of weapons of mass destruction, another round of searches that yield no fruit. That is a dangerous combination, but life in this camp has remained relatively the same. Each family has a decent space as far as camps go. There is no overcrowding; but I cannot imagine why this place, this valley, is peaceful. It is as though the world forgot this camp exists. I don't know if this is good or bad, but I suspect that it is bad.

I think I'll see them again: the women and children I befriended years before I left last time. But no. These are new people. Rafiq's face sags a little too. We have come so far and yet have returned to the place where we desperately want to see the old women from before, their faces covered for more than half a century. Who knows what they do inside their homes? Who knows what happens at night in bed with their husbands and lovers? I try not to presume. I hope they have some measure of happiness and freedom outside the confines of their black robes and the rules imposed on them. Who knows what has happened to the children I saw playing here two years ago? It is likely that some of them are dead, and it is also likely that some of them have been fortunate and moved away. Hopefully they have another place to play and a peaceful place to sleep.

On the way back, we notice changes. Some of the walls have been painted over while others have been left written with the language of bullet holes, mortar shells, carnage, and wreckage. Some have been painted over and repaired so that you can never tell there was ever a war, and some have been painted with murals that proclaim there will always be a war. The whole day is much like a poem in Carolyn Forché's *The Country Between Us*, "Letter to a City Under Siege," except that I am in the war across the seas and not in the Americas. I think of Virginia as Forché's words echo in my head: "And what else, what more? Even the clocks have run out of time." The poet and my dead best friend will always be linked in my mind. I think of our innocence in college, I remember the shine in Virginia's eyes when she won the contest and garnered the poetry books as a prize.

I step out of the hotel compound and almost immediately hear comments from a group of younger men with intense stares and beards, some sort of insignia on their matching armbands. Two break from the pack and follow me as I walk down the street toward the shopping area and my vendor. Since the Hostage Crisis in Iran more than two decades ago, there has been a general shift in modesty standards all around the region. The latest decrees from Tehran echo as each government tightens what they deem appropriate attire.

So far, if a woman's hair is covered and there are long sleeves for her arms and legs, it is acceptable. The white reporters, mostly men, are given more latitude. The local reporters are targeted more harshly; some female anchors in parts of the region have been asked to cover their faces. In solidarity, one male anchor joined them one night. A single, vivid effort to show gender inequities and censorship.

I check myself in the mirrored window as I cut across the plaza that houses an abandoned American oil and gas company office. I look okay, and I'm feeling confident until I realize I left my press badge on top of my nightstand.

I look at the mirrored window again and notice that the pair of young men have picked up their pace. I walk faster and faster, my heart galloping to my feet's trot, until I reach the area where the vendors have gathered. I wave to the candy vendor, who asks loudly how I am, and I answer in Arabic that I'm well. I reach my vendor, out of breath.

"Shab teek ache, Didi?" he asks, and he looks over my shoulder, presumably at the pair of men who had been following. Everything all right?

I nod, panting. I turn my head and they have vanished. Not even ghosts. I almost call Rafiq to ask for a ride, but then I decide against it. I buy what sundries I need and thank my vendor. As I walk home, I put on my sunglasses even though the sun is in its decline and I keep my head straight as my eyes dart all around. The streets are empty save for a few motorists, and I'm more than relieved. Last time around I held my own hours: I took power naps. I went everywhere. I made up the sleep on those infrequent days off and I somehow survived it and thrived in it. This time around a small being controls my every action. I must sleep as soon as the deadline is over, I must rest to quell the nausea. I must eat regularly. I have become trapped by the daytime hours, and now of course there are armed police everywhere watching, there are cameras everywhere watching. During this part of the war everyone has become suspicious of everyone else and their allegiances and loyalties and affiliations. The hotel staff cautions me that it is not wise to go outside in the dark.

Still, on the nights that I know Rafiq is visiting his wife in her fabulous compound far away from the war, I drink a glass of juice and steal a cookie from the mezzanine business office and venture outside. Sometimes I catch my vendor as he's closing shop and I walk with him to where he boards the bus or catches a carpool ride back to his home.

Tonight, he thanks me. My letter of reference helped. "My niece has enrolled in school," he says, beaming.

What isn't said is that she escaped the all too familiar fate of marrying too soon, of having to take care of a sixty-year-old husband and his eighty- or ninety-year-old mother.

"I told her about you," he says. "She has drawn you a picture. When it arrives, by post, I'll give it to you."

I smile.

Two nights later, even before the first call to prayer, there are sirens and warnings and all the reporters in the hotel spend a few hours in a shelter underneath the building. It is like a tornado drill except it's not a drill and there are no tornadoes. These are man-made disasters heading our way, the war is spreading. Then the morning breaks open and we retrieve our things, get dressed, and go to work.

Rafiq and I go to the very street where we know people have disappeared (after Hanan): mostly women, some young girls. It is a normal street, there are vendors, there are street shops. Some are open all day, some are closed after lunch. Mostly, there are men in the storefronts even at the women's clothing store. I spy the shopkeeper's daughter behind the counter: I don't recognize her. What has happened to the girl who was there years before? Maybe she has been married off. Surely some of these people have seen those who were taken and recognize the manner in which they disappeared—but no one says anything to us when we ask. There are people out walking but I notice that this is different. The children no longer walk to school on their own, they are now accompanied either by a gaggle of mothers and aunts and grandmothers or by their fathers and uncles. The children of the war still go to school, but they do not attend unaccompanied.

There is another Forché poem, "San Onofre, California," one that I mutter to myself thousands of miles away from the people I once knew and grew up with: "We would lead our lives with our hands tied together." That is true. Isn't it the job of the journalist to write a rough draft of history, and yet our hands are tied together? We are told to be objective, but it is impossible because we are, after all, human. Our eyes may be cameras, but they are cameras that can cry real tears and sometimes the salt water produced blurs our vision. Sometimes the wind kicks open the windows where I stay, and the pages of the newspaper rustle, and the pages of a book flip open, and the wind reads. Sometimes the wind rustles through the trees, lemons fall to the ground. Sometimes the wind smells and stinks of hot breath or something gone wrong. Often the wind smells of roses because even in this war the gardeners have their subterfuge, and they still grow flowers.

The bookkeeper for that textile company still takes in the stray dogs—there've been many more this time around than what I noticed before. He takes them in one by one, leads them gently off the street and offers them food, brushes their coats, applies ointment in the open wounds, and soon those dogs are unrecognizable: barking, happy, healthy. His landlord I'm sure has complained and threatened action, and yet he continues to take in the dogs one by one. The birds (and the butterflies) still return, their cycles not yet broken. I hear the birds' familiar calls, and for a short time I believe everything will be all right.

Adam has left two messages, one in the New York newsroom and one at the hotel. I don't remember telling him the name of my hotel, and I'm impressed with his research. I tell him so when I call him. "You're going to put me out of a job, Brother."

He laughs. "I saw Dad . . . and Mom."

I sit up in my seat in the business office and look intently at the black phone in my hand. Outside the hotel, horns blare and voices carry. An uproar over a fender bender. "What? When? Tell me everything," I say, asking what seem like a hundred questions.

"I took Jen with me," Adam says. Sam's directions were perfect, and they matched also with what Dad had said. "We saw him right away." A big cemetery, with a slew of Kepplers buried there, going back several generations. A lot of people named Adam, Elena, Elizabeth, Dorothy, Karl, Ann, Mary, Steven, David, Samuel, John. Kepler spelled with a single p, Kepplere spelled with two ps and an e at the end. Dad, standing in front of Mom's gravestone, a bouquet of pink roses in his hand. "He looked older," my brother says, his voice suddenly hoarse.

"Was he surprised to see you? What about Mom?" I ask again, gripping the phone receiver tightly. My knuckles are white. I can scarcely breathe.

Adam says, "He was surprised you weren't there. He figured you'd come before me. Overjoyed to see Jen again." He coughs. "Mom was where he said she'd be." Adam describes the chiseled gravestone: CHAMELI D. KEPPLER, BELOVED WIFE OF KARL, BELOVED MOTHER OF ADAM AND ELENA.

Butterflies float in my stomach and I cannot think ahead to ask him what happened afterward. Finally, the churn in my stomach subsides. "Did you talk to Dad for long?"

Adam laughs quietly. "He was desperate to keep talking to Jen. We ended up driving him back to his cousin's house. He gave us a phone number of the place where he's staying until his house is ready. He is hoping you'll call."

I exhale. 'What did he say, exactly?"

"He said, Please give Rita my number. I'd like to hear her voice." Adam's voice breaks at the end.

I *humph* the way I'd heard Dad *humph* for years. "He doesn't speak that way, Adam."

Silence. Then Adam says, "I paraphrased."

I want to laugh but instead sink into the chair. "Which part?"

Adam sighs again. "He does want to speak with you, he made that clear."

I take the paper I was going to write his number on and crush it into an uneven ball. "This is what you want. I bet he didn't even ask about me." I hold the ball in my hand and wish with everything in my heart our mother was still alive.

"He did ask," Adam says. "Please, just take down his number."

A single tear runs down the length of my face and drops onto the collar of my blouse. "Tell me what he said, exactly."

Adam says, "He said he wanted to talk to you. He said he shouldn't have sold the house without talking to us first. He's . . . changed, Rita."

I hear the desperation in Adam's voice. I take the ball and open it up, smooth out the wrinkles. I wipe my eyes and reach for a pen. I exhale. "Okay."

After I take down the number, I thank my brother and promise to call soon. I look at the wrinkled paper and the number scrawled on it. London, Wisconsin. I do the time zone math and almost reach for the phone. But I don't—instead I ball up the number again and toss it into my satchel.

I think this is going to be routine, a quick story about a baker and his bride, his father's store, how it is a neighborhood institution that everyone in a square-mile radius has taken great pains to help keep open. A bakery adjacent to the camps. Calamitous water shortages—demand far exceeding supply. How the groom and bride rise even before adhan and knead dough that has been resting overnight, how they bake their morning loaves before they join their elders in worship. But the war shifts like a fire-breathing monster, teeth chewing through everything without mercy.

At the start Rafiq looks bored: The baker and his bride both studied in America and their English is excellent.

"How long have you been home?" I ask after I learn they met in the university library; they had been searching the stacks for the same book. Poetry. The Persian poet Hafiz.

"Five months," Sonya says, beaming at her husband, Naseer.

There is a rumble in the distance. It is low at first, as if it were thunder clapping miles away. But the noise turns into a roar: Something is edging closer to the camp.

We look around briefly but see nothing. Then we talk about the bakery routine and the influx of refugees coming into the region from North Africa: how the famine and the climate change have forever altered the landscape. They talk about their efforts to feed the hungry and the displaced, how husband and wife are gathering what's unsold from other food shops every two or three days and finding volunteers to drive to the camps and donate the food. There is never enough food, there are always so many gaping mouths to feed, Sonya says. There is never enough water.

"We won't stop trying," Naseer says, his face somber.

A crowd has assembled in the small square in front of us, as if by magic. They hold up signs and chant. They protest the government's indifference to their thirst; these are people who cannot access water consistently. They protest the ongoing war in the region, and how much the war has cost them—in lives of loved ones. They protest America's invasion of a neighboring nation-state. From my peripheral vision I see reporters at the rear, I see photographers snapping photos. I turn to Rafiq and raise my eyebrows. He excuses himself and walks quickly in the direction of the square.

Husband and wife fall silent. Then Sonya uses her hand to indicate the presence of soldiers. They too have arrived at the square, guns at the ready.

Without warning, sirens sound and the children around us put their hands to their ears. Then bombs whistle and the mothers and fathers and uncles and aunts and grandparents and neighbors and friends start to run. The screaming begins, but there is a group of protesters who stand their ground.

Naseer and Sonya gather whoever is nearby, mostly women and children, and hustle them into their shop, they take cover.

No one gets far. Buildings shake and, like broken bones, shift. Dust plumes like mushroom clouds on the next block and many fall to the ground. Rafiq runs back toward me, and we look at each other and yell to take cover. I move toward his car and then, like out of a B-movie, part of the restaurant balcony overlooking the street breaks off and falls on top of the parking area. I run toward Rafiq but the smoke obscures my view.

The protest continues—despite the convergence of ambulances and military police vehicles with men in faceless helmets and olive-green uniforms holding weapons. The protest continues despite these soldiers and police marching in unison and undeterred by those who have gathered in the square.

The protest continues despite the tear gas on the neighboring street and the billows of smoke clouding our vision.

The open windows from top floors of the buildings are being closed—there are no more children looking in between the slats and metal gates.

A woman shouts "War is death!" and the crowd of a hundred or so answer in return. Someone else shouts "Down with the government!" and the crowd pumps its fists collectively and answers back. Someone fires a round of bullets from his gun and the heart of the crowd remains intact even though the ones standing at the margins, on the outskirts, begin to disperse.

Sirens scream in the air. It is deafening.

People scream as they run past me and their screams echo in my head.

I inch along the boulevard and crane my neck to keep the woman who shouted the first slogan in view.

Even from this distance I can feel her anger. What started as a peaceful protest is ending in chaos and violence.

The woman opens her mouth and shouts again "War is death!" and the heart of the crowd responds in kind, loudly, hands raised in defiance.

Now there are the sounds of multiple guns being employed, and the screams and the bullets and the marching soldiers merge into the sound of a large machine churning out chaos. This is the noise of a war machine at work. I take my eyes off the woman in the pink headscarf for a moment to look at the bodies strewn on the ground.

The gunfire continues sporadically. People run and the heart-shaped crowd shrinks, and then I think I spot Tom Barnes. Or someone who is wearing his trademark navy vest with the word PRESS taped on his back. He is lying facedown and his camera is some feet away, the lens pointing toward the sky. I make my way toward him, the edges of my headscarf covering my mouth and nose. I don't have to turn him over. I recognize his hair and the clothes he wears. I find myself sitting on the ground next to him. No matter how many dead bodies I've seen, each is a fresh wound, tearing off the scab from the first time. I am thousands of miles away from the Kolkata enclave where I witnessed a man being hanged. And yet it is all fresh before my eyes as I hold Tom's bloody head in my lap, people screaming all around me, the wail of ambulances and the street, peaceful only a minute ago, filled with dust and carnage. The stretcher comes and an ambulance, one of many. I crane my neck and see Rafiq a short distance away, but it could have been the moon. He sits up against a wall, his clothes covered in dust and grime, his head in his hands. I try to call out to him, but I cannot make a single sound. Finally, he looks up and I beckon with my hand, but he does not move. His glasses appear to be broken, askew on his face, as if the wire rims have been twisted with violence. Some medics come to look at Tom, and after, I point to Rafiq. They go to Rafiq, and he waves them off. He stands slowly and stumbles toward me. "I want to go home," he says. "I will find my way." I try my voice, but nothing comes out, so I squeeze his hand. The medics are kind and insist both Rafiq and I hitch a ride with them to the hospital. I look back at the bakery and I see Sonya and Naseer are okay, they are shepherding children into the bakery. One medic looks us over and asks

Rafiq questions. We are okay. It is too late for Tom. The medic uses his fingers to close Tom's unseeing eyes. At the hospital, I hear people in the waiting room shouting, saying the government had launched bombs on its own people, on its own unarmed dissenters. I hear others saying it was a copycat action of some splinter group trying to sow dissent. I think of Sonya and Naseer and the shock and sorrow on their faces.

Hughes sends me a message, asking me to call. We talk about the story I am still trying to file, the baker and his wife, the protest and what followed. I tell him that Rafiq has a few cuts and bruises but that he will be okay, that I have sent him home to Zahra. I tell him about Tom. I tell him that I've been asked to officially identify his body.

"But why does it have to be you? Why can't someone take your place and do the identification?" Hughes asks. Tom's editor saw the video on cable news, no doubt, and wanted my word that it was really his reporter. "What is it about you and Tom that you are not telling me?"

I shrug and then smile—grimace, really—at the telephone receiver and realize he cannot see my face or read my body language. The emergency room at the hospital here is chaotic. Still, one of the nurses was kind and I had an alcove to myself—really a storage closet—so I could call Hughes.

"We all had dinner together," I say. Just before the latest conflict, I say. I was the designated ride coordinator. I had volunteered to be the one not drinking during dinner and to make sure everyone got into a safe taxi, and I would have done this for Tom Barnes. It was all for nothing, as Tom was staying in the hotel next to the restaurant and he simply stumbled next door.

"Why you?" Hughes asks. "You love their lemon martinis, and it's one of the few places where you can get a drink you like."

I know I must be careful because I cannot tell him the truth, but I cannot stray so far into the world of fantasy that I cannot retell the lie convincingly.

"That's a lecherous crowd," I say. Which is true. Ford's in that crowd when he's in town. And that's how I get into trouble, hanging out with the wrong sort. Hughes knows that all these reporters are on their third marriage at least. Occasions like these are fertile grounds for someone to stray. "I'd rather liked my husband on the day we were out to dinner," I say, meaning I was neither in the mood nor the market for something new.

Hughes grunts, sighs. "When do you have to do the identification?"

Later this morning, I say, but what I don't tell him is that I must eat, vomit, eat again. That I cannot view and identify a body on an empty stomach like I normally would, that I felt the butterflies of the baby's kicks this morning as I rose, that I finally understand there is a change coming—one that I cannot skirt and run from. I miss my mother. In this moment, in every moment.

"Well, I won't keep you on, then," he says.

I promise him I'll be in touch soon when I'm done with the story. I plan to include an obituary of Tom in my next story. Tom wasn't the story, but he became part of it when he was promised safe passage and the promise was broken.

No one is taking responsibility for the incident. There are at least three groups in the region whose signature fits the shootings and the bombs, fits the widely known intent to gun down reporters. But no one is taking responsibility. There's so much speculation in and around the government offices, and in and around the cafés and produce markets, and around the movie theaters—the ones that are still open. The air is all abuzz with speculation and whispers.

And then suddenly there will be a press conference. I call Rafiq but he does not answer. I head out alone.

The concierge sees me walk across the lobby and we exchange nods as I leave the compound. He follows me out again. "Will you be all right walking by yourself?" Mr. Haddad is wearing suit trousers, a white shirt, and navy tie. His jacket is off.

"I'll be fine." I'm walking toward the parking lot, and then on to the street toward the kiosks.

"Would you mind if I accompany you?"

I wait for him just outside the hotel doors.

Moments later his face looks shiny and his jacket is back on.

"Won't you be hot?" I ask.

"I represent this hotel so I must be dressed well when I leave here, even if it's just for a few minutes."

He already has a five o'clock shadow, but I say nothing about that.

He begins to ask me why I am here in the nicest way possible.

I smile and say it's my job.

"Are there many women at your newspaper?"

I say yes, there is a fair number of women, though it's not fifty-fifty, it's not equal. There are not enough women on the foreign desk and not enough of us covering government and corruption and crime and war.

We speak of the places that I sometimes go, in the evenings, when it is dark, to meet my sources. Inside and hidden away.

I want to write so many stories, I say carefully: on inequity and violence against women. All across the region there are whispered stories of rape and assault, of violence against women and girls. Across the region there are whispered stories of subjugation and trafficking and patriarchy, of violence against women and girls. Across the region there are stories of intimidation and stalking and kidnapping and murder, of violence against women and girls. Across the region there are days when none of these stories are written or aired. Across the region there are not enough voices calling out the violence against women. Across the region there are voices speaking the truth about the violence against women—but these voices are being drowned out.

His eyes brim with unshed tears. "My sister," he says. "Murdered."

I stop and put my hand on his arm. "I'm so, so sorry."

He pats my hand. "It was so long ago. But it feels like yesterday."

"I know that feeling, though it is not exactly the same." I pause. The sorrow weighs on the back of my neck and shoulders, a steady and heavy pressure. "My mother died from illness. Almost two years ago and it feels like it happened in the last hour."

Aren't we the sum of all the things we eat and all the things we watch and all the things we tolerate and all the things to which we are accustomed? The scene now at the war unfolds in front of me like a police drama I used to watch with Ford before I met Sebastian and married him. It is too normal. Just like the opening of the show, Thursday nights at ten o'clock. All my memories are of the stiff green couch and wooden chopsticks resting over the open flaps of nearly empty takeout cartons of shrimp fried rice and Hunan beef on the coffee table. The repetition.

Today all that is missing is the ominous music at the busy intersection in the new neighborhood just outside the heart of the city, outside the sightline of the war. Here pedestrians walk freely and shop at the street-facing stores, tiny boutiques that remind me of the nice streets in large American cities. Rafiq meets me at the guarded entrance to a huge compound. Unfortunately the compound is at the top of a rather large hill and there is a steep staircase to overcome.

I want to stop, find a comfortable chair, rest my aching shins; I want to stop panting like an old dog. I want to be there already, the hilltop compound of this affluent, powerful politician. The air-conditioned press conference. It is the first time I've ever climbed this hillside staircase between the parking lot and the gated garden and felt so nauseated, so weak. I am typically the first person up the stairs, and impatient with my guide. I'm typically in charge of the time and the schedule and the boundary conditions of the interview I'm planning to conduct. But today is different. The sun is above us, Rafiq and me, like the inside of a tanning booth, and it is hardly even the lunch hour.

I catch Rafiq's hard stare. "Rita," he says, panting a little as well. "What is wrong?" He takes out a handkerchief and wipes his sweaty brow. Usually he has water, a reusable bottle, tepid but clear liquid that on a hot day like today would still feel glacial going down the throat. But his hands are empty save for his encased camera, the strap dangling from his scarred wrist.

I don't know which lie to say right now. Truth be told, I cannot remember all the lies I have told him in the recent months. I think about the truth, the consequences of what I've done before my reassignment. "I'm pregnant," I blurt out.

Rafiq nods in recognition. His face wears a knowing look. "I knew it," he says. "You look just like my cousin Saira did when she was expecting."

I grunt. "What's that?"

"Glowing," he says.

I wait for him to offer congratulations and ask about my husband. But he is silent, and his face is pinched into a look of intense concentration.

Glowing, Rafiq says, and the word echoes.

I once knew a woman who glowed, so the joke goes. She won a pair of Nobel prizes and immortality but died too soon. Marie Curie. *Radioactivity* and *radium* are among the words she coined. I also knew a woman, a much younger friend of my mother's, who, when she was expectant with her son, glowed, skin shining. She died in childbirth and her son and husband moved back to their hometown, some village miles outside of Iowa City. I remember my mother's face after she came back from the funeral. The sadness contained but chafing the skin from the inside. I was fifteen years old, and it was summer, dahlias bloomed wildly in the backyard.

Now I would happily sell Rafiq for a bottle of ice-cold orange soda or sparkling water.

Rafiq says something but I don't quite catch it. "Pardon me?"

"We should turn back," he repeats, hesitantly. "You don't look well."

Although this is something I desperately want to hear and have wanted him to voice for the past fifteen minutes, upon hearing it, my resolve hardens. "No," I say firmly, in between pants. I channel the tenacity of Christiane Amanpour, I channel the determination of Sylvia Poggioli. "I'm on deadline, and Hughes will not take no for an answer." What I don't say is that I'm on deadline and I will not take no for an answer.

"Does he know?" Rafiq asks, gripping the camera strap and placing his left foot on the next step.

"You're the first person I've told in [--------]," I say, and I am suddenly elated to be telling the truth again.

"No one knows?"

"My doctor, in New York." I pause.

Then Rafiq overtakes me on the staircase, so that when he turns around, his body looms. "And your husband?"

I stifle an urge to groan. I think of Sebastian, I think of Ford. I am a woman officially above approach and unofficially without compass. I am a woman who cannot pinpoint the moment of her baby's conception and, therefore, does not know who the father is. I am a woman in dangerous proximity to being labeled a whore, especially in this non-Western part of the world. My mother, if she were still alive today, would be deeply disturbed. By the same token, if my mother were still alive today, I don't think I'd be in such a predicament. I remember everything in flashes now: our first few happy months until the wars broke out, until Sebastian and I were assigned to different parts of the world, until our calls and infrequent reunions were just a jumble of bitch sessions and office politics, until we stopped laughing.

And that is the sad truth of everything I do, that I cannot follow every story to its logical conclusion, that I must stop one thing the minute I've covered it and learn something new so I can tell the public. It is the same with my marriage. And now I've ruined it with my uncontrolled anger—I'm left holding exhaustion and regret. Rafiq's question was worth $100,000, wasn't it? "No," I say. "We are speaking in two days' time when he returns to his home."

We get to the top of the stairs and Rafiq helps me to a chair and someone miraculously appears with a bottle of ice-cold water. He plops down beside me. After half an hour my body is sufficiently cool, and I am ready. I look over at Rafiq and his face is relaxed. I avail myself of the bathroom. Everything is cold to the touch, and I pull the compact out of my purse and fix everything up so that it looks like I sailed here on a catamaran even though this particular area is landlocked, not even a river. I wonder how they get all the water up to the top of this mountainous hill; it must be some hidden source, otherwise the flowers would die. I look through the window and see how the lushest parts of the garden are cordoned off as if this were a golf course. I finish pinning my hair back into a tight bun and step outside.

I sit at a lavish banquet table, without food but with a dozen or so reporters all trying to understand what they are witnessing. We watch the richest man within five hundred miles about to dine alone while expounding on the war, his position in the government, his power. I'm the only woman in the room, and his eyes land on me, this war-happy government official with money. "Why are you here?" he asks.

I consider what Marie Colvin would do if she were here. "You are preparing for yet another war," I say.

He wrinkles his nose a little, and he sits down to eat. He talks for a little bit about the modernizations that need to be made, about the people he must help when he has consolidated his position in the government. He does not like me, and yet he invites Rafiq and me to join him for a short walk. Some of the male reporters look at me and mouth "Will you share?"

I nod.

He says to me, his English British, "You are the most trustworthy of the lot."

"Why?"

"You do not hide your disgust, but you are . . . diplomatic," he says.

And I still ask questions. I see Rafiq trembling, I see his hands trembling, but I continue to ask questions. That is all I have in this moment to keep us both safe: my voice. These are all the questions I'd ask a firefighter putting out a major fiery incident, only I substitute for *fire* such words as *war* and *government* and *people* and *human rights*. He answers readily enough, and then we return, and his secretary arrives accompanied by his wife. I am very relieved to see her. Because she is there, I think we will not be jailed at the end of the evening. We share with the other reporters. Rafiq shouts in glee when we finally get down the hill and get into the car, free.

We enter the hotel, bedraggled from the long day and this car ride. The cable news guys stop Rafiq and me in the hotel lobby, and we are asked to provide analysis of the meeting with the rich government official, the one who plans to take over the country and perhaps the country next door. It would air in a week, as part of a longer series on the region and its conflicts.

"Should you call Hughes?" Rafiq asks before I go on camera.

I shrug.

As we talk, there is breaking news: that the camps are hit again. The camps that are housing all those displaced from the countries to the south, that are suffering because of catastrophic famine. There are two competing stories, I say: troop movements and a military buildup as the Americans are embedded in another regional conflict, another war; and the humanitarian crisis, how the climate change is causing famine, which is causing starvation, mass migration, refugees. How the pictures of bombs falling plays better on TV than pictures of children starving to death. How the mantras have become "If It Bleeds, It Leads" and "Better to Be First Than Right."

Twelve

[JUNE 2003] — HANAN CALLS AND WANTS TO MEET ME AT THE hotel. "I can be there later this morning," she says.

She sounds weary. "Why don't I come to your apartment?" I ask, wanting to inspect her place again. Two years have passed since the black cars whisked her off the street and she disappeared. I look around my hotel room and settle on the window, how the light coming through is slanted, how the light and shadows appear like abstract art on the nearby wall.

"Oh no," she says. "That would be so inconvenient for you."

I know when I am being handled. "Not at all," I say as soothingly as I can.

She clucks her tongue. "When I returned," she says haltingly, as she carefully plucks words from the air, "my father . . . my parents invited me to live with them again."

Ah. Yes, that makes sense. I don't want to offend her by laughing but I do appreciate her diplomacy. She was the independent daughter who had been taken; now that she is back, she is more closely supervised. More likely than not, her stepmother and father have locked her away. "What are you telling them, to come see me today?" I ask. Truth is out of the question. I know that whatever happened, her father and stepmother would not approve of her speaking with me.

"I do have an appointment, a checkup today," she says. "I can come to you before I return home."

Ah. "Are you sick?"

"No," she says.

I wait for her to say more, but the silence grows between us. Finally, she says goodbye.

Hanan shows up at my hotel on time. She accepts a glass of

water, and we sit in the business office on the mezzanine. It is early in the day. We sit in more silence until she finishes her water. She puts down the glass and presses her lips together. "I need your help."

I think of the story I wrote and how far from the truth that was or is. I don't know what the truth is. I look at her closely, and she is somber. Still, I see a sparkle in her eye. "How did you return home? How long have you been back?"

She murmurs something I don't quite catch. "It was a misunderstanding," she says, louder. "I went to Jordan. I want to return." She needs a letter of reference from me, she could secure work like Zahra but in the Jordanian capital.

I need some kind of confirmation though I don't know why: Hughes will never let me write another story about her. "It wasn't a kidnapping?"

She shakes her head.

I sigh. "What happened?" I ask.

"I can't tell you everything," she says. Her eyes dart to the windows and the wall behind me and then refocus again.

I smile. "You haven't told me anything."

She bites her bottom lip. "You helped Zahra without knowing everything."

I lift my own glass and bring it to my lips. I take a sip. I put the glass down with a thud and I see Hanan's eyes grow big. "I'm sure I did." But what I didn't know was as important as what I thought I knew.

Hanan sneezes. "Excuse me."

I reach for the box of tissues, offer her one. "You are sick."

She blows her nose. "My heart is broken."

I think of Rafiq, of course. But there seems to be so much more to this story. I want to take her hand in mine and console her. Instead, I just look at her and remain still.

It is a test of silences and will. I know I can win this test, but I don't know what the prize will be and what consequences will result from this meeting. I can hear the hotel staff bustling about on the lobby level below us. Voices ring out in greeting, and birds chirp and cars honk their horns in the distance. Several minutes fly by this way, and I almost open my mouth twice to ask her more questions. I'm stopped by the pain visible on her face, her down-turned mouth, black pouches of sleeplessness pooling where her eyelashes end.

She rises and looks at me with big brown eyes, crinkles forming in the corners. I detect sorrow as well as determination. "Zahra said you might help me." Her voice drops to a whisper. "Please consider it."

I call Rafiq and ask him to pick me up, and when he arrives, I give him the address. He stares at me for a moment too long, says nothing, opens the car door for me.

I approach the shopkeeper again, the one who witnessed the purported abduction of Hanan and her nieces. I say hello and introduce myself.

He appears to recognize me. "It has been a long time," he says.

I nod and Rafiq materializes beside him. I introduce them and the gentleman seems to know Rafiq well, there is something sweet about the way he greets him, slaps Rafiq's back with his frail hand.

We talk again about the day when Hanan disappeared two years ago. Can he remember anything odd or unusual?

He stops and scratches his head. "I think I said it before," he says. "They were smiling."

"Who?" I ask. "The abductors?"

He shakes his head. "No, the girls. They were screaming but with big smiles on their faces."

I think back to what he said before: "The little girl in the pink dress with a big smile."

I had misunderstood.

Rafiq's mouth opens and closes a few times after the shopkeeper stops speaking. I cannot stop looking at him. Rafiq cannot meet my eyes.

I thank the shopkeeper and then Rafiq and I return to his car. I shut my door but don't fasten the seat belt. "You've been lying."

"Not then." He shakes his head as he locks the door and points to the seat belt. "Only now."

"You didn't know that this was a ruse?" I know there is incredulity in my voice.

He fumbles with the car keys, then starts the ignition. "Not until Hanan's nieces came home."

"You lied to me," I repeat.

He turns left sharply at the light and stops the car by the side of the road. "You've never lied before? You've never tried to help someone who was in trouble?"

My lips tremble. Not out of fear, exactly, but more that I'm startled. This Rafiq has undergone transformative change. Old Rafiq would never have used that tone with me. This Rafiq is combat-ready. Old Rafiq would have looked at his watch and sighed, then slunk off.

"I just want to correct my mistake," he says now, his voice considerably cooler, more polite. He hesitates for a few moments, and then he reaches into the inside pocket of his suit top and pulls out an envelope.

A pair of Polaroids: He gently places them on my lap. One is of a baby swaddled in a blue and white blanket, with a tuft of dark hair and a strong baby nose. The other is of an older woman holding the baby, wrapped in the same blanket.

"Oh," I gasp. "He's beautiful."

He smiles. "Hanan left our son with my friend's mother."

The riddle becomes a puzzle, and the last pieces fall into place. "A kidnapping to hide a pregnancy."

He nods. "Zahra wanted . . . Zahra wanted Hanan to have a new beginning. And Zahra wanted a new beginning with her new husband."

This I understand. An unwed mother would be ostracized, and her family would be shunned. And Zahra didn't want the baby around as a constant reminder. But Hanan now wants to be reunited with her son. Rafiq and Zahra want to help her. "What changed?" I ask. What changed?

"Zahra and I cannot have children," Rafiq says, his voice nearly drowned out by the passing cars. "Hanan will share him with us, but we cannot do that here."

How much the war has cost us all. Yet Zahra came around, she solved a childless riddle. For Sebastian it is a different riddle, but perhaps he would want to solve it too. Perhaps there is a way to apply their solution to my complicated situation. I touch the Polaroid again. "What's his name?"

He reaches across my seat and fastens my seat belt. "Ashraf."

I cannot remember where Sebastian will be and what his schedule is at all. I try to recall but what flashes before me is him clad only in a towel, kissing Layla. I remember I'd sent him an email, saying I'd call at this time, but I don't know if he replied. I see flashes of him hovering over me before I fainted. I dial the phone to the New York apartment and there is no answer. I remember the scowl on his face as I answered that phone when his mother had called. I try his office in New York and there's no answer. My mouth goes dry. Then I try his apartment in Spain. He picks up after the fourth ring. "Hello?" He sounds out of breath.

"It's me," I say, hope in my throat. "How are you?"

He pauses. "How can you ask me so casually, as if we speak every two days?"

I feel my face go hot again, grateful in the moment that he can't see me. "What should I ask you? 'How's Layla'?"

He scoffs. "Why didn't you tell me you were back in [--------]? Why did I have to learn about it like everyone else?"

I take a sip of water. "I had to get away," I say. "I had to get some distance." In this moment I recall our honeymoon in Venice, the gondola, the waves rippling away from us, his easy laugh at my every joke.

"From what? It's not just me." Frustration punctuates every syllable. "You didn't leave New York until April."

The heat courses over my face and neck again as I recall Ford. "You're the one begging to talk," I snap. Then I sigh. "I'm sorry. I don't know how to say this . . ."

He is silent for maybe a minute. "What is it?"

I recite with numbers: 1. I am pregnant. 2. I had been staying with Ford after our last fight in New York on your birthday. 3. I don't know if it's your baby. My hands and feet begin to tingle, and a fog of numbness descends.

His response is anything but orderly. "My god, Rita!" and "What are you thinking?" His response is filled with half-uttered sentences: "I can't believe anything about us anymore," so much anger, so much disappointment—"I don't know if I can speak to you again."

I try to defend myself but have no defense. I try to bring up Layla, but then who am I to say anything about Layla since I have Ford squarely in my corner, occasionally beckoning? I should apologize more but then I find that even those words are stuck in my throat. What I have done, because of my anger and blame, cannot be wiped away in an instant.

Eventually a wall of silence consumes us for a long while. Neither of us speaks but neither of us hangs up. We listen to each other breathe. The rhythm subsides into a regular pattern, occasionally one of us sighing. I remember my head on his chest listening to him breathe as he slept the day after we eloped. I couldn't keep my hands off him then. Only a few years have passed but it feels like I am looking into a telescope, surveying the nebulous past. I hear the doorbell ring at his apartment, and with a click the line is cut. I'm left holding the receiver to my ear, a rapid busy signal droning on and on. After a while even that noise stops, and I finally replace the phone in its cradle.

Two hours later, the phone rings again. I hope against everything I know to be fact that Sebastian is calling back. I walk over to the nightstand but don't sit on the newly made bed. If by some miracle Sebastian is on the line, I know what I'm going to say. It's going to start with an apology.

"Hello?" I ask into the receiver. My voice comes out scratchy, hoarse.

"Rita, is that you?"

Not Sebastian. Hughes. I stifle a groan. Maybe my marriage is over, but at least I have my job. At least I have this.

"Yes," I say, then clear my throat. "Sorry."

"Were you asleep?" he asks but doesn't wait for a reply. "We need to talk."

I gasp. I know that tone of voice. This is Hughes at his angriest. I sink onto the bed, the pillow compresses under my weight.

I hear papers being shuffled on his desk. "New York. Tomorrow," Hughes says. There is no lava in his voice, just volcanic ash. It coats everything and leaves everything dark, homogenous, without nuance.

I can tell just from the way he says "tomorrow." Every second of our relationship as colleagues is being studied from a different perspective. "There's a night flight that lands in Charles de Gaulle in the morning with a good connection. Be on it."

I can be Elena here, be the persistent reporter, be savvy, make a tense situation a tiny bit lighter. I try one last time. "There's a slow boat to Hong Kong Tuesday," I say. "Why don't I jump on—"

But Hughes is having no fun now. "The M.E. hates to be the last to know," he interrupts. "You embarrassed him," he shouts. "I vouched for you." He calms down, apologizes for shouting but not for what he said. "I'm sorry," he repeats.

My toes and fingers tingle, and the numbness washes over me again. "Wait, I'm being fired?"

"No," he says, toneless. "We are . . . expecting . . . you in New York."

I pause, confused for a split second: My thoughts about the famine didn't embarrass the managing editor. Then I look down at my stomach, still flat but starting to round. The way he said the word "expecting." He isn't mad about the cable news interview. He is mad because I had transmitted to him through the magic of TV that I am pregnant. He seems to read my mind from thousands of miles away.

“How long have you known, Rita?” He takes a deep breath.

But that’s not the important question, is it? “How long have *you* known, Hughes? When did you tell the M.E.?”

I hear him shuffling papers, like cards. “You looked just like Charlotte did when she was expecting our son,” Hughes says, softer now.

“How long?” we ask each other in unison.

“I suspected when I watched the TV interview,” he says. “But Ford . . . confirmed it. I got a call from him last night. Your ob-gyn is trying to reach you. You missed an appointment.”

I want to howl. “Ten weeks,” I mumble. I clear my throat. “Twelve weeks. Maybe fourteen.” Outside, the shelling resumes, and the screams resume, and the light bulbs flickering off and on like fireflies resume, and the ground being unstable resumes.

“You could have told me,” Hughes says. “You should have told me.”

Really? I want to ask. But it’s silence I’m transmitting now. Loud and clear. I hope Ford is listening to this transmission as well: I’ll never speak to him again.

“I’m not firing you,” Hughes says, his voice still raw. “I can’t fire you for being pregnant. But there are consequences for lying to your boss.”

I gulp. “I didn’t lie.”

Hughes sighs. “Lying by omission is still lying, and you know that.”

He is going to park me at a desk and I’m going to be writing obituaries or typing wedding announcements for the rest of my life. I open my mouth to argue, but no sound escapes.

“Tomorrow night, Miss Keppler.”

My heart rattles inside my rib cage like a metal ball in a pinball machine. I hang up and begin to pack.

I see only strangers as I print out papers in the business office and stuff them into envelopes. I check out. Mr. Haddad is not working. A new girl, Hala, with long dark hair twisted in an elaborate bun, wishes me a pleasant journey. I almost forget to do my one good deed for today, and I turn around in the lobby and find her again. "My friends will come by and pick up these documents later today, if you call them," I say, handing over three envelopes, labeled with the names of Rafiq, Zahra, and Hanan and their phone numbers. Their letters of reference, so they could start over. The letters of reference are the culmination of hours of frantic phone calls, pressuring contacts and diplomats; they represent examples of my best persuasive writing; they represent a means to an alternate future for Rafiq and his family. Hala is kind and says she will take care of it. A driver, a stranger, picks me up from the hotel, and we head to the airport. I look around but find no traces of Rafiq and Zahra, no traces of anything. I've been recalled twice now, and my job is in jeopardy, if there even is a job awaiting me in New York. Not because I couldn't do the work but because I couldn't tell the truth to my editors.

The driver—whose name I cannot remember, though I've asked twice—is kind and wishes me a pleasant trip after he pulls my bags out of the trunk. I thank him and enter the passport verification line. Several minutes later I'm inside and I begin to queue up for the airline check-in and the first of six hoops I'll have to jump through to head to Paris, Amsterdam, and then New York. I audibly sigh, feel the dread work its way down my back and into my legs. I am among the first to board and I offer my window seat to a young girl traveling with her mother, seated next to me. I close my eyes and sleep almost instantly and dreamlessly.

When I finally arrive in Amsterdam, I find myself walking away from the long queue for the New York flight and walking slowly toward the airline information desk. I find myself almost wondering aloud if I could just not go to New York and go somewhere else. I could just quit. I could just go to India by myself, as Elena Indrakshi Keppler, private citizen. I could finally do a follow-up on the story that had the biggest impact on my life: the hanging. Twenty-eight years ago. I could talk to Adam. I could report on a story that has been haunting me for most of my life.

There are several people in line ahead of me, and there is something oddly familiar about the man who is at the front of the line, his back to me, a baseball cap covering his hair, his stance, his cream-colored shirt. I gasp. It is my husband. The agent he is speaking with raises her voice, "Sir, you must produce your wife. I cannot change her ticket without her being present." She motions for him to step aside so she can help the next customer.

He doesn't budge. "Look, she'll be here in a moment," he says. "I know she will."

"Then come back here when she arrives," the agent says.

"I'm trying to do something nice for her," Sebastian says, and he looks over his shoulder. He smiles broadly and turns back. "See? I told you. She's here!"

He waves me over and I stand before him, heart pounding but in a fog. "Why are you here?" And then I remember the promise I made to myself in my hotel room yesterday: "I'm sorry, Seb. You have no idea how . . . how sorry I am."

He turns from the ticket agent and grins; he too looks as though he's been crying and worrying. "Look, I know this is a surprise." His words come fast and faster still, he is painting a portrait of a marriage in record time: We took a chance and started strong. He is sorry for the strife, he wants to accompany me home to the United States, he wants to start over. He has ended it with Layla. He wants a family. He wants this baby. "*We* will work this out," he says. His voice is low but fast, and there is an urgency in every syllable. "I will do anything you want."

I stand there, vaguely dizzy and studying his handsome face; I catch most of the words, but I am too tired to practice diplomacy. "I won't go to the United States with you." I surprise myself with my emphatic tone.

Sebastian's face pales. "Please, Rita, don't say something that you'll regret . . ."

I put my hand on his chest to steady myself. I open my mouth to voice the wish that is growing inside. "I have to show you where my family . . . changed, where it happened, where it took root." Then: "Will you come to India with me?" The question comes out a whisper.

He gathers me close and says, simply, "Anywhere you want. You are my home."

Epilogue

[KOLKATA, JUNE 2003] — I LOOK OUT THE WINDOW AND, OUT OF habit, count the baggage as handlers unload it from the conveyor belt onto a baggage cart, and I keep an eye out for ours. My mind races as I think of all that I need to say now that we have landed in Kolkata. I think of the phone calls I need to make, of the other apologies that must be made. I start my spiral of anxiety and then I stop—I exhale and force my eyes away from the window and onto the top of the airline magazine peeking out of the seat pocket. The headline for an article about home renovation techniques from a well-known TV personality.

I smile, remember Mom and how much she enjoyed his TV show, how the renovator brought a large crew of designers and construction workers and, over the course of a weekend, gave needy families "a facelift." The before and after pictures were always stunning, a sharp contrast. I remember that sometimes I didn't want to watch the show, and that I'd say "Let's watch the next one together. Later."

This is what we squander when we think we have tomorrow, when we save things for another day, when we don't say what we need to say in the moment, when we act from a place of fear or failure or impostor syndrome, when we don't think: Hey, I have to see this moment now because it might not be back again tomorrow. This is the fall of the youth when they think that there is tomorrow and a future, and their youth will last forever, and they are in such love with their immortality, and they can't imagine growing old or not having the world at their feet or not getting what they need or want. We all become orphans eventually and we learn to be our own house, we learn to be a roof over our own heads and four walls for the next generation. Maybe that's the lesson I've been trying to learn and that's the lesson my mother had been trying to teach me all these years: that one day I would have to be on my own and she wouldn't be there to be my proudest champion, to be my collaborator.

Even through the air-conditioning, the air is stale. All the things that are left unsaid pepper the forced cold air. It is almost evening, it is the moment of our arrival, it is time for me to let go. I catch Sebastian looking at me and I wink at him. He crosses his eyes and I smile, so grateful in this moment for this second chance.

I think of my last phone call with Adam. "Before we leave the airport, I need to make a phone call," I say to Seb.

"Hughes?"

I shake my head. "Dad."

Later, I sit behind the driver, an older man with cloudy eyes and a turban, and Sebastian sits beside me a few feet away. We each guard our doors with our bodies. We do not touch.

Sebastian makes small talk with our driver and the old man says this is his second career driving taxis. He had been a farmer and later an office worker for quite some time, but after retirement he was bored. "My wife suggested I drive in the city with my electric oxcart," he jokes.

"This is why electric oxcarts will never go out of style," Sebastian says. "Our wives will never allow them to be put to pasture."

I laugh even though I have promised myself I wouldn't respond—that I would be content to be a passenger and not a player in the day's drama. I am proud of myself for not cringing when Seb and the driver banter using the word *oxcart*. I am still basking in the light of my brief airport lounge call with Dad. "I'm in India," I told him, "with my husband." He apologized for his behavior after the funeral, just as Adam predicted he would. He apologized for selling the house. "Promise you'll come and see me, Elena, and visit . . . your mom."

I could hear the tears in his voice. "I promise, Dad." We have a long road ahead, but Mom would be happy in this moment, to see us try.

Now in the taxi, Sebastian reaches over and squeezes my hand.

I squeeze back. I turn my head and he smiles.

I blink twice as I'm prone to do when I want to express affection in public.

"Where are you from, if you don't mind me asking?"

I look away from Sebastian and lock eyes with the driver. He had picked us up in front of the international airport. Curiosity stamps his eyes, and his eyebrows are raised in a quizzical expression.

I grip Sebastian's hand a bit tighter. "I'm Bengali, but from America," I say, as lightly as my voice allows. "I make my home in New York."

It is Sebastian's turn to laugh. "I'm just a city boy from Los Angeles." He winks at me.

This is both true and false. Sebastian was born in Pasadena and lived there until he was five, when his parents moved for work. He spent the next thirteen years in San Diego until he left for college on the East Coast and now goes back to California for holidays and special events. His father, now retired, divides his time between Southern California and Madrid.

"I knew it!" the driver says. "I can spot Californians from a great distance."

I grin at the pride in his voice.

"What about them gives them away, do you think?" It is now my turn to wink.

"They're so glamorous, they all act like they're movie stars," he says.

A few minutes later we are at the bus depot, and there are many men and women and buses and taxis milling around. Nothing has changed and yet everything is different. The same shops and their blue-washed walls and flickering fluorescent bulbs, the smell of incense from the Kali mandir in the air, the statue of Swami

Vivekananda stares impassively, arms crossed. Sebastian gets out of the car and offers me his hand. "Here we are," he says.

"The starting line," I say, as I take hold of my husband's hand and let the rush of adrenaline settle in my veins. I step out and look ahead, remembering Adam on the cusp of adulthood, in his pullover shirt trying to mimic our father; and Dad, who unintentionally gave me the best gift in that tragic moment as he tried to shield me from danger, when he hoisted me up on his shoulders. He gave me an unobstructed view and sparked the desire for me to always seek the truth. I look around and see my young mom, a bright yellow flower, blooming, beating back the darkness with every breath.

This book is dedicated

to

Shireen Abu Akleh

1971–2022

&

Daniel Pearl

1963–2002

&

to the

2,545 journalists and media workers

killed since 1992*

* This data was taken from the website of the group The Committee to Protect Journalists (CPJ). As of January 10, 2026, the number of journalists and media workers killed was listed as 2,545.

Acknowledgments

I didn't think this part would be so difficult. I know whose tireless efforts once again helped me finish this book. I feel it's insufficient to just say "thank you" and be done. My hope is that you understand how grateful I am for all your kindnesses, big and small; and that we will strive to see each other in person to catch up and to celebrate.

Enormous gratitude to my champions at Mariner Books and HarperCollins: Rakia Clark, Ivy Givens, Mary Interdonati, Martin Wilson, Bob Castillo; and Mumtaz Mustafa for the marvelous cover art. Thanks for everything to my beloved agent and friend, Reiko Davis at DeFiore & Co., as well as Brian DeFiore and Adam Schear.

Many, many thanks to my dear friend and writing partner Elizabeth Stark, without whom I would not have finished this book. Much gratitude to Maureen Fan, Korinne Lassiter, Sejal Patel, Lisa Taggart for their careful, close reading and invaluable advice over the past few years. Gratitude to my champions, Alka Joshi, Nina Schuyler, Meg Waite Clayton, for their generosity and support.

Love to the extended Laskar, Chakravarty, Dasgupta, and Sen families, especially Joy Laskar & Gauri Sen. Love to all the amazing cousins. Thanks to the multitude of friends, teachers, family and chosen family for the inspiration and unconditional support over the years. Special love to Anjini & Ellora & Devrani Laskar, Ru & Kimmy Sen, Nabin Laskar, Chandra Bagchi, Parna & Aloke Roychowdhury, Malaya Gupta, Subrata Dasgupta, Elizabeth Rosner, Angie Powers, Parna & Tesha Sengupta, Dorothy Hearst, Nanou Matteson, my classmates at Book Writing World,

UTV, Tin House, FMWG+B & CWOV Crazy 8s, my VONA family, especially Karineh Mahdessian, Zeyn Joukhadar, Sarah Gonzalez, Cinelle Barnes; Brett Hall Jones & Lisa Alvarez; Deborah Krainin, Pete & Patricia Apostolakis, Gloria & Juergen Hoefler, Tanya & Jay Kruse, Kathy & Dean Brewer, Shankar & Ruma Sengupta, Faith Hoople, Robin Holtson, Eric & Helen Graben, Vi Pham, Anjoli Roy, Sunanda McGarvey, Aya De Leon, Faith Adiele, Misha Chowdhury, Amanda Gersh, Lucille Clifton, Elmaz Abinader, Molly Fisk, Samiya Bashir; Chris Evans, Amanda Scacchitti, Dave Nast, Jill Leonard, Vicki Ferris, David McKinnis, Beth Lyon, Monique Truong, Anjali Enjeti, Kathy McDonald, Dani Chiofalo, Jeff & Cheryl Gramling, Shikha Malaviya, Lee McLees, Ellen Sussman, Ewa Chrusciel; Pam Mosley, Mahlet Tsegaye, Vijaya Nagarajan, Susan Ito, Karen Goelst, Debi & Mithu Chaudhuri; Helen Bhattacharyya, Evelyne Accad, Lucy Jane Bledsoe, Sabina Khan-Ibarra.

Thank you to the multitude of journalism colleagues, friends, teachers, and mentors over the years, especially Luchina Fisher, Lane Mitchell, Lisa Allen, Suzanne Jeffries, Rhesa Versola, Kathy McAdams, Harry Amana, Joyce Fitzpatrick; Linda Hosek, Greg Ambrose, Cynthia Oi, Terry Luke, Stirling Morita & Rod Ohira; Bahbra Boykin & Larry Smith; Louise Windsor & Anne Valentine; Katie Orenstein, Christine Larson, Kelly Nuxoll & Zeba Khan; Ellen East, Kathy Scruggs, Joey Ledford, Duane Riner, Moni Basu, Louie Favorite, Deborah Scroggins, Maria M. Lameiras, Laura Wisniewski & Scott Marshall. Deeply grateful to follow the reporting of so many brave, dedicated reporters in the United States and around the world; and to the investigative works produced by such groups as Human Rights Watch, Amnesty International, and the Council on Foreign Relations. Grateful for the works of Cathy Park Hong, Valarie Kaur, Christina Sharpe, Chimamanda Ngozi Adichie, Hala Alyan, Sonia Faleiro. Special thanks to Christiane Amanpour & Sylvia Poggioli, their tenacity is in part the spark for this novel; and for the truth-seeking work of such fearless journalists as Jamal Khashoggi, Marie Colvin, Anja Niedringhaus, Kathy Gannon, Lyse Doucet, Clarissa Ward, Arwa Damon, Jane Ferguson, Lulu Garcia-Navarro, Saira Shah.

Remembering the ones who would be especially proud today, but are gone too soon: Pranab K. Sen, Amulya L. & Renu C. Laskar, J.R. & Nilima Dasgupta, Kalyani Sen, Gautam Dasgupta, Susan M. Freiburg.

ABOUT
MARINER BOOKS

MARINER BOOKS traces its beginnings to 1832 when William Ticknor cofounded the Old Corner Bookstore in Boston, from which he would run the legendary firm Ticknor and Fields, publisher of Ralph Waldo Emerson, Harriet Beecher Stowe, Nathaniel Hawthorne, and Henry David Thoreau. Following Ticknor's death, Henry Oscar Houghton acquired Ticknor and Fields and, in 1880, formed Houghton Mifflin, which later merged with venerable Harcourt Publishing to form Houghton Mifflin Harcourt. HarperCollins purchased HMH's trade publishing business in 2021 and reestablished their storied lists and editorial team under the name Mariner Books.

Uniting the legacies of Houghton Mifflin, Harcourt Brace, and Ticknor and Fields, Mariner Books continues one of the great traditions in American bookselling. Our imprints have introduced an incomparable roster of enduring classics, including Hawthorne's *The Scarlet Letter*, Thoreau's *Walden*, Willa Cather's *O Pioneers!*, Virginia Woolf's *To the Lighthouse*, W.E.B. Du Bois's *Black Reconstruction*, J.R.R. Tolkien's *The Lord of the Rings*, Carson McCullers's *The Heart Is a Lonely Hunter*, Ann Petry's *The Narrows*, George Orwell's *Animal Farm* and *Nineteen Eighty-Four*, Rachel Carson's *Silent Spring*, Margaret Walker's *Jubilee*, Italo Calvino's *Invisible Cities*, Alice Walker's *The Color Purple*, Margaret Atwood's *The Handmaid's Tale*, Tim O'Brien's *The Things They Carried*, Philip Roth's *The Plot Against America*, Jhumpa Lahiri's *Interpreter of Maladies*, and many others. Today Mariner Books remains proudly committed to the craft of fine publishing established nearly two centuries ago at the Old Corner Bookstore.